139 Years to the End of the World

Aden Ng

To my mother and father.
Maybe I'm not doing what it was wanted of.
But I am doing what I was raised to.

Year One, Part One

Mist Poisoning. When the doctors told me those words, I knew. I knew it was over. Of course, my right leg had been paralysed from the knee down for a year by then. I had also been blind in both eyes for nearly a month so I had a pretty good guess I was dying. The disease caused cells to mutate, slowly shutting down nerves in the body from the bottom-up, like the ones that are connected to my legs and eyes. After a while, you'd get this nifty ability to stop feeling pain.

By the time they diagnosed my condition, it was already too late to treat. Though it was not like there was a cure either, so it was more about buying time with therapy and medications. I had, according to the specialists, about three weeks left to live. Time suddenly became as precious as family to me. I couldn't imagine living without it. Given my situation, I don't think I can.

For the first few days, I had resigned myself to living without my sight and had accepted my death. But from out of the blue, my family and I received a sponsorship from a government affiliate for bionic implants. I went through emergency surgery and got a new pair of robotic legs and a new set of mechanical eyes wired to a hard drive and processor in my brain that reworked the information into optic nerve signals. That same hard drive is responsible for what you're reading now as well, as I can record thoughts as texts straight from my mind to it. Of course, I was still dying. The Mist Poisoning can't be cured. But I can at

1

least see the faces of my family and friends in my final days.

And that brings me to my predicament. As I sat in my clean white hospital bed after the surgical transplant succeeded, enjoying colours after a month of darkness, I had expected my family to be the first by my side. My wife, Joan, and my beautiful adopted daughter, Leila. Of course, that was not the case. If it was, I wouldn't be recording like this.

Beside me sat a bald man in a black suit lying against a chair, wearing sunglasses despite being indoors, soaking in the bright white fluorescent light of the room. Everything about him screamed of 'government agent', like the ones in those classic 2D spy films I watched as a kid.

The entire room was empty saved for the two of us. No nurses or familiar faces. Just me, the bald man-in-black, and the beeping of my ECG. I could not tell if the man was awake since his sunglasses covered his eyes. So I just stared at him, pondering my next move. There were no buttons to call for assistance either. No windows to open or curtains to draw. Just a small, white, clean, empty hospital room with a door in the corner.

Suddenly, the man spoke in an expected gravelly voice. "Milton Jones?" His lips barely moved. The man's body was still as a statue in his seat.

"Yes?" I answered to my name. That's right, I haven't introduced myself yet. Milton Jones. I'm thirty years old this year. Geography teacher.

"Son of Stella and Jason Jones? Grandson to Sally Sparrow?" the man asked again.

"I am." I wanted to ask 'What is this?'. But I felt I would find that out eventually in this strange conversation. Everything appeared like a dream. The whiteness of the room was disorienting for my newly reacquired eyesight. The smell of alcohol disinfectant punched into my nose.

"My name is Agent Matthews from the East Forum Administration," the man introduced himself. "Our files says you're not a man to beat around the bush with so I'll get straight to the point. We need your help." His voice was as rough as sandpaper, if sandpaper had a voice that was.

"The E.F.A?" I replied, slightly surprised but still collected. "What do you need my help for? Learning how to write better introduction speeches?" My mother always said I was a lot like her father. Witty in

2

the face of dangerous and odd circumstances, never knowing when to keep my mouth shut. I'd like to think that I'm just really stupid at conversation-making and very good at pissing people off.

Agent Matthews sat silently, my ECG beeping the seconds away. Breaking the silence, he said, "I did not expect this."

"What?"

"Witty banter," the man took off his sunglasses, revealing his jade green eyes. "For a man on the edge of death, you have a sharp sense of humour."

"Gotta have a little whimsy in life," I replied, adjusting my seating. I don't know what for though. Ever since the poisoning spread to my spinal nerves two months ago, I stopped feeling any pain or discomfort in my body. Perhaps it was just muscle memory, doing stupid things. "So, what does the E.F.A wants with me?"

"Straight to the point. Long story short, the world will end in about a hundred and thirty-nine years and you are the only person capable of stopping it. Possibly," he paused, as if to emphasise the word possibly. "So we're offering you the chance to be cryogenically frozen for that period of time."

Wait, cryogenically frozen? "As in, like, an ice pop? For over a hundred years?"

"Yes."

"What in the world makes you think I'd do something like that?"

"It's actually a pretty good deal."

I cut in quickly. "How? How in the world could being frozen for a hundred years be a good deal?"

The agent leaned forward and rested his elbows on his knees. "You're dying."

"Yeah but—"

"You have less then two weeks to live," Agent Matthews said without pause, preventing me from replying. "You can't feel it right now because your nerves are all fucked up, but your body is breaking apart. You have a daughter. She's ten. You'll never even make it to her wedding at this rate."

An anger rose up within me. I could not feel heat, but I'm sure I was boiling with it. Gritting my teeth, I replied, "What's your point?"

"My point, Mr. Jones, is that you have at best, fifteen days to live. Aside from the ten or so days we'll take for maintenance and possible

3

emergency situations, we're giving you a chance to live the remaining five at any time of your choosing in the next one hundred and thirty odd years. Who knows, maybe there'd be a cure in that time. But in any case, you can be there for your daughter's graduation, her wedding..."

"Her death?" I cut in.

The agent took a deep breath and sat back up straight. "If you so choose, yes."

Time was precious to me, I knew that the moment the doctors diagnosed me with my own death day. But now, it was a commodity. It had a value of quality and quantity, and I'm being given the chance to trade one for another.

Agent Matthews continued, "The freezing process has been refined. We can guarantee a ninety nine percent success rate. The only thing that can prove lethal to you are freak accidents and your own illness. You won't even feel a thing. In fact, once you go under and wake up, it'll be no different from a night of sleep."

My mind felt blank, stunned, unresponsive to my thoughts. Hazily, I slowly pulled away the blanket that covered my leg. New bionic legs, covered in attempted skin coloured plastic, moulded to the shape, but not the look of a human leg, laid there. I instinctively tried to wiggle my toes, but found none, as my feet were replaced with just a rubber piece resembling a shoe.

I asked, "Did you guys do this?"

"We paid for this," the man replied. "But in general, yes, we did. The leg's a little off in colour and too solid in looks, but the eyes turned out pretty good."

From his shirt pocket, he took out his glass phone. He tapped on it and slid his index finger in a zigzag pattern across the screen and the back of the phone slowly turned reflective. He held up the device to my face's height.

Looking at myself in the mirror, I realised just how pale my skin was. My short, messy hair, usually maroon, had half of the strands greyed out. My eyes, once a faint teal, were now dark black, the lens of the implanted cameras adjusting faintly where my pupils once were. Their movements were unsettling, but proved they were real, functioning bionics, and not just my eyes miraculously healing themselves.

After staring at my reflection for what felt like hours, I asked, "What if I refuse your offer?"

"You go on with what's left of your life," he replied matter-of-factly. "And we'll still let you keep your implants as well, if that's what you're really asking. No catch. We're asking you to do something no one else has ever done before in the history of the human race. At least, not for as long as you are about to."

Matthews lowered the phone and I met his gaze. I sized him up. A well-built but not too muscular man, the agent had the rough and rounded head you'd see on stereotypical soldiers. His jade eyes being the most prominent of his features. They were piercing, but honest and strong, like that of a teacher. I thought the man would have made a fine educator had he not chosen his current profession.

I said, "Okay, I'll take it."

"Take what?"

"Five days in a hundred and thirty-nine years to the end of the world. I'll take it." I paused, my mind suddenly remembering something important. "To go of course," I added the take-out joke. No point facing the apocalypse without some witty one-liners.

Year One, Part Two

We left the hospital as soon as I got changed. Long black jeans hid my new prosthetic legs and a fresh set of blue shirt and grey cotton jacket warded against the breezy temperature. Though the robotic legs are functioning properly and I was capable of standing, they moved too slowly as they had not fully synchronised with my neural pathways yet. Thus, I ended up leaving the front door of the hospital in a wheelchair.

I had thought the world was bright upon waking up, that the light in the room was blinding. Once outside though, I realised just how wrong I was as my senses were bombarded with the colours and luminosity of the pale, azure-tinted sunlight.

Agent Matthews walked next to me. At his full standing height, he was a towering 2.1 meters, a full 30 centimetres taller than I would be when standing, the top of his head whistling just under the arch of the entrance. He had offered to push my wheelchair but I declined, saying I should do such simple things myself.

"As you wish," he had replied. His tone and manners reminded me of a butler, complete with a suit.

A black sedan was pulled up at the entrance with another man-in-black waiting by the car. This one had a full head of brown, ruffled hair. Instead of shades, this other agent wore a pair of horn-rimmed glasses and had deep brown eyes and a scar across his lips.

As we approached, Matthews introduced, "My partner, Agent Golph."

"Call me G," Golph cut in. He was audibly friendlier than Matthews. The standard good cop, bad cop. Mutt and Jeff. The sticky and the stickler.

"Agent G," I replied with a childish grin. "Now that's a spy name."

G opened the passenger side door for me and offered to help me in. I waved his hand away and slowly stood from the wheelchair before gently pushing myself into the back seat. I lifted my new, heavier legs into the car with my hands. Matthew loaded the wheelchair into the trunk and took the driver seat while G went the long way around and sat beside me. In just a few seconds, the engine was started and we were out of the hospital's vicinity.

The engine was relatively quiet and the car's radio was turned off, dragging out the silence that had fallen in the vehicle.

Breaking the stillness in the air, I turned to G and asked one of the millions of questions on my mind. "Does my family know about this? I know we're under time constraints but I would like to see them again before going under."

G, his voice with a hint of southern accent, replied, "Your wife was told an hour before you. She's on the way to the lab with your daughter now." He removed his glasses and cleaned it with a piece of cloth from his shirt pocket. "Your mother and father are being escorted there as well."

"And they're all okay with me doing this?" I asked a question which, in hindsight, I should have brought up the moment the proposal for turning myself into an ice-pop came up.

Agent G stopped cleaning his glasses, put them back on, and kept the cloth. "I think that's something you should ask them yourself."

I turned away from G, pondering the decision I made to be frozen, in order to save the world from a future I was not sure was going to happen. The city buildings of New Roagnark scraped the skies. Each one with their non-reflective solar panelled windows glowing under the setting sun, bathing the cityscape with a light teal. Hundreds of cement towers, held up by metal, wrapped in glass, unwavering even as they touched the heavens themselves.

Another question popped into my mind. "How did you guys know?"

G replied, "Know what?"

7

"That the world was going to end in a hundred and thirty-nine years? Kind of a specific number if you asked me."

Matthews took a left turn onto a ramp and up onto the highway. "Your grandfather wrote a song that predicted the future," the bald agent said nonchalantly.

At first, I thought he was telling a joke and I waited for the punchline. When I realised he was serious I replied, "Wait, what?"

I looked to G who returned a look that said, *Crazy, I know. But it's true.*

Still disbelieving, I said, "You guys expect me to believe that my grandfather, a car mechanic, predicted the future with a song?"

Matthews with his eyes still kept on the road, replied, "Doesn't matter if you believe us or not. Truth is the truth. We don't know how he does it, or why it only appears in songs, but he has never once been off. And technically, they're not songs either. They're hymns."

"Wait, this isn't the only prediction he's had?"

G stared at me with a looked as if I've gone insane, which he reiterates when he says, "What are you? Nuts? The Forum wouldn't trust a guy for just one prediction."

Oh sure, I sarcastically thought. *Predictions of the future are like job experience after all.*

Matthews continued, "What we know is that he was there sixty five years ago when the Mist came in. You know, the blue gas that's been hanging in our sky since we've been born?"

"Yeah," I replied, nipping. "I'm dying from 'Mist Poisoning' aren't I?" The Mist had become a staple of our lives. A blue, high altitude gas that hangs in their own atmospheric layer, covering the planet. It was poisonous to anyone who inhales it in large quantity, though not common as they never dropped below their altitude enough to reach most of our noses. I was just unlucky, stumbling onto an air pocket of it by accident during a stroll through the park.

"Right," Matthew answered. "After that, your grandfather predicted over a dozen events that are said to have been pivotal turning points in the history of mankind and prevented millions of death. The Battle at Orion. Little Haven Power Outage. The financial crash two decades ago. He got them all."

"You're kidding?" I asked to no reply. I assumed that the two agents were tired of explaining something they themselves felt was the truth so I moved on to my next question. "And what's this hymn that has supposedly predicted the end of the world?"

Matthew said, "G? I'm driving."

"Urgh...fine. Let's see..." G gave a few seconds of thoughts before starting the hymn to the familiar tune of The Chosen Way, the old boy scout hymn I used to sing as a child.

Lost to the Father upon the end of days
The years will be coming where he will lose his way
For all the darkness that covered all men's reign
A light will shine, with my blood in his vein

Time will cease when the days turn into years
My son to son will quell all your fears
From limped till the end in one-three-nine days
He'll lead us through the last turns of the maze

Don't say it, I told myself. *Hold it in,* I reinforced. "That was a gay-ass song." I hate me.

"I didn't write it," G replied. "And before you ask, I don't know what the hell it means either. That's up to all the smart people to decide."

"He means the decoders," Matthew cut in. "We're here by the way. You've got any more questions, you can ask Professor Hullway when we see her. She'd be able to tell you more."

I leaned to the side of my seat to look out the front window as a building rose from the horizon. A clean, dome-shaped grey structure stretched from end to end of the wind-shield. Like all the other buildings of New Roagnark, the E.F.A Headquarter was covered in non-reflective solar-window panels, glowing a slightly blue hue under the Mist tainted sun.

Matthews took the next exit that came up, and from the cross junction after, took a left turn onto the empty road towards the building. Chain-linked fences surrounded the land; with only one concrete, arc-shaped guard house at the end of the road that doubled as the entrance with a metal mesh gate.

As we drove up to the guard house, Matthews took a card out from inside his jacket pocket and held it out the window. A red light beamed from one of the security cameras of the building, following and scanning

9

the card he held. Once the light disappeared, the metal mesh gate rose and Matthew drove through without slowing down.

We drove up to the parking plate in front of the lobby entrance. G got out of the car first to retrieve my wheelchair, followed by Matthew after popping open the trunk. I opened my passenger side door and lifted my prosthetics out, dangling along the edge of the seat like a child on a swing. I stared blankly at my new limbs, still unsure of how exactly I should feel towards them before looking up to the front entrance of E.F.A HQ. The darkened glass automated door extruded a foreboding aura of what laid beyond them.

As G rolled my wheelchair to me, the glass doors parted ways and a woman in a white lab coat walked out.

"Professor Hullway," Matthew greeted her before pointing to me. "This is Milton Jones. The subject for Project Dawn."

"Yes, Agent Matthews, I can guess that," she replied, not with snide, but a sing-song happiness. Her long golden blond hair waving behind her lab coat, a pale lemon yellow under the blue sky, her black flats kicking up dust as she walked.

As I heaved myself onto the wheelchair, she stepped passed the two agents and knelt on one knee, levelling face-to-face with me. "Milton Jones, I'm Professor Leah Leslie Hullway." She had slight a foreign accent, akin to those from the Northern cities. Underneath her lab coat, she wore a knee length black skirt and a yellow frilled shirt of similar colour to her hair. "I'm hoping the two agents have briefed you on why you're here?"

I adjusted my seating position, though again I was not sure why. With my nerves as good as dead, I couldn't feel discomfort. I replied, "Yeah. But I still have loads of questions though."

"Understandable," she replied, getting to her feet. "But I think it'd be best if we answered all that once your family has arrived."

Matthews took out the remote control key to the car and clicked the lock button. The vehicle's light flashed and beeped twice before the parking plate began lowering itself into the ground to the automated parking lots below.

As the car descended, slowly revealing the view hidden behind it, I noticed a familiar sight forming over the roof of the lowering black sedan. A blue mini van had been halted at the metal mesh gate, with guards walking out of the guard house to inspect the vehicle. It was my wife's car. I wondered if that was the last day I would ever see her again. My next two weeks would be a long, long time away.

Year One, Part Three

Apparently, my wife was named after a saint called Joan who was from an arc. I had never heard of her in all my lifetime and had no idea why she would be from under a doorway. According to my wife, Joan the saint lived a few hundred years before the Mist even came into our world. A lot of information before the time of the Mist was lost. Despite it being just sixty five years apart, only fragments remained from the knowledge of the older generations. Only now, when the world has regained stability are there any concentrated efforts at rediscovering and preserving them.

I don't know about this Joan of Arc, but my wife was definitely a saint. I can only imagine the doubts and fear going through her mind right then, but her strength to look at me with a smile ceaselessly amazed me. Professor Leah left us alone in a room to make the decision of whether I wanted to freeze myself while my parents took my daughter, Leila, to have a quick tour of the facilities with Agent Matthews.

They had left us in what seemed to be an employees' lounge of sort. There was a small, circular, plastic table surrounded by chairs that appeared to be a place to eat. Beside it was a simple counter topped with a microwave, mini-fridge, and a coffee machine. A single potted plant in a corner provided the only sense of colour to the otherwise dull-white walls and colour scheme. Even the floor, while carpeted, was a boring

12

shade of office blue.

The two of us sat in an out of place maroon couch beside the plant, Joan leaning her head against my shoulder. She was still in her work clothes. As a herbalist working in the Sun Dome, her white shirt was stained with patches of dried mud, as was her denim shorts. She had obviously rushed down from work as part of her hands had dried spots of dirt left, meaning she did not get a chance to wash them properly. Since the Mist came, plant life on the planet had dwindled drastically. People with knowledge of plants and nature became well-sought after specialists in an attempt to revive the world's greeneries.

"So what are you going to do?" she asked as I brushed back the fringe of her short dark hair. She was just shy a year older than I was at 31, yet her body, petite and lithe, was so much smaller than mine, her head at my shoulder at standing height. Sometimes I wonder how could such a small, fragile looking woman be strong enough to support me, especially at times like that, and I thanked everything from the sky to the earth for bringing us together.

I contemplated silently as she patiently awaited my answer. "I want to take the offer." It had been barely ten minutes since we sat down together, and already it felt like I've had years to think it through. My wife had that effect on me, clearing my mind, calming my soul. "I don't want to live for two weeks, just to leave you and Leila behind. I want to be there, for the important parts of your lives."

She looked up at me, my face reflected in her clear, hazel eyes. "Then go," she said gently. And as if she read my mind, she continued, "You don't have to worry about us. There's less you can do in the next two weeks than you can in your next five days."

"I'm just thinking, what about money? I have insurance that you can claim if I die, but I don't think 'cryogenic freezing' counts on anything."

The look of concern on my face must have been crystal clear, for her lips were pouted in annoyance. "I told you not to worry. Besides, the Forum's willing to leave us with enough money to last for a whole generation."

"Wait, really?" I replied in disbelieve.

"Yeah, so go. Freeze yourself!" she said excitedly, jabbing me playfully in the arms.

I squinted my eyes in wary, "You just want the money don't you."

A devilish smile stretched across her curved face. "Of course!" She

13

laughed a playful laugh. A mesmerising laugh, continuing her coltish jabs.

I could not feel her punches but I played along, raising my hands in a feeble block. She stopped suddenly, looking down at her lowered hands, fingers gripping each other tightly. Then I saw a drip of tear land on her wrist and I instinctively brought her into an embrace, her face buried in my chest.

Her sobs hurt me more than the Mist Poisoning ever did. More than losing my legs or my eyesight. More than the thought of being frozen in time. She let out a muffled, "Go."

"You cannot wait for me," I replied. I wanted to cry but no tears came to my robotic eyes. I had not asked about it, but apparently a trade off for my new eyes were the ability to cry. I wished they removed the ability to feel sad too. I repeated, "You cannot wait for me, understand?"

I felt her head nodding against my chest followed by a soft, "Got it."

Burying my face in her hair, taking in the smell of fresh grass and flowers that had practically fused with her body and soul, I told her calmly, "Let's go get Leila."

She took a few seconds to collect her breath. In between sobs, she nodded her head. When she raised her head to face me directly, her eyes were red from crying. In an attempt to cheer her up, I gave her my best smile. A lopsided grin she repeatedly told me was stupid. She chuckled and kissed me. She pulled apart and I leaned in again to steal a quick second one.

"I love you," she said, her breathing steadied. Her strong gaze returned.

I couldn't help but smile. "I love you too."

Three knocks on the door turned our attention to it. Professor Leah's voice echoed through from the other side, announcing, "I'm coming in!" Making good on her words, the door swung opened without hesitation or any consideration to our privacy and she walked in in strides. Agent G followed close behind.

Joan and I had struggled to untangle ourselves from out little cuddling session and I had a feeling my cheeks were reddening as the professor and the agent approached, an insinuating grin on her face.

"I see you two are making the best of this precious day?" Leah said. But her smile quickly faded as she apathetically continued, "But we've got to get to the point now. We don't have a lot of time. Being frozen doesn't mean you'll have any more than the estimated fifteen days. You'll still die once that time runs out."

G, who was carrying two chairs over from the dining area cut in, "Hells, Prof, you don't have to go all doom and gloom on them."

It hadn't really hit me just how dark and depressing her words were until G stated them. I must have flashed a look to convey my sudden 'enlightenment' for my wife tapped against my skull and called me a "Blockhead."

"Anyway," Leah pulled us back on track, "You have to choose five days for us to pull you out. It doesn't have to be specific dates. It can be events like your daughter's graduation or the day Game Station Ten comes out."

"Do I have to make a decision on all of it now?" I asked. "Can't I just give one, go under, wake up and give another?"

She replied, "You don't have to decide all of them now but I recommend you have at least two or three. We don't know in what order events will unfold and can't guarantee it even will," she held out a pen and a piece of paper. Simple equipments I felt for such an enormous undertaking. "But at the end of the day, when you wake up, let's not make it just to tell you your dreams have failed and you need to choose a new one, cause it'll take at least half a day to put you back under."

The situation seemed to engulfed me like a fog. I reached out and took the paper and pen from her, mind a blank. On the way over in the car with Matthews and G, I had a definite list in mind. Now though, with the act of writing them down, I hesitated like the day I asked Joan to marry me.

Leila's college graduation. Her wedding. The 20th anniversary for my marriage. My parents' nearing their death. Those were the five dates I had chosen previously.

"Milton," Leah said. I looked up from the empty paper that I had been staring at. "You have to choose."

I'm sure someone, somewhere, is asking the same question. If you could choose to live only X days in your life, which days would you choose? And someone, most likely drunk, will answer something stupid or joke about it. Why wouldn't they? It's an impossible thing, which makes the answer impossible as well. Yet there I was, in the break room for a government branch about to have my body frozen colder than the poles, and I have to make that impossible choice.

15

Joan took my hand in hers and I look to her smile for guidance. With that gentle expression, she said, "The first thing that comes to your head."

"The first thing," I repeated.

I looked down and I had my answer. Written in black on white.

Leila's college graduation

I traced my fingers over my daughter's name. I felt disgraced for writing something that beautiful in my ugly handwriting. I took a small breath and jotted down two more lines.

Leila's 18th birthday
Leila's wedding

Looking to my wife, I let slipped, "Our anniversary-"

"Don't you dare," she cut in. "Don't you dare waste a day on something otiose like that."

I couldn't help but grin at her words. "Since when do you use otiose?"

"Shut up!" She playfully pushed me away.

I laughed. She laughed. When I looked back forward I was met by G's crooked grin at our antics. On the other side of the fence, Leah's eyes were filled with what I'd come to know as pity.

My smile slipping, I handed her the piece of paper. "This will do for now."

Leah took the paper and pen from me and asked, "We'll have to do some paperwork."

"No need," I replied. "I'm gonna be dead in two weeks either way. Not much to lose at this point. Besides, I thrust you guys for some reason. And I'm sure my wife will kick all your asses if you don't hold up your end of the bargain."

Joan backed up my words with, "I will, you know. But in all seriousness, you can leave the paperworks to me after he goes under. Time is of the essence right?"

Leah and G stood up from their seats and my wife and I followed suit.

Then G announced, "Let's go find your daughter."

Year One, Part Four

They called it the Cryo-Tube. That's the name of the machine they'll use to freeze me. It sounded like some exotic dildo if you asked me. Joan and I walked hand in hand as we followed Professor Leah and Agent G down a long, white, spotless corridor. Even the floors were tiled white. A small black spot marked the end in the distant. Fifteen stories underground, the temperature chilled and the environment felt damp. Joan shivered and I took off my grey jacket and gently wrapped it around her.

"Your daughter and parents are waiting in the main chamber," Leah explained as our footsteps echoed down the hall. "That's where the Cryo-Tube will be stored at."

About two minutes into the walking; we could see a metal door at the end of path. Though from the distance, I judged we were only halfway there. It could have just been me and my new legs slowing everyone down. They were strong enough to walk now but moved stiffly, with a little wobble in the left with every step. I'm sure the plastic grating against my flesh would have hurt, but without the ability to feel pain, it became just a minor thought in the back of my mind.

Joan asked, "It's quite a walk isn't it?"

"Apologies," Leah replied. "We needed to access the underground river for the energy needed to power the Cryo-Tube. And this depth meant a more stable surrounding temperature, allowing us to better control the freezing temperature."

"Good, good," I replied blankly, nodding my head in a dumb daze. I didn't fully understand the explanation but the professor sounded really confident. I like that in people attempting to preserve my life.

We walked the rest of the way in silence. I admit that by the time we had reached the end of the hallway, I was panting a little. Can't really blame my stamina for that though. I'm dying. It's the way that works.

Leah placed her palm flat on a scanner on the left of the metal door and G did the same with another on the right. A soft beep from both machines cleared us to enter. The door made a rough grinding noise and descended into the ground, coming to a thumping halt once it levelled with the floor.

G bowed exaggeratedly and directed us in with a cheeky grin. "This way."

Once across the threshold, I heard the sound of sandals slapping the floor and found myself assaulted by a pint-sized girl, no taller than my chest. Her long auburn hair flailed wildly as Leila, my seven years old precious foster daughter came charging into my chest for a hug.

Expectedly, I began to fall backwards, my legs not strong enough to hold her weight. Joan however, placed a supportive arm behind me. I looked to her and she smiled reassuringly. Stabling myself with her help, I grinned back like an idiot.

"Daddy! This place is so cold!" Leila exclaimed excitedly, looking up at me with her hazel eyes and bubbly chin, her smooth white face like that of soap. She had her hands wrapped in pink cotton mittens, and wore an oversized leather jacket that reached down to her knees. The sleeves were rolled up to her elbow and she looked like, well, there's no other way to say this, a cute little hobo. "It's like Hillbury."

I bent over and snuggled my nose in her hair, "Your favourite-test place ever!"

We had taken a trip to Hillbury last year and saw snow for the first time. Leila was ecstatic. Even in the freezing temperature, she would drag me and Joan out to build snowmen and have snowball fights.

She giggled as I jokingly blew into her scalp. Softly, she repeated, "Favourite-test."

Looking up, I saw my parents walking towards me followed by Agent Matthews. My father, James Jones, wore a white singlet and jeans, having given his jacket to Leila. His whitening hair had receded to the point where half his scalp was visible. Unlike most men, he made no attempts to hide it, leaving his hair sloping to the sides. The muscles that once held up his rugged face had loosen, his skin having tightened till it outlined his bone structure. Thin but not frail, his hardened construction worker frame still lingered.

My mother on the other hand was quite chubby for her age. I suspected it was from the habit of sampling her own dishes from the time she was a cook. Stella was her name. She took after my grandmother with her rock brown hair and tendency to wear light dresses, as was the bright and green floral dress she had on that day. She looked no older than forty if you asked me, but both my parents were well into their late fifties, an age that many people of the time could never reach.

My father nodded to me with a smile, but I could see the indication behind his eyes that said he wanted to talk. I nodded back and, with some effort, pried Leila loose from her hug. With a smile, I reluctantly told her, "Why don't you show mommy around the place?"

At the thought of playing tour guide, she enthusiastically replied, "Okay!" and quickly reached over to grab Joan by the hand, impatiently dragging her away. "Come on mommy! Let's go!" G and Matthews followed after.

I smiled as I waved them off, and for the first time, I managed a good look at my surroundings. We were in a large square chamber, the walls lined with the same white that preceded us in the hallway before, with glass windows on the walls to the left and right, likely leading to rooms beyond them. In the centre was a large, metallic grey, well, rice cooker would be the best way to describe it. The Cryo-Tube had pipes running into it, with a large tank of liquid coolant at its side. A stepladder by its side was what I assumed the only way to get in. The thing was about twice my height and two meters in diameters. Consoles surrounded it at a distance, connected by wires and tubes, with scientists in spotless lab coats behind them. The entire scenery blinded me with its whiteness.

"Milton," my father greeted grumpily. "You're late as usual."

"Sorry dad," I replied. "Things are not exactly 'usual' though, so cut me some slack. Besides, I just found out grandpa was psychic."

Distressed, he rubbed his hands over his temple, nursing that fake headache he's always having. "It's not that we didn't want to tell you, it's just that your grandpa told us not to."

19

"That's just like that old fart," I mused. I used fart affectionately, like how some people call their friends pieces of shit. Or maybe I'm the only one that does that? I looked to my father again and asked, "Is there anything I should worry about with this place?"

My mother whispered to Leah, just loud enough that I could hear and be embarrassed. "That's just like Milly, always looking at the details."

"Mom..." I sighed under my breath.

She came over and gave me a hug, one which I nevertheless returned despite the offhand embarrassment. "You're just like your grandfather like that. Always into the details."

She pulled apart and I found myself reconnecting with my father's steely gaze. He continued, "Everything we see here seems good. Nothing 'shady' or the like. I know these guys when they were working with your grandpa. They're good souls. You can trust them."

The thing was, I didn't. But I did trust my parents. They had always been, in my eyes at least, great judges of characters. Not to mention the fact that my grandfather worked with these government blokes as well so that must have meant something.

I turned confidently to Leah, her lab coat and general bright dressing seemed to camouflaged her into the background. When I tried to look her in the eye, I felt like I was speaking to a floating head. "Okay, let's get this done."

She wheeled her head back a little in shock. "Really? No questions or doubts?"

"Plenty. But..." I shook my head. "My parents trust you. My wife has an eye on things. That's all good enough for me."

"This is a big decision. Are you sure you don't want to-"

I cut in, "I have two weeks left to live. Let's not waste more of that time," I looked over my shoulder to Leila showing Joan one of the control panels. "I want to be there for the days that matters."

My father said to Leah, "And if anything happens to my son, I'll personally find all of you and make sure you get what's coming."

My mother broke a grin, before pretending to sternly reprimand him. "Come on James, we have to be civil." She turned to me with another of her trademarked sassy smile.

I nodded back before turning to Leah, "You guys can fill me up with all the boring stuff when I wake up for whatever maintenance. Right now though, let's get this over with."

"Okay," Leah replied. "Let's get you prepped for freezing."

Year One, Part Five

The oversized grey shirt and long grey pants they had me wear handled like silk. I can only describe the feeling of wearing them as being hugged by water, smooth and fluid, rubbing each other without much friction. Leah explained that the clothings were made from special materials designed to help regulate and properly distribute heat while I was frozen to prevent any nerve damage from body parts being cooled separately. It sounded fancy enough that I just straight up trusted the explanation without question. The shirt had a hood to cover my head; and the sleeves and pants legs were made to be buttoned up to encase my body entirely in the material. Unbuttoned, they were slightly longer than my arms and legs and I looked like a child in a grown man's pyjamas.

I walked out of the changing room, pants legs dragging slightly along the floor, to the laughter of my family. Leila said I looked like a blue stick insect. Even my dad, serious as he was, cracked a chuckle. I must have looked really ridiculous, but I was okay with that as long as my family was happy.

"Milton," Leah called out to me from the giant machine that is the Cryo-Tube. "It's time."

With those two words, the light hearted daze that had lifted our spirits dissipated from the room almost instantaneously and a fog of grimness settled in its stead. I nodded to Leah and approached my family, my feet dragging the ground more than my pants.

I went up to my parents first. My ever cheerful mother and stern-faced father. "Thanks for getting me here," I told them from the bottom of my heart.

Whatever held up my mother must have snapped, for she broke into tears and embraced me. "Take care of yourself, Milly."

Returning the hug, I looked up to my father who could only manage a nod, one which I returned. I said, "I'll see you again."

She pulled apart from me, wiping at her tears. Once her eyes were relatively dry, she said between sobs, "I love you son."

"Love you too," I replied.

I ripped my gaze away from my parents, the pillars that raised me and groomed me to the man I am today. I could not have been more indebted to anyone else in my life. I faced my wife Joan, the light of my life.

She smiled to me and said, "Hey you."

"Hey yourself," I replied. Those were the first words we said to each other when I accidentally knocked into her on the streets all those years ago.

Joan placed her hands on my cheeks and I closed my eyes. Even though I could no longer physically feel, the memory of her touch welled up inside my head and I could imagine the warmth of her hands spreading through my face. I opened my eyes to see tears slowly rolling down her cheeks. I wiped them from the familiar curves and creases and gently kissed her.

With my best smile, I said, "See you soon?"

She smiled back, though holding in her tears made her squint. "Not if I see you first."

And then it was time for the most painful part of the day. I knelt down and turned to my daughter. I'm impotent, which meant I could never have a child. But Joan and I talked about it when we married and wanted one anyway. We went to an orphanage and there she was. Leila, my daughter with her auburn hair, scribbling drawings on paper after paper.

I looked at my little girl, a frown that never suited her worn on her face. She asked, "Are you going now, daddy?"

"Yeah," I replied, choking on tears that can never surface. "I'm going away for a long while now."

23

"When will you come back?" she asked.

That question tore at me. I had requested to be back, by earliest, her eighteenth birthday. But there were no guarantees if the freezing process would even work, or if the uncertain future would prove too uncertain to even happen.

Instead, I redirected the question, "When I come back," I said softly, "We'll go to Hillbury and play with snow again, okay?"

It worked. A small smile crossed her face as she lighted up slightly with an enthusiastic nod. It was a blatant lie though. Hillbury was, by flight, almost half a day away. To go there and return back to the Cryo-Tube in a single day was impossible. But I wanted the last image of my daughter to be a smile instead. A little selfishness on my part.

She wrapped her small arms around my neck and hugged me. I returned the hug, tighter than any I've ever given before, kissing her tenderly on her forehead. Painfully, my heart wretched as I pulled her apart. That was more painful than any other form of hurt I could ever feel physically with my nerves.

I smiled at her and said, "Take care of your mother okay?"

Without a verbal reply, she nodded her head. I got to my feet and turned to face the Cryo-Tube.

"Okay," I mumbled to myself. Agents G and Matthews came to my side. I nodded to them to show I was ready. "Let's do this."

The short walk to the machine felt longer than it looked. By the time I reached the stepladder, it felt like I had left a whole lifetime behind, yet I could only wish that I had more time to spend walking there. Up close, the machine was about twice my height, which was towering in scale. It was large, rounded, and metallic, like a boiler that had expanded. Everything seemed to have been made with stainless steel, even the foreboding looking ladder.

With the Agents' help, I slowly climbed up the ladder. My prosthetic legs fought to hold my weight as I ascended. By the time I got to the top of the machine, I was panting slightly, but otherwise fine. It might have been due the cold temperature underground but I did not sweat either. G and Matthews followed me up and we stood on the platform above.

Matthews pointed to a noticeable, one meter in diameter circular plate on the top of the Cryo-Tube and said, "Stand over there if you will," I followed his instruction.

"Okay man," G said, "Once the Prof gives the green light, the plate will lower you into the machine. Don't panic when that happens okay?"

I replied with a nervous, "Okay."

"Milton," Leah called out from below us. She was standing beside one of the control panels to my right with two other scientists. "When you're in the Cryo-Tube, a panel will seal you in from above. Once inside, there will be an oxygen mask. Put it on and press the button."

"What button?" I asked.

Matthews answered for her, "You'll know it when you see it." He took what I recognised as a palm sized ECG from his pocket and said, "This will hurt a bit," he pulled my shirt collar down slightly and placed the ECG in the middle of my chest. My body jerked as the device latched itself to my skin with a needle and suction, but I felt nothing.

Slightly surprised, G said, "Maybe not."

Leah continued, "The chamber will start to flood with the preservation liquid. Don't worry though. Your mask will pump in anaesthetics and oxygen once you are half submerged. Just tell me when you're ready and we'll start."

I looked to the two agents who gave me light nods of acknowledgement of what I'm about to do. Buttoning up my clothes and pulling up my hood, turning my hands and feet into wrapped up stumps, I turned to my family. All of them, including my daughter, gave me the smile that one puts on their faces when at a funeral. The look meant to support the loved ones who lived while they buried their dead. I found myself in the position of being both.

Without taking my eyes off my family, I gave a firm, "Ready!"

"Lower panel!" Leah shouted across the room. The people on the other side reacted, and the platform jerked and started to rumble and descend.

In seconds, I was knee deep in the machine. Waist deep. Chest deep. The last image I saw before my vision was blocked was of my family, standing hand-in-hand, strong smiles on their faces. With the same jerk as it had when it started, the panel came to a stop. A circular button lit up green in front of me, the oxygen mask, with a tube connected to it, placed in an alcove beside it. I picked up the mask and stuck it to my face. It was one of those with surgical glue that allowed it to be sealed tightly against the skin, but easy enough to remove with minimal tearing. A little like a bandage really.

"Milton," G called out. I looked up to the opening above to the agent peering down. "Good luck," he finished. I saw him pushed something – a button presumably – to his side, and a steel cover slowly slid shut overhead, covering the last shred of light I have to the outside world.

With no other source of communication, I looked to the glowing green button, my only source of light in the otherwise fully sealed tube. I could hear my own heart pounding, echoing and reverberating within the sealed container. With my wrapped hands, I pressed the button and the glow disappeared, plunging me into completes darkness.

I could not feel the liquid filling the tube but I could hear it sloshing around me. It must have been cold, for my body shivered and teeth clattered. Perhaps it was out of fear. I started breathing deeply in an attempt to calm myself down.

And a sudden thought came to me. *Did I turn off the kitchen stove when I left home for the surgery?*

Before I could get further into that thought, the panel above me slid opened. The light from the outside was blinding after being submerged in complete darkness, and my prosthetic camera eyes took much longer than a real eye would in adjusting to the change in brightness.

The shadowy figure of a man popped his head over. "Milton?" I recognised the voice as G's.

"G? What happened? Did something go wrong?" I asked, feeling slightly disoriented.

"What are you talking about?" he replied confused. I imagined him talking in my head. The ruffled brown hair. The horn-rimmed glasses. The scar on his lips. "Did something happen?"

"That's what I'm asking you," I replied, slightly irritated now. My eyes finally started to settle into the light and I saw G clearly. With a buzz cut. Another scar across his nose added to the one on his lips. His glasses were still the same though. "What the-" I mumbled in surprise.

I looked down and realised I was slumped against the corner of the tube, my body and clothings soaking wet with light blue liquid. As the situation started to dawn on me, I looked back up to G who seemed to have pieced together my thoughts from my reaction as well.

Unsure of what to do, I peeled off the oxygen mask – painless, of course – and awkwardly said, "So uh...long time no see?"

"Yeah," G replied, equally clunky in tone. "Seven years is pretty long."

Door to Tomorrow, Part One

The future is terrifying for any person, let alone an everyday school teacher like myself. When faced with just the talk of the future, most people recoil in uncertainty. Yet, when presented with the physical manifestation of it, we give either wonder or fear. Or sometimes, both.

As the platform rose from from the Cryo-Tube, I got to my feet, unbuttoning the custom pyjamas made for me, freeing my hands and feet from their silky prison. When the view of my surroundings came to light, I was awestruck by the sight of them. Not by the differences, but lack-thereof. The walls were still pearl white, and every machine and consoles were exactly where they were when I last saw them. Nothing had changed. There's no way I was seven years in the future, *Impossible!* my mind screamed. And yet, my gut knew it was the truth. The tone of the colour of the floor, the small scratch marks on the shells of the machines, the slightly shadier tone of the environment, every minute detail jumped at me. It was dizzying.

The platform screeched from its old parts – unmoved for three quarters a decade – as it came to a bumpy halt.

G stood beside me, scanning the entirety of my face, ignoring the fact that my body was soaked to the bones with the blue liquid used to freeze me. I looked to him quizzically, asking, "What's wrong?"

He cracked a smile, "You haven't age a day."

27

"Why do you sound more surprise than I am?" I asked. "You guys are in charge of this project right?"

"Heh, you're right about that."

I took a step forward, only to have G reach out and grab my arm as my legs buckled.

"Take it slow," he said, also removing the paste-on ECG from my chest in the process. "Your body's seven years ahead of your mind."

"Right," I replied, suddenly feeling the daze. With G's help, I descended the ladder, followed by the agent himself. I glanced around the chamber, scanning through the men and women in lab coats working at their respective consoles, not even once looking me in the eye. "Where's Professor Leah?" I asked.

"The freezing canister malfunctioned so we had to pull you out on short noticed," G replied, "She's at home and just got notified."

Up till that moment, I had assumed the agents and the professor had just lived at E.F.A Headquarters. I have no idea why I thought that. I guessed the trio just had that air of professionalism and work centric personality about them. It didn't even occur to me the possibility that they had lives outside of work. Then the question hit me.

G passed me a walking stick, which I waved away, and paced himself beside as I walk, directing me to the changing room with his steps. I followed, leaving a trail of blue goop behind. I casually asked, "What about Agent Matthews? Home with the wife and kids?"

As soon as the question left my mouth, I could tell something was wrong. G slowed his pace and stared down at his feet. "He uh...passed away last year," he choked out.

"What?" the news hit me harder than it should. "I just saw him ten minutes ago."

"Yup," G replied grimly. "It would seem that way to you."

That was the first mistake I made in my short, fifteen days journey. One of many I admit. Hindsight is twenty-twenty, but foresight we have none. From where I stood then, what I had said was not only selfish, but stupid. In turn, my solution seemed equally retarded in answer.

"Sorry about your loss."

The agent took a deep breath through his nose and changed the subject. "We've notified your wife that we're bringing you out. She's got something planned for you. I'll bring you to her location. Professor Hullway will be there as well."

"Okay," I replied, nodding blankly as he opened the door to one of the rooms.

"I'll meet you at the entrance once you're ready." He handed me a plastic card attached to a blue lanyard. The card had my face, from what I recalled as a photo I took eight years ago. "I hope you remember where that is?"

After digging deep into my senses, I replied, hopefully, with wit, "Like it was just yesterday."

G bid himself off with a soft nod of the head. I turned away from the agent and entered through the door into what seemed to be a medical bay. Though I had mostly dripped myself dry of a significant amount of the freezing liquid, blotches or water still formed when I walked into the room. The place was small, barely 4x4 in meters. There was a white gurney to one side, cornered by an ECG machine and a counter top filled with medical equipments, sided by a single chair. From a stethoscope to swaps, to syringes, to pills, and bottles, even a set of surgical tools on a tray, the table seemed fully stocked for a small emergency.

From behind, the gruff voice of a man said, "If you would take a seat on the bed, Mr. Jones."

I turned just as a man with a blond crew cut, dressed in one of the many lab coats, cuts by me through the door, a clipboard in hand. He pulled out the chair and sat down. When he realised I had continued to stand in front of the already closing door, dumbfounded without moving, he lowered his clipboard and pointed to the white gurney, gesturing me to sit.

But that is so white! What if I dirty it? I wanted to ask. Stupid question, I know. And I know there were more pressing queries. But my mind's not known for being serious. Pushing back the urge to be a complete ass, I dragged my drenched self over to the bed and sat awkwardly at the edge of the mattress.

Once I was settled, the man introduced himself in as monotonous a voice as I've ever heard in my life. "I'm Doctor Parker, I'm just going to check to see if you're showing any negative feedback from the freezing process." The man had a young face, free of blemishes, and deep hazel eyes. There was no doubt in my mind he was just in his early twenties.

"Uh...okay," I replied casually, staring around the room to take in more details, including the eye chart I now saw behind the door. Not that it helped me understand the surrounding much. It was as boring as any

29

clinic. There was even a poster on the empty wall that had a cat hanging on a branch with the bolded words, 'Hang in there!' underneath. "Ask away."

"Do you feel cold?" the doctor asked in his blank tone.

I replied, "I uh...don't feel anything." I of course, was talking about my fucked up nerves damaged by Mist Poisoning.

He looked up at me with that annoyed look that teenage girls gave. You know, the one where they roll their eyes as if they're talking to a retard? The doctor just gave me one and said, "I meant, do you feel like your body is shivering?"

Admittedly, I was kind of pissed at his tone of voice, but I kept it together and replied, "No. Why is that by the way? I don't seem cold at all."

Again, Doctor Parker lowered his clipboard. But this time, he openly gave me the face that read, Are you retarded? Before answering, "We lowered your body temperature back to normal before bringing you out." He added the cocked eyebrow that said, *dipshit.*

"Oh," was what I replied, though I had half a mind to punch him now.

He continued with his next question. "Do you feel any discomfort?"

"Like?" I asked.

This time, he sighed audibly. "Like any migraines or feeling of nausea?"

"No," I replied. However, I added on before he could continue, "And could you not be such an asshole?"

"What are you talking about?" he replied, a visible look of anger on his face as he scrunched his brows at the accusation.

"Like your tone and that eye rolling," I flailed my hands exaggeratively. "Was that really necessary?"

He took a deep breath and, finally, the sound of emotions entered his voice. Though what his anger sounded like was not really that much of an improvement to apathy. "Listen, Mr. Jones, this is my job. I've worked here for the past two years, looking at your vitals twenty-four-seven. I'm not Professor Leah. I don't have any emotional attachment to this work. For me, and most of the others, this is just another job that we will do for a few years before getting moved to some other field."

He had not really answered my question though, so I pushed on, "Your point?"

30

Parker let out an angry grunt. "My point? I don't care who the fuck or how special you think you are. To me, you're not special. You're just a job. You don't get to act all high and mighty just because you're the 'subject' okay? After what? Five years? I'm moving on again. You're a passing phase. So sit down and answer the fucking question you pampered twit, and you can go off and enjoy all the money the government's giving your family."

I got up to my feet, now furious myself. "You think I'm doing this for the money?"

"Yeah," he replied without hesitation. "Why else would you volunteer to become a guinea pig like this?"

I had never been as angry at anything in my life up till that point. I raised my voice, which I was sure boomed even outside the sealed room. "How about for my family? How about to be there for my daughter in the future instead of leaving her fatherless? Huh? Have you ever thought of that?"

Parker backed into the corner in shock and fear, staring at me wide-eyed as if he had seen a demon and was about to be eaten. I'll admit, I was kind of hungry.

Despite his visible terror, I continued anyway. "Or maybe," I lowered my tone. "Just maybe, and hear me out on this crazy theory here. I just don't want to fucking die!"

My breathing was heavy, and I was sure my mechanical eyes looked just as crazed as psychopathic biological ones.

I took a deep breath as I ended the conversation with the speechless doctor. "I'm feeling much better now Doc. Thanks."

Without looking back, I exited the medical bay.

Door to Tomorrow, Part Two

On the list of weird things I had ever done, walking through the halls of the E.F.A Headquarters after waking up would have been in my top ten; along with being cryogenically frozen and that one time I ate a broccoli blindfolded and somehow managed to guess sausages instead.

For me, I had walked through the halls in the same black jeans and blue shirt just a few hours ago. Yet, everything seemed foreign in one way or another. The once pearl-white walls had a grey tint of age to them that, to people who saw them everyday for the past few years, would not have noticed. Nor would they have noticed the fade of the blue of the carpeted floors. The stain on the windows hit my senses and memories hard, but definitely not as strong as what I saw after them as I walked out the sliding glass door to G, standing beside a black sedan just as when I first saw him.

Still looking up as I walked to the car, I asked, "What happened to the sky?"

G turned his attention upwards, only to show a short look of puzzlement before realising what I was talking about.

"The Mist has been getting lower," he explained. "And as it gets lower, it gets denser, since there's not as much surface area around its atmosphere level."

I remembered the last time I saw the sky, it was a light teal. At that moment though, standing there with G, it was noticeably sea blue. Though light still managed to shine through, the surroundings were slightly darker in exposure.

"Is that what I'm trying to stop? The Mist from engulfing us?" I thought of my own predicament with Mist Poisoning and how exposure to the gas had led me on a path to certain death.

"Maybe," G replied. He headed around to the driver's side as I entered into the passenger's. "But I highly doubt it," he finished as we both closed our doors behind us.

He started up the car and we both buckled up. I asked him, "Why not?"

As the car revved out from the pathway and onto the road that lead through the guardhouse, he replied, "Cause the Mist will be on ground level in about a decade. Nowhere close to your hundred and thirty-two years."

"Thirty-two?" I replied, confused. "Right! Seven years in the future. But won't everyone just end up dead in ten years at this rate?"

"Don't worry your time travelling head about that," G said as the guardhouse raised the gates for us to pass through. "We're already working on something for that. It's quite cool actually."

"And what 'master plan' is that?"

"Oh, you'll see when we get to the city."

"And where are we going exactly?"

"That's..." G's tone of voice softened considerably. "That's um...you'll know it when you get there."

The city had expanded over the years and for a moment, while we drove through the refurbished outskirts, I could not believe my eyes that we were in the same New Roagnark that I grew up in.

"It's just Roagnark now," G corrected. "We got rid of the 'New' a few years back."

The city had expanded by over a dozen streets, with much more pedestrians on the road than there were before. I wondered how many of those walking around were my students from half a decade back. How many of them are people I could have met had I not been terminally ill. How many were living the life I could otherwise had.

We crossed back into the part of the city that was familiar to me. The older inner portions had buildings that were around my time, and suddenly the streets and roads were as clear to me as the back of my hands. One detail stood out from the older buildings though. Hundreds of glass covered walkways connected each of the structures, spanning over the roads like human delivery tubes.

As I scanned the sights in wonder, I asked G, "Is that the 'solution' to the Mist?"

"Yeah," the agent replied, "That, and the underground road that's being dug out right now to extent the infrastructure below."

"Amazing. And all this happened in seven years?" I asked, astounded at the progress.

"A lot of things happened in the past half a decade Milton. The team assigned to research a method to protect us from the Mist initially wanted to build a giant glass dome over the city."

"That's stupid," I replied without thinking.

"That's what they thought as well. So they came up with this instead." He turned the vehicle up one of the familiar highways out to the eastern suburbs. "We're in the process of connecting the ventilation system of the entire city to the Sun Dome. And we're building more of them plant domes around the city as well to provide clean air for everyone once the Mist settled down."

My wife, Joan, worked as a herbalist at the Sun Dome, researching ways to repopulate the dying plant life around the globe. Her knowledge of plants and their chemicals from making medicines ended up being used to research on which plants were better suited for growth in different areas of the polluted world. "Did my wife help with any of this?" I asked. Something in me already knew the reply.

"Helped?" G laughed at my words. "She's one of the people leading the team on the project. Just five years ago, she got a Doctorate in Environmental Sciences and made a few high profile breakthrough in both medicine and plant growth research. It was her idea to build more domes and connect them to the city as well."

I couldn't help but smile. My grin must had stretched from ear to ear. A small part of me couldn't believe just how amazing my wife had become, only to be overshadowed by the part that knew she was fantastic to begin with.

G continued, "In a way, she's saving the world. Her ideas are being adopted by the rest of the Five Cities and construction progress have been beyond smooth." He passed a quick glance of pride my way. "Must run in your family, saving the world. First your grandparents, now your wife."

"We usually don't let people into the family until they've at least stopped a falling plane," I joked.

G laughed, "You'll be up there with them in a hundred odd years. Saving us from the end of the world, fire burning across the lands, monsters attacking helpless damsels. You'll ride to their rescue on a hover bike with a plasma blasters, shouting out one-liners with hordes of demons chasing you down."

"I'd more likely hit them with a walking stick at the rate my body's going."

"Ah, you'll be fine," G waved off my walking stick idea. "You're here aren't you? That means you're a survivor!"

As we continued down the road, I recalled the path would lead us pass the old graveyard. A question hit me. "You mind if I ask about Matthews."

There was a short pause from G before he replied, "Sure."

Making sure to be more sensitive in my questioning, though unsure just how sensitive one can be in asking questions like that, I asked, "How did he, you know..." I didn't finish.

G took his eyes off the road for a second to look at me and nodded, indicating he was comfortable with talking about it before returning his attention to the streets. "There was um...there was a robbery at this restaurant. When the cops came, he and the rest of the people there were held hostage, including his family." He paused and took a deep breath after that. I sort of knew where the story was going. "Him being him, tried to talk the perps out from the whole situation. From what the hostages said, Matts almost succeeded too. But cops got anxious and charged in at the wrong time. He got caught in the crossfire. Dead at the scene."

"I'm..." I managed to pause my body before I finished my sentence, running over the words to make sure they were right. "I'm sorry. For your loss." It was the same sentence I said to him back at the lab, but nothing else seemed to fit.

"You know, after that day we met you and put you to freeze, he talked about you a lot," G continued, shooting right pass my condolence. He must have heard them countless times by then. "Said you inspired him to a be a better person. Started going out more, making more friends, and doing more charity work and all that."

"But I didn't do anything," I replied truthfully.

"That's what I said when I asked him. What about you made him want to change?" G answered, a tone of surprise at the similar reply I gave. "He said you were a symbol of hope for him that things will be better. He reasoned that...believed that, you were going to make it to year hundred and thirty-nine. That meant the world would last at least that long as well. You were his hope that there will be a future."

I was unsure how to reply and could only sit in silence even when he finished speaking. It seemed G didn't knew how to continue from there either, and we rode the rest of the trip in quiet contemplation. At least, that was the case until we reached the graveyard which earlier, I thought we were going to pass. Instead, I let out a small gasp as G took a turn into the road that led up to it.

We called them graveyards but that's not entirely accurate. They were more of an underground catacomb made to look like a 'yard'. The road we turned into lead up to a building, a church atop a small hill in the middle of a suburban forest of houses.

As the car pulled up the drop-off point, I asked numbly, "Who are we visiting?"

G turned off the engine and as the noise winded down, replied, "I think it's best if you see for yourself."

36

Door to Tomorrow, Part Three

One thing I've never believed in was divine powers. God didn't create the world in a week and the Day of the Mist certainly wasn't a way to punish sinners. My grandfather once told me that we had just one life in this world, and that was it. No afterlife or happily ever after when we pass. And because we had just this one chance at living, we had to make each and every second of it count. What we leave behind after we're dead is our legacy, and it's our responsibility to make that shine as brightly as possible. I think that idea's much more beautiful than anything a deity could represent.

I left G outside as the large, oak double door of the church closed behind me, the dimness of the building settling into view. There was only one pathway from the entrance pass the marble stoup. I crossed the container of holy water without interacting with it and into the main hall of the small church.

Long wooden benches lined the aisle that lead to the bema, the extended platform from which clergymen would preach from. The body of Jesus Christ was portrayed into the stained glass window behind the podium. The only source of light came through the body of the son of God. Christianity was one of the few things that made it through the Day of the Mist. In the face of almost certain destruction, I guess some people needed hope and spiritual support more than food or shelter.

Sitting nearer to the aisle on the left front bench were the silhouettes of two people. A tall, pony-tailed woman in a glowing white lab coat, and a shorter figure with clipped and wavy auburn hair. There were no guesses needed to know who they were.

"Joan," I called out to my wife in a nervous, almost inaudible whisper. "Leila."

My heart skipped a beat when the pony-tailed woman twitched at my voice. A wave of insecurity drowned me in a flash flood. What if she doesn't recognise me? Does she even remember my name? All my worries were moot however, when in less than five seconds, she had crossed the length of the church and ran into my chest in a tight embrace, face buried in my chest.

She lifted herself off and stared face-to-face with me. Her hair, once dark like the night sky, were now lighter, akin to charcoal. Thin creases, barely visible, ran through her forehead. Aside for the length of her hair, Joan looked almost the same as she did seven years ago. Her lab coat was ragged with patches of dirt, as I had assumed it would, and she still wore her patented style of shorts and dirt stained white shirt underneath.

As her hazel eyes scanned my face as frantically as I scanned hers, our stares met and she broke out with a smile. Though not openly weeping, balls of tears rolled down her cheeks. "Hey you," she croaked.

My heart melted at the familiar voice, soothing me both emotionally and physically, and I let out a breath I didn't even knew I held. "Hey yourself."

On the way over, I had dozens of questions deluging in my head to ask when I met her. *How are you? Is Lelia doing good in school? So you're a hero now?* But with my wife in front of me, all those questions disappeared, and it felt as if we had not parted for more than a day. For me at least, that was the truth. I had after all, just woken from what was basically a nap.

I asked, "Where's Leila?"

The smile slipped from Joan's face. Just slightly. Barely noticeable. But I could tell. I had always been able to know. It's one of those things about loving someone deeply. Something was wrong and she was putting up a strong front.

She turned to the other figure that remained on the bench and called out, "Leila, come say 'hi' to your dad."

If I was any older, I would probably have had a heart attack the

38

moment the girl stood up. Dragging her feet across the aisle, my daughter was the epitome of proof that I was, indeed, seven years into the future from my previous day.

Leila was at the height of my chin, almost twice what she was when I last saw her. Her auburn hair had a slick glow to it, kept short and combed into a neat wave, an ocean of red. She wore a black leather hoodie, a white shirt underneath it, and jeans so blue it really should just be called black by then. She wore glasses too. A pair of sharp-edged, grey browline spectacles that fitted gently on her nose. Since the day she was adopted, it was known that she was slightly myopic and would need glasses one day. I was just glad that they had enhanced the sharpness of her hazel eyes instead of negating them.

Almost warily, she looked up to me, and with a tone so apathetic that I felt my heart clenched in sudden, overwhelming sadness, she greeted, "Hey."

Holding back the croak that attempted to make its way up my throat, I replied, "Hi." That was not a greeting between a parent and child. That was how you'd greet a stranger. "How are you?"

"Good," was her one worded reply as she directed her gaze to her white sneakers.

I squatted slightly so I could be exactly at her height and tried, "How's school?"

She looked back to me with a quick snapping stare of annoyance before looking away, "Okay I guess."

Without noticing, I had raised my shaking hands and cupped them around her shoulders. She jolted with shock when I did so and pushed my arms aside, stepping back as a look of rage flashed across her face.

Joan cried out in shock, "Leila!"

And in returned, my daughter, the same one who I had raised for the first four years since her adoption, snapped at me. "DON'T TOUCH ME!" she shouted, her voice echoing throughout the empty church, tears streaming down her hazel eyes.

In that split second of distraction, whatever subconscious part of my mind that controlled my mechanical legs gave way and I fell to my knees, arms still held out in shock. I could hear Joan sobbing silently behind me. I wanted to cry, to ball my eyes out, but my implants would not let me.

"You were gone!" Leila screamed, sweeping her arms in an attempt

39

to wipe me from her vision. "Just like that! You climbed into that stupid machine and you were gone for seven damn years, just like that!"

"Lei..." I attempted to wheeze out her name.

Another burst of anger crossed her face. "Don't 'Leila' me! Do you know what it's like? People asking me, 'Where's your dad?' and I have to tell them you're dead!" Her tone softened as she was overwhelmed by her crying. Between the incoming sobs, she continued, "You ju-just decided to go and you think y-you c-can just come back and every-everything will be okay? Just come back a-and treat me like I'm seven and everything will be fine?"

"I didn't think...didn't know you were..." The words caught the tip of my tongue with a pick and wouldn't let go.

She wiped away a round of her tears only for another gush to cover her cheeks again. "Didn't t-think what?" She took a deep breath to calm her sobs. "T-that I would miss you? My friends talk about how their dad's don't understand them. How they're old and don't know what it's like to be a kid. I'm fourteen now, dad. You've been gone for half my life. That's half of me you've never met!"

I stared at my daughter, unable to reply. Finally, she shook her head, disappointed at my lack of a comeback and headed for the door, walking past me in the process.

"I can't wait for you to come back," she murmured just as she passed.

Joan called out, "Leila!" We watched her walk away. Putting a gentle hand on my shoulder, she told me, "I'll be right back." She went after our daughter.

I looked up at the stained glass image of Jesus, the man who was said to return at the end of days to judge mankind. In the between, he inspired hope and dedication in his followers, something which I was unable to do even with my own daughter. But I'm not God or some divine being. I had never claimed to be. Just human, that's all I ever was and will be, and something such as indisputable devotion is something I can never expect from people. Like all other humans, I make mistakes, and climbing into the Cryo-Tube might have been the biggest of my life.

I wished there was some important life lesson that I learnt then, knelt on the floor alone, unable to cry or feel physical pain to numb me. The only thing I got out of the experience was that at the end of my one hundred and thirty-nine years, I would likely have to face the end of the

world as I did the aftermath of that outburst.
    Alone.

Door to Tomorrow, Part Four

As the elevator descended to the basement of the church to the graveyard below, I contemplated the metaphorical descend as similar to my relationship with my daughter. On a way down to hell. I shared this thought with Joan, to which she said I'm being melodramatic and Leila was just going through a phase.

Professor Leah Leslie Hullway had joined us shortly after my daughter's outburst. "She's right. You're just over-thinking it," she agreed to Joan. Her blonde hair had lost some of its shine in the past seven years and she had chosen to forgo the lab coat ensemble in favour of a yellow sleeved dress and a thin white cotton jacket, colouring in a shade of perkiness to the otherwise moody atmosphere. "Give her some time."

With a sigh, I could only reply, "Yeah." I thought of how Leila had requested to return home first without even saying goodbye. After some discussion, some gritted words, and more crying, Joan relented and had G escort Leila home.

A ding signalled that the elevator had reached its floor. Though we called it a graveyard, the place was more of a crematorium. The expanding Mist meant less places to build and bury bodies, forcing the five cities to expand downward to sustain the slowly increasing population.

Stepping out into the graveyard which stretched for almost two hundred meters in all directions, we were greeted by rows and columns of urns placed squarely on marble-white pedestals, each unique in their own designs. Some were vase-like, with intricate patterns etched into the ceramic, while a few styled themselves as busts of the deceased's heads. Long fluorescent tubes lined the ceilings, bathing the room in bright white light. The floors were covered by stone slab tiling.

"Who are we visiting?" I asked as we walked down the aisle of the dead, even though I already knew the answer somewhere within me. "Is it my parents?"

The ensuing silence from the two ladies confirmed my suspicion and I knew immediately which were the two urns the moment they entered my sight. Settled in the middle of a field of painted ceramics and carved stone urns, were two plain ones placed side-by-side. No special designs or elaborate details. Just a pair of round urns, plain clay brown and grey.

I stopped right between the urns, the women not questioning how I knew. I just knew. I guess it's like those people who were blinded when young and their hearing improved as compensation. When your entire body loses the ability to physically feel anything, emotionally, the mind tries to balance things out. Maybe. I'm completely grasping at straws here.

Looking down on the golden name plate with 'James Jones' etched into one and 'Stella Jones' into the other, I found my legs wobbling and placed two hands on the pedestal of my mother to steady myself, Joan supporting me with a helping hand on my elbow.

"When was this?" I asked.

Joan answered, "About a year after you went under," she paused, sensing I needed the short time to centre myself after the news. "In their sleep. Same day. Peaceful."

"I should have been there," I said to no one in particular. Well, that was a lie I guess. I was trying to talk to my parents, knowing full well that such a thing was not possible. "I am a selfish asshole. Leila's right. I didn't think anyone would miss me. Not her. Not you. Not even my parents."

I recalled how as a child, my father would come back late from work and, despite his fatigue, would tutor or play with me. My mother would wake up early in the morning, earlier than I did, just to get me up and ready for school, never once a peep of objection on her part.

"What kind of son am I? Can't even take care of his parents in their

43

golden years." To me, it felt like my illness, this Mist Poisoning, was just an excuse to be lazy, even though the logical part of me was yelling that it would not have made any difference. "I should have just died seven years ago."

"Okay," Joan cut in, a tone of mixed annoyance and concern in her voice. She dragged me by my arm and turned me to face her. "Listen to me Milton Jones, you are my husband, and I love you. To the death. But this is not your fault!"

"But—"

"No buts!" she raised her voice just slightly, loud enough to shut my advances. "Not your parents, not Leila, not even Matthews. None of them is your fault!"

Leah cut in, "She's right. You were going to die in two weeks anyway. You wouldn't be here to know about all these things if that was where you ended."

Still rejecting the reasons of logic, I fought my case, "But if I died then, at least it would have been the end of a chapter for everyone. You will mourn me, you will miss me for awhile, but at least everyone will know that I'm dead!"

"Milton..." Joan tried to put a reassuring hand on my shoulder but I took a step away in hesitation.

I looked at my wife beseechingly. Pleading for what though, I do not know. "I'd rather die and be a memory, than live and be someone's false hope."

Leah cut in, "They were proud of you." I turned to face the professor. Her looks conveyed both pity and regret, and a certain understanding that I wasn't sure where from. "Your parents were so proud of you. Their son, about to save the world."

Again, Joan, turned me to her and I stared into her strong gaze, sharpening my own strength in the process. "It's not your fault. Things change, people die. But we keep walking."

No longer able to hold her stare, I turned to my parents' urns and placed a hand on each of them, "I love you both. So much." Had I kept my ability to cry, tears would likely pour out of my eyes with enough to fill a bucket. The lack of physical pain also meant that heartache was not possible.

After catching my breath and composing myself, I turned back to my wife and was surprised again by how well she knew me, ever after all these years. "You're going back aren't you?"

"Yeah..." I replied warily.

She took my hands in hers and leaned in for a deep kiss. "You don't want me to come with you, am I right?"

Initially, I could only smile in acknowledgement. Somehow though, I managed to find the strength to speak. "You should go take care of Leila. She needs you more than I do now."

She smiled back reassuringly, the ones you get when others are trying to tell you everything will be okay. "I love you."

We kissed again. "I love you too."

And with no more from either of us, I turned away from my wife of six years for me, and thirteen years for her. I could hear Leah discussing with Joan about my transportation, guaranteeing the latter that she would bring me back to E.F.A Headquarters safely.

The professor caught up with me as we neared the elevator, leaving my wife to pay her respects to her parents-in-law while I reminiscence about my childhood with them. The scrapped knee that my father tried to disinfect with his whiskey before my mother took over for a gentler approach. The phone they had refused to get for me unless I scored A's for my exams, but ended up buying it for me anyway.

"The thing about elevators," Leah said in her musical foreign accent as we stepped into said contraption, snapping me out of my trance. "Is that they go up as well." She pressed the button for the ground floor and the door closed behind.

I replied, "That's one way to look at things."

"I know how you feel; you know," she said with her eyes to the floor, scanning her snow-white shoes, perhaps for stains or blemishes to rid, given her immaculate look. "The insecurities, the fear. The confusion of seeing the world passing by you in leaps and bounds with a single blink."

Without meaning to, I let out a derisive snort. "And how could you possibly understand that?"

Calmly, not sounding the least bit insulted, she replied, "Because I'm twenty years older than my body."

Confused at her proclamation, I turned to look at her and our eyes met. I still exclaimed, "What?"

Holding onto my gaze, she explained, "I was the initial test subject for the Cryo-Tube prototype," The elevator doors slid opened noiselessly.

45

The light from beyond the stained glass Jesus crystallized her face in a disco of colours which made her blissful smile all the more strange. "I'm like the monkeys that went to space."

Door to Tomorrow, Part Five

There are two kinds of people. The ones who had their path in life chosen for them, and those who don't. The destined and the blank page. Perhaps you were born into a wealthy family, meant to take over the family business, or a child genius who always knew you were going to live a life of science. Maybe even someone born with some mental defect that prevented you from doing anything, destined to live a life constrained by your disability. Personally, I think those are the lives that are easy. For those of us that are set down a course we would need to chart ourselves, we are given the heavy responsibility of making decisions. It doesn't matter if we were derailed from our destined path or were born a blank slate. Once a life of decisions is chosen, we must expect to live with regrets.

Professor Leah Leslie Hulway was one of those that had her life set from the get-go. She was born to nothing, with null to her family name. She was destined for obscurity. "We were simple folks, just trying to get by everyday," she said as the church disappeared from us in the rear-view mirror, the setting sun behind it. "Dad was a grocer and mom a housewife. Had a baby sister two years younger than me who couldn't attend school for a year since we did not have enough money."

The bug-like yellow car she drove turned tightly as we headed back onto the small road that would lead us back to E.F.A Headquarters.

"How did you end up here?" I asked, looking at her rather solemn face.

I found the professor easier to talk with compared to the others I've met since I woke up, even more so than my wife. There also seemed to be a mutual attraction, though neither sexual or romantic. If I had to put a finger on what it was, I'd say it was more of curiosity.

She lingered on the question a moment, opening and closing her mouth as she attempted to form words before replying in an almost musically sad tone. "In the end, we could only afford school for one of us. At first I wanted my sister to go, but she practically cried me into submission. Said that I was always the smarter of the two of us."

She drove silently for a few minutes, and I waited intently for her to continue her story. The sun cut off at the horizon, bathing the surrounding suburban buildings with shingles that seemed aflame.

Just when I thought that perhaps the topic was too sensitive for her to want to elaborate, she continued, "So my sister gave up her bright future. She had all that potential and she decided to past all of that to me. One thing let to another, and I ended working here, at the E.F.A as the decoder for your grandfather."

"You knew my grandfather?" I exclaimed in genuine surprise, before remembering that her entire career had been built around deciphering his predictions.

"Before that I was just an intern. Then one day, your grandfather walked in, pointed to me and said, 'She'll be my translator! Which was weird at the time, cause he was speaking perfect English by my standard." She laughed at the memory and I could not help but smile. That was how my grandfather was as a person after all. And my fond memories of the old man had not faded, even after the discovery of his secret life. Leah continued, "You can imagine my surprise when I realised who he was. Back then, the E.F.A just got started. Barely a decade old, and this guy was already a legend, and I was to decode his visions."

"I know it's rude to ask," I said nervously, "But how old are you?"

"Physically, I'm thirty-four years old, same as you. Physically at least," she replied matter-of-factly. "But I've been alive for fifty-four years now."

I did the quick math, coming to the conclusion she had been frozen for twenty years total. "So you're actually older than me?"

She chuckled as I said so, "You're kind of rude, aren't you? First you ask a girl her age, now you're calling her old?"

"I'm an asshole," I replied. "It's in my blood."

"Oh, I know. It was in your grandfather's blood too. Old man wouldn't stop insulting people even when we begged." We were now on the main road back to the headquarters, circling around the city instead of going through. G must have taken the long route to show me the progress of the construction. Leah continued, "But yeah, I am older than you. I was born eighteen years after the Mist entered. I started working with your grandfather the same year you were born."

"What was he like back then?" I asked suddenly, too entranced by the tale to think properly about my interruption.

However, the professor trailed onto my topic without even skipping a beat, as if her words danced from track to track. "He was kind of a big deal. All these stories of how he saved the world from death and destruction. How he helped rebuild the city after the Mist. Of course, I was barely an adult back then, and the population of the world was so small after all the natural disasters that I took all those stories as just that, stories. Didn't stop him from embellishing in them though. The man had some ego."

I recalled as a child how he would often tell exaggerated tales of his youth. "Sounds about right."

"Anyway," she continued, "We worked together to decipher his latest premonition. The one you're part of right now. See, the lyrics said, 'with my blood in his vein'. That meant someone who carried his blood. And 'My son to son' meant you, the son of his son. But you were already born by then, so there was no way you would live for over a hundred years. Unless we clone you." She stopped for a moment, as if reminiscing on that idea before saying, "But that was too expensive they said. And 'From limped till the end', well, that's self explanatory. When you become disabled."

"So you guys knew I was going to be crippled?"

"We knew it was going to happen, but not the how or the when," she defended, still focused on the road as the large dome of the headquarter building came into view. "All we knew was your disability would be the starting point. We didn't know it was going to be Mist Poisoning of all things. Once we deciphered the song, we started a think tank to find a solution to preserve your life for the hundred plus years. Within a few

49

months, the Cryo-Tube prototype was created. I volunteered, turned myself into ice for twenty years, and here I am."

Pulled back to the initial question that got us sidetracked into the conversation in the first place, I asked, "So what happened to you when you first came to?"

She took a deep breath, as if gathering strength for what she was about to say next. "I was like you, in and out every few years for maintenance. But it was always for just a couple of days before going in again. At first I was frozen for a year. Twice. Then three. And five. And finally ten."

The car slowed down as we pulled up on the side of the highway. The topic apparently not just sensitive, but draining for the professor. I placed a hand on her slim shoulder, and in what I thought was a pretty weak attempt at comfort, told her, "You don't have to tell me anything you don't want to. Like maybe you were all wrinkly when you came out. I can't live with not knowing."

She laughed with a genuine smile, teeth shining through and all. "You really are an asshole, you know that?" She laid her head against the headrest and wrapped her hand over mine, as if to gain strength. "After that five years gap, I came out and found out my parents had passed away. They didn't want to wake me cause they thought my work was more important than them. I argued with my sister about that whole incident and I went back in with our relationship in pieces."

I wanted to ask what happened afterwards, but as if reading my mind, she took a grip of my hand and brought in down to be wrapped in her other, cupping my single fist in both of her palms.

With a voice so gentle that it could only be trumped by that of my wife, Leah said with two drops of tears rolling down her cheeks, "Give it time. I know it may seem like your daughter hates you now, but trust me when I say hate doesn't last forever."

"Your little sister—" I began asking.

However, she cut me off. "We're fine. She's not so little any more but we're fine," she shook my hand as if confirming the situation. "We have lunch together every month and I go to her place on the holidays. Turkey dinner. Every time. No idea why. You just have to give it time. And you have all of that in the world right now."

"Turkey dinner," I said, smiling.

She let go of my hand and returned to the wheel. "Yeah."

50

The car started again and we were back on the road in a matter of seconds. We drove the last few miles in silence, listening to the hum of the engine as I contemplated on what to do next. As we headed up the road that let to the guardhouse, Leah held her card out the window, with the same beam of light as before scanning it, the grates rising to let us in.

"I've decided," I began. "I'll leave the decision of when I wake up next to my wife and daughter."

"Okay," she replied without questioning further. A gesture I was thankful for, as I wasn't sure I could reply with an answer for my decision. "We will arrange for that."

The car stopped in front of the building's main entrance and we both got out. Locking the doors with a press of her remote control key, the yellow bug-vehicle descended into the automated parking lots below.

Without further conversation, we headed through the lobby, with people greeting the Professor as we went. She returned the greeting with graceful smiles and gentle nods, her sylphlike personality and figure seemed to charismatically charmed anyone who knew her. Down the elevator. Through the long corridor. Into the Cryo-Tube chamber. Not a single delay in our steps.

I'd like to think that the period of silence was both of us reflecting on our lives. Uniquely different in so many aspects, but similar in more ways than one. I was born to a blank page, with a myriad of possibilities for a future. Yet, I ended up on a predetermined path in the past forty eight hours of my life with one single decision, full of regret and possibly, and even more pain in the future. Somehow, the two of us convened at the same place, at the same time. Different reasons, different lives, different people. But we were there with the same feelings. At least, that's what I'd like to think.

There were no formalities this time. I got dressed in the special pyjamas, stuck a new ECG on my chest and headed to the machine. Leah waited for me at the bottom of the steps, now dressed in her lab coat.

I approached her and she said, "You know, Milton, this might sound selfish but, I'm glad you got frozen. I've waited seven years to share the experience with someone who might even remotely understand."

"It's not selfish at all." I smiled back. "I mean, 'Hey. Do you remember the one time I got cryogenically frozen?' isn't exactly a relatable dinner topic."

Leaning in, she gave me a full-on hug and I returned the gesture.

"It'll be okay," she said again. "I know it will."

Not having much left to say, I simply nodded in confirmation. We parted and she headed to the controls while I climbed the ladder, this time without G or Matthews by my side. I stood on the panel and took a long scan of the room. Just a day before for me, I was watched over by my entire family and a room full of scientists as I was lowered into the Cryo-Tube. That day, only the scientists remained. Just a room of scientists and one friend. No agents. No wife. No parents. No daughter.

I gave Leah a thumbs up to show I was ready. The panel started its descent and I wondered when, if ever, my family would want to see me again.

Life Goes On, Part One

If I had to describe the sensation of being cryogenically frozen, I'd say it was like blinking really hard. Similar to blinking, it happens so fast that you don't consciously sense you're doing it until your eyes had already reopened. The only difference between blinking and getting frozen, aside from the obvious, is that the world around you changes, months and years at a time. That's not exactly a good description, I know. But that's about as close as I can get to the actual experience in brain text. You blink hard, and the world changes.

Once more, I found myself in the dark containment of the Cryo-Tube, with only the hum of the machine to soothe my confused soul. Here's the thing with being unable to feel pain, or any physical contact for that matter. If you close your eyes, you don't know if you're standing or sitting. My eyesight and muscle memories made up my abilities to move about and not hurt myself unintentionally. Not to mention I had a few days to train on living blind before my prosthetic eyes were put in.

The darkness was disorienting and I moved my hand as far right as I thought possible before gently knocking at the steel container. The resulting sound was music to my ears and proved I was still in the confinement of the tube. Echolocation is the ability to discern our physical surrounding and positions of objects by sound alone. Though it sounds like a superhuman ability, it's something everyone can do to some level. It's why our brain can decipher if a sound is behind us or in front of us.

A red light flashed on beside me, illuminating the place. Looking down, I was once again slumped against the wall, my dressing soaking wet with the freezing liquid. I balled my hands in a fist and banged slightly harder against the wall, the echoes lasting longer in my ears than I thought it would.

I removed the oxygen mask and yelled, "Hey!" I waited a second for a reply. But when none came, I continued shouting. "What's going on out there?"

A beep resounded from seemingly every corner of the tube and a voice came through that I recognised and somewhat loathed to hear. "Milton? We're experiencing some problems with the hatch. Just wait awhile while we try to crank it open manually."

"Doctor Parker," I replied sardonically, unsure if he could hear me or if there was even a microphone in the chamber. "How many years has it been?"

I waited and the seconds seemed to pass in a matter of days. Concluding that there might not have been a microphone after all, I admittedly felt quite silly for basically talking to myself.

Then, "Three years Mr. Jones. The doctor sounded slightly despaired in his reply. "It's been three years."

"Ten years total..." I mumbled to myself before returning my attention to the doctor. "Weren't you supposed to be gone by now?"

Another long silence from Parker's end. With really nothing to do until the hatch opened up, I could only wait for a reply. When it finally came, I was somewhat stunned by the soft and humbled tone in which he spoke with."I know we got off on the wrong foot Mr. Jones, but three years has been a long time. I'm not proud of what I was and I've changed quite a bit since then."

"Really?" I replied, wondering if I might have been too harsh with my words before.

"Yes. Really. I've applied to, and have been assigned as your permanent physician. And I know this is over a thousand days late, but I just want to say I'm sorry for how I treated you three years ago," he apparently awaited my response after that. But I was still unsure how I should act and continued staring at the grated floor. He continued, "You don't have to reply immediately. I just wanted you to know."

I mumbled, "Right." Unsure if he even heard me.

"Anyway," the doctor continued. "Could you stretch your body around? Move your joints a little, and check if there's anything wrong? Any weakness or dislocation? The liquid should have kept your muscles from entropy, though your arms might feel slightly weak for the first few minutes."

Doing as instructed, I stretched my back and arms, and even my legs though there was no need for it as they were prosthetics. It was more of a habit than anything. "Everything seems fine."

"Good. Good," I could hear the scribbling of pen on paper as he jotted down what I hoped to be positive tidings. "We're turning off power to the Cryo-Tube, except for the ventilation to power down the magnetic lock so we can open the hatch manually. The cooling liquid should continue to keep your body temperature stable so you don't have worry about it getting too hot."

I wanted to remind the doctor that I can't feel heat but held back thinking the thought might have just slipped the man's mind. Instead, I simply replied, "Go ahead."

"Okay, turning off power in three...two...one." The red light bleeped off as the machine quietened down.

Only the ventilation from the grate underneath me remained active, the fan spinning softly while pumping fresh air into the chamber. In the sudden darkness, my mind began to clear as I recalled everything that happened the day, no, three years ago. My daughter, practically disowning me being the most pronounced event and my thoughts lingered on how she was then. Had she forgiven this useless father of hers?

And thoughts of my grandfather lingered, on how his double life had lead me to the predicament of being stuck in a metal container in complete black space. How it had indirectly led me to perhaps lose the most important person in my life. And why me? Why had my father not been chosen? I wondered if Leah knew the answers but something in my gut told me she did not.

The death of my parents continued to loiter around the same area. Not surprisingly though, it was not at the forefront, though there were still pangs of sadness. Though I regretted not having been able to spend their golden years with them, the fact that they had lead a life longer and more fulfilling than most people of their time brought me some

55

consolation. At my grandfather's funeral, my mother told me our family had always coped relatively well with deaths. Even before that, on their deathbeds, my grandfather and grandmother had both assured me that they were going to somewhere safe and loved. I had never understood how they knew, since we were not religious people, but they had said it with such confidence that I've never questioned them. Surely, my parents, especially my mother, felt that way to. And that confidence of theirs to face death had brought me comfort in the battle against it.

With nothing to hinder my senses, neither sight nor pain or sound, my mind was free to wander as I thought back to happier days. Time spent with the whole of my family at barbecues and gatherings. The joy on my mother's face the day I brought Joan home. The joy on her face when we got married. And the first crack of a smile from my father I've ever truly seen when Leila came into our lives.

The hatch above started to creak and a beam of light shone through the cracks that formed. Slowly, it got dragged opened, the rust screeching every so often as it did so. Slowly, my eyes adjusted as the the light outside got brighter and brighter. A familiar figure poked his head over the hatch.

"Hey G," I greeted. Again, the agent was the first face I saw. "How's it going?"

"Oh you know, fine. The lift's turned off so you'll have to climb out of there." He reached his hand down the chamber.

Accepting his offer of aid, I grabbed his arm and after a moments struggle with him finding it hard to grip my slippery skin, we managed to get me out of the Cryo-Tube and back on the platform.

"What happened?" I remembered telling Leah that the next choice I get to come out would be decided by my family. With hope, I asked, "Did Leila want me out?"

"Sorry Milton," G replied, wrinkles and lightening of his hair showed his age. "It's just a malfunction."

Though disappointed, I tried to keep my hopes up, even though my wife always said I was a pessimist. I thought I'd try it her way for once. "If we keep having these malfunctions, my days are going to number down real fast."

Needless to say, I was failing at being optimistic.

G replied, "That's what we thought." He pointed to the corner of the room where a pile of mechanical parts had been stacked aside with a dozen engineers standing by them. "We're overhauling the hardware."

I nodded at the notion, though in truth, it was details I could care less about. "So, what awesome future stuff do you have for me today?" I looked around the room and saw no other familiar faces. Even that of Doctor Parker having gone and disappeared from the room. I asked, "Where's everyone else?"

"The professor and Joan got called off to Hillbury for an emergency. One of the dome malfunctioned and, well, lots of technical mumbo jumbo."

"And Leila?"

G took a deep breath as if preparing me for some harsh news. "She decided to go with them."

Though the sentence seemed innocuous, it unexpectedly stung at me emotionally. "Right..." was all I could reply.

"Don't worry though," he tried to comfort as we climbed down the stairs, me with his help. "We're setting up a webcam conference for you guys. Joan's got something important to tell you."

He walked with me to the changing room as I left another trail of blue liquid behind. The thought occurred to me as to who was in charge of cleaning that up. "Sounds like you know what it is though," I deduced.

"I do," he replied reluctantly. "But I think you should ask her yourself."

Though the walk to the changing room was less than ten seconds away, my ability to pester others must have gotten better during my unconsciousness for by the time we got to the door, G had already caved.

"Milton," G said. "She's engaged."

"Who? Leah?" I genuinely replied.

"No. The professor's married. Joan's the one that got engaged."

"Oh..." For a few seconds, my mind processed the information as 'The professor married Joan' before splitting the sentence up again. "That is news."

Life Goes On, Part Two

G brought me to the conference room. A ten meters long and wide room with a ceiling twice my height and walls bland enough that they painted them beige. The floor was also carpeted with the same furry blue as the rest of the building. What looked to be chair-desks were arranged in a large circle in the middle of the room. Each desk had an in-built computer, sleek and glowing with blue neon at the edges. The chairs looked more like the seats from a first class plane, fully wrapped in comfortable looking brown leather with enough arm space to fit an elephants' trunk.

I told him, "This looks nothing like a conference room."

"It's for V.I.Ps," he replied. "We usually don't get to use this place."

I circled around the desks and spotted a large, metallic torus in the middle of the circle. Made of a shell of glass, the torus had wires running round its shape with four projectors joint in a cross at the perpendicular inner edges. An arms length away, it was connected to a black platform surrounded by four cameras which were stuck onto metal poles drilled into the ground.

"Does that make me a V.I.P?" I asked.

G followed me around into the circle and sat casually into one of the sofa-chairs. "You actually have higher security clearance than I do." He turned on the laptop on his desk and settled back as he waited for the

58

system to boot.

"Why would I have higher clearance? That makes no sense."

"Something about you needing access to high security places in case of emergencies." The computer finished booting and he began working on it. "I guess the higher ups thinks we'll still be here in a hundred and twenty nine years and whatever it is you're suppose to save us from will need clearance." He laughed.

The glass torus lit up and a blue neon glow emitted from it along with a low humming sound. Small red dots lighted up on the four cameras as the equipments turned on.

"And what does these things do?" I asked about the torus shaped machine.

G wiped off a speck of dust that had settled into his glasses with a flick of his nails before replying, "Hologram projectors. Really expensive apparently. There's only one in each of the five cities."

"Are you serious? Holograms?"

"Yup. That's the meaning of progress, man. It's still a prototype though. They're trying to make it more marketable but it's really costly to build. Joan will be using the one in Hillbury to contact you." He then pointed to the black platform surrounded by cameras. "Stand over there. Once the machine starts up, she'll be able to see you as well."

I did as he said and stood on the platform, feeling a little silly.

He continued tapping away at the touchpad of his computer. "Looks like Joan just activated hers." He hit one of the keys harder than I thought he should, letting out an audible clack. The projectors in the torus powered up, lighting up the space in the centre of the circle with a block of red, green and blue lines. "Once she sets up her side, you'll see her in that," he pointed to the psychedelic coloured block.

"And she can see me?"

"Yup. Just like a normal conversation really." G got to his feet. "I'll leave you two to it then. Just come back to the Cryo chamber once you're done. I'll get someone to come up and turn off the machine. You have all day to talk this time." After the instructions, he headed for the exit, turning off the lights before closing the door behind him noiselessly.

Alone in the dark room, save for the glow of the hologram torus and its projection, I was suddenly overwhelmed by nervousness. Joan was engaged. She was getting married. To someone who was not me. I rummaged through the thought of it as waves of unending questions

59

beats into my mind.

The projection flickered and the wall of colours slowly faded. A chair, shaded and formed by the red, green and blue colours took form in what used to be a coloured wall of nothing. From off-screen, Joan walked into view. From the angle, she seemed to have circled around my projection before coming into my sight. She stretched out her arm towards my face, her hands disappearing as they left the cameras' field of vision, but I knew she was cupping my holographic face in her hands. I closed my eyes, imagining her doing so, and imagined the warmth of her touch through my nerve damaged skin. All my anxious thoughts swept away.

I heard her voice, echoing out from the speakers of the torus. "Hey you," she greeted.

Opening my eyes, I locked vision with her and smiled. "Hey yourself."

She let out a breath of relief, retracting her hand. In my mind, I could feel her touch leaving my face. Smiling, she sat down on her chair, her hands cupped in her lap. She wore a lab coat which covered a shirt, vest and shorts. I was relieved that her style in dressing had yet to change over the years.

She did not worry or react when I stepped out of my cameras' view. I circled her closely, taking in as much details of her as I could in spite of the odd RGB colour tone. Though the resolution wasn't clear enough to show wrinkles on the face, I could tell immediately she had aged slightly, her hair slightly less thick than it was before. Though not a major change, it was a glaring difference for someone who stepped out of a time from years ago. I squatted down at her side and gently controlled my hand to be placed over her digital ones.

As if she could feel my action, she smiled and said playfully, "I hope you're not doing something perverted."

I laughed and replied sarcastically, "Use your imagination."

Getting to my feet, I searched the room and saw the outline of a stool in a far corner. I jogged to it and brought the furniture back to the platform. I took a seat in front of her as she traced my action.

Face-to-face then, I asked, "How are you?"

Still smiling gently, she said, "Good. Can't complain. There's still some work to be done before the Mist reaches us, but we'll still be here for you to come back to."

Slightly concerned, I told her, "You don't have to worry about me so much you know?"

She looked down to her hands as she fiddled with our wedding ring on her left ring finger. I noticed a second ring on her right hand. "I can't help it," she said. "I'm so afraid that you'll have nothing left to come back to one day. A hundred years. I can't live that long. Not even Leila."

"Is that why you started the project to counter the Mist?"

Letting out a chuckle, she looked back up and met my stare. "You see right through me." A short pause followed as she took in my face and put together her sentences. "You have two weeks to live, and yet, you'll outlive all of us. I have to make sure you have a place to come back to."

I couldn't reply. I felt helpless, the burden of my life shouldered by the woman I loved. Even with contemplation, I could only manage a weak, "Thank you." Before going silent, a thought then occurred to me and I asked, "Where's Leila."

Her smile faded slightly and I could see her struggling to maintain it as my pillar of strength. I didn't point it out as she'd never admit it, and I wouldn't give her even a seed of doubt in her incredible spirit. "She went shopping with Leah," she answered. "I don't think she's ready to talk with you yet."

You were gone! Just like that! You climbed into that stupid machine and you were gone for seven damn years just like that!

My daughter's words to me all those years ago rang out loud and clear in my day old memory. I could only nod in reply to Joan's words.

"Milton," Joan said my name. "There's something I need to tell you."

"You're engaged," I replied without hesitation.

She didn't look shocked, managing to maintain her calm nicely. "Did G tell you?"

I nodded and smiled back. I genuinely smiled back. "Congratulations. Is it someone I know?"

"Yeah. You know him."

"It's G isn't it?"

She cocked her head to the side. Again, not shocked, but merely the look of curiosity. "How did you know?"

"I'm guessing in ten years, everyone I knew either moved on with their lives or had forgotten about me. My students are too young and we didn't really have a large social circle or anything either." A thought

61

occurred to me, "What was the cover story for my disappearance by the way? I never asked."

Joan took a second to remember the decade long story before replying, "You died during your prosthetics surgery."

"Right..." I was surprised how calm I was at hearing the tale of my death. Instead, I put the new information to my deduction. "There was only a few people on the project to begin with. They'll be the only people who knew both of us after my 'death'. It could be one of the other guys but G's the most obvious choice."

"You're amazing, you know that?"

She had said that to me before and I could never take it to heart. I was, after all, just a dead schoolteacher. "I'm very normal."

Another gentle smile to calm me. With an uncharacteristically apologetic tone, she softly said, "Sorry."

"For what? Getting married? Finding happiness?" I leaned as far forward as I could without my body crossing the border of the platform. "You don't have to be sorry for that. Never. Ever. Sorry. I love you to the end of the world. Even if that means you'll get married to another less funny, uglier looking man to be happy, so be it."

She laughed at my joke and wiped away unseen tears from her eyes. Looking away from me as she cried, I patiently waited for her to gather her composure.

After a minute, she took one last deep breath before finally asking, "Do you have time to talk?"

I grinned widely and replied, "All the time in the world."

Life Goes On, Part Three

None of the mechanics that left the Cryo-Chamber did so much as look at me when I passed them in the long corridor. I was reminded that for many on Project Dawn, I was but another job, and the small group of people with an emotional attachment to me are possibly the only friends I had left.

Entering the chamber, I got my first look at the new Cryo-Tube. Installed on a raised platform, the new tube – well, more of a box – looked much more similar to a science fiction machine than the bulky metal monster before. The cumbersome tanks of preservation liquid remained around it, but the main part that housed me had been replaced with a sleek, metallic, rectangular container with a half cylinder glass door.

I instantly recognised Doctor Parker as he was the only blond in the room. He stood by one of the control panels with what looked to be an ECG monitor. His hair had also grown out into a ponytail which I thought was kind of an untidy hairstyle for a doctor but perfect for a slightly arrogant hippy.

"This is more like it," I said as I approached him. "Now it's starting to look sci-fi."

The doctor looked up from his work and, in a completely unfamiliar fashion, smiled at my presence. "Yeah. No more climbing up and down

63

for you."

"I'm sorry about earlier," I blurted out.

"For what?"

"For not forgiving you."

Parker nodded solemnly and turned his sights to the machine in the middle of the room. "I started talking with the professor and G after that day. They told me the little things about you that I never thought to look into myself." He pulled up a chair and sat down. I leaned against the console and listened to his story. "That's the thing about being a doctor. When I worked at the ER for my internship, I saw so many patients that they just become a number to you. A job. I numbed myself and forgot that they were human as well."

Unsure of how to reply, or even if I should, the better part of my social abilities, which there wasn't a lot left of, redirected the conversation. "What's new with the Cryo-Tube?"

Jumping on the bandwagon away from the awkward topic, Parker explained, "Well, as you can see, we have a door now so all you have to do is step into it. And we can monitor your physical status by sight as well." The doctor got up and headed to the machine. I followed. Knocking on the glass, he explained, "High density magnesium aluminate spinel. One of the hardest transparent ceramics we have. It'll help keep in the pressure when we fill up the liquid while giving us visuals of you."

"I don't know. That's kind of weird, you guys watching me as I sleep."

"It beats us not knowing your physical condition. At least this way, we won't just rely on the ECG. We'll be able to use other methods to help preserve you better." I found it weird speaking of myself as an experiment, but figured the term was required for them to properly do their jobs. Too much emotional investment can sometimes lead to bad decisions, no matter what the doctor thought of professional stoicity.

I leaned into the glass. Well, the doctor called it a spinel-ceramic-something but I'm a layman and if it's hard and transparent, it's glass. On the other side, I can see the enclosed space as just slightly smaller than the previous metal one. The floor was a metal grate, probably to drain out the liquid. There were about half a dozen of what looked to be medical instruments – from tubes to plastic suction cups – placed on the white interior wall, including an oxygen mask. A shoulder harness was connected to the ceiling and left dangling in the middle.

Parker continued the explanation. "The holes in the walls are used to better regulate the liquid." Sure enough, there were four holes that wrapped the wall at waist height. "With that, we can control how active your body is. We can adjust the pressure and the amount of the liquid, basically letting your body 'exercise' in a way. Keeps your body healthier and active. Lot's of sciency medical stuff you won't understand."

I felt a pang from his last sentence, a slimmer of his arrogant personality surfacing for a brief second. However, he wasn't wrong in that I had no idea how any of the stuff he explained was supposed to work.

Stepping away from the glass, I asked, "So do I need to go change into that stupid pyjamas now?"

"You don't have to do that anymore either. We've got a new system that will rinse, disinfect, and warm your body dry before you even wake."

"Seriously?"

"Yeah!" he announced proudly. "I'd dare say our engineering team has outdone themselves with this new design."

"That's pretty convenient," I said. "What about G? Is he here yet?"

"He should be on his way down. You want me to hook you up while we wait? I'm sure you two have a lot to talk about."

Without reasons to do otherwise, I agreed. With a shout to one of the other lab hands, we stepped back and watched as the Cryo-Tube depressurised with puffs and hisses. As the gears of the machine clicked and chugged into place and movement, the glass door began retracting into the walls.

Parker instructed me to step in and strap on to the harness, with my shoes being the sole exception to the clothings I was allowed to wear. I did as I was told.

The shoulder harness hung by an tensioned rope that extended to my height when I pulled. I slipped into it and felt slightly lighter as my body weight lessened with the stretch. The doctor squeezed in after me and began to fit the instruments from the walls onto different parts of my body. A wired ECG was attached to my chest in favour of the wireless ones from before, and a few sensor patches were stuck onto the back of both my hands and my forehead. I felt like I was being connected to a computer where I would become its brain.

"Alright, we're done," Parker finished, stepping out of the Cryo-Tube just as G came into view. "I guess I'll leave you two to your talking." The doctor greeted the agent and turned back to me with a, "See you next time." He walked out of sight past the walls of the machine.

G stepped into his place and asked me, "How does it feel in there?"

I looked around, getting a sense for the space. "It feels bigger. Guess it's the colour. They say white makes things look larger you know."

"That's why I don't wear white. Don't want people thinking I'm fat." He laughed at himself and I smiled.

I said, "Congratulations by the way."

Looking me in the eye, I saw a gleam of apologies in G, even as he said, "Thanks."

From inside my round enclosure, the world outside looked indescribably larger than I knew it to actually be. I felt isolated, and knew that in just a few minutes, I would be frozen, suspended in animation while the world around me moved forward with its life. And part of the life would include Joan's marriage to Agent Golph.

The mood turned serious, as if we were about to host a ceremony to past on some sacred mission. In a way, that was true. "You know, G, I don't even know your first name."

When the realisation hit the agent, he grinned broadly and chuckled at the revelation. "You're right. I can't believe we've went ten years without you knowing my name." He let out a sigh. "It's Randolf. Randolf Golph."

"Well, Randolf, you take care of her." I smiled. Though I had made peace with their engagement, I could still feel emotions welling up within me and was sure I would cry if I physically could. "Give her a good life."

"I will," G nodded in reply.

"And don't let her work to hard."

"Gotcha."

"She's not young anymore," I informed him. "Make the rest of her life a good one."

I could see the shine of waters welling up in the agent's agreeing stare. He continued to nod at my instructions and let out an audible sniff as he held back his tears.

"And take care of Leila. Don't let her date anybody without vetting them through The Forum's criminal database. Make sure you take her to

Hillbury when it snows. She may say she doesn't like it anymore but that's a lie." The words poured out of my mouth as the realisation that I was passing on everything I cared about into the hands of a man I've only known for three days dawned on me. "And bring Joan to Tikika for your honeymoon. She loves it there. And please, for all's sake, don't—"

G stepped into the Cryo-Tube and embraced me, no longer able to hold back his tears. He sobbed quietly as he confessed, "I'm sorry for replacing you."

Limply, I lifted my right arm around him and patted him on the back. "Thank you. For replacing me."

After a minute, he finally managed to get his crying under control and stepped away from me and out of the Cryo-Tube. "Look at us. Two grown men, acting like kids watching a sad move." He laughed, and after a moment to regain his cool composure, he said, "See you."

Taking the oxygen mask off the wall, I placed it over my nose and mouth and it automatically sealed itself against my skin. I nodded back at the agent, "Be happy for me. Do what I can't."

G looked to the side and with a thumbs up directed outside my view, the glass door slowly closed, shutting me inside the soundless box. This time though, I could see the outside, just as much as they could see me. I watched as G walked away from me and towards one of the consoles to begin his work. Doctor Parker rushed to another panel to monitor my vitals. Two friends. I found that a much better viewership for my freezing than the day before. I could only hope that better scenes laid in the years ahead.

A puff of white mist shot out from the holes in the walls. They smelled of disinfectant and old folks home. The rope of the harness retracted into the ceiling, lifting me off my feet. I dangled in the air as clear water poured out from the gaps in the wall, probably to wash me off before freezing. In seconds, I was completely submerged in water. It was then that I found out that not only could I see clearly underwater due to my implanted camera eyes, but that my mechanical legs were heavy enough to prevent me from floating.

I mused, *Guess I can't swim anymore. On the other hand, I'd be great at diving.* Internally, I laughed at that insight.

The experience of being frozen was different with sight. For one thing, there's actually a memory to show for it instead of instant darkness and immediate dawn. I could see the blue cooling liquid being released

67

into the water and watched as it mixed and misted, snaking it's way around the currents as it slowly surrounded me.

My vision blurred as the clear liquid was replaced by the murky blue, yet I kept watching until I could no longer stand the mind twirling sight of the dancing liquid and closed my eyes. When it felt like the dizziness was gone, I reopened them to find myself hanging in an empty Cryo-Tube, bathed in an orange light that I assumed was warmed. As promised by Parker, my clothes were dried and on the other side of the glass door stood Joan.

Despite knowing full well that my voice would not reach her through the soundproof glass, I asked, "How long?"

She got my question anyway, as I knew she would. She held up her hands and extended all five digits and I knew immediately why I was awoken.

It was my daughter's graduation.

The Healer, Part One

I was made a suit while I slept, which was one of the many perks of now having a glass door instead of being stuck in a metal can. Though the idea that people watched me while I was unconscious had a certain level of creepiness attached to it, and was even more unsettling know that someone actually came along and measured me for a suit without my knowledge. Scarier was that the suit was a perfect fit, which begged the question of how they measured me within a sealed container.

"You look good," Joan commented when I met her again in the lobby after changing. She had changed into a green cotton dress and heels for the occasion of Leila's graduation. For me, seeing her wearing anything outside her tomboyish ensemble was a rare and beautiful treat.

"I always look good," I joked and adjusted the knot on my bow tie. "But seriously? I didn't know bow ties still existed."

She walked up to me and flattened the creases in my shoulders. "Of course they do. Bow ties are awesome." Our eyes met and the years between us felt like days. She placed a gentle hand on my cheek. "You're so young."

"Not as young as you," I said and kissed her forehead.

The last time we met, she was but a hologram. Now, in the flesh, I could tell she wore her age nicely. Her wrinkles barely showed, and her hair, though faded slightly was still a definite black in shade. At forty six

69

years in age, Joan would be considered as starting her golden years by the lifespan of people of our time, though she seemed healthy enough to continue living for decades more.

From behind me, the familiar voice of Professor Leah Hullway called out, "Milton! You're awake."

I turned to see her walking calmly across the empty hall towards us, wearing her lab coat over a yellow-themed babydoll dress. It was at that moment I concluded she was simply addicted to the colour yellow.

"Oh, Leah," Joan greeted with a wave. "We were just about to leave for Leila's graduation."

"I know. But I need to borrow Milton for a while."

I asked, "Can't this wait? I mean, it is sort of my day off," I ended jokingly. Joan nonetheless nodded in agreement with me.

Leah clapped her hands together in a friendly plea. "Just for a few minutes. The skies are clear over the portal and it would be much better to show it to him while its active."

Joan looked visibly disappointed, a rare frown on her otherwise bubbly face. But she agreed to let Leah take me. "Fine. Just get him down in half an hour or we won't make the ceremony." Her allowing me to go on such an important day in our daughter's life told me how important the 'portal' had to be. "I'll see you later, Mil."

I waved her goodbye and followed the professor to the lift lobby. I reiterated how empty the building seemed as we entered the elevator.

"It's the weekend," Leah told me as she selected the 5th floor from the column of buttons. "Plus, there's a new movie out today that everyone's been dying to watch."

Suddenly, I felt out of the loop, as if the entire world had an in-joke that I was not a part of. "Right. Right. You know, this is my forth day as a... whatever it is I am. Sometimes I forget that the world around me continues to move, even if I'm not in it," I unintentionally confided my feelings on the matter as the door closed behind us. "I don't know if I should be happy or sad about it."

Realising that I was basically pouring out my personal emotions to a person I've known for less than four days, I tried to apologise but was cut off by her reply. "It must be weird for you, isn't it?"

Going with her flow, I answered, "Yeah. A little." I felt at ease in her presence, feeling more like a friend who was just meeting up to hang out rather than a terminally ill, time travelling, stranger from the past.

As if reading my mind of the subject, she continued, "You feel it too don't you? That even though we've only technically known each other for less than ninety-six hours, we're close." Unsure of how to reply, I simply nodded. "You know, the only people who actively participates in your project now are myself, Agent G, Joan, and Doctor Parker. We've read your case files and followed you for years. G's even a part of your family now."

"I just feel out of place sometimes," I admitted to her. "Every time I wake up I wonder if our relationship's still the same."

She placed a caring hand on my shoulder. I looked to her and she smiled. "We're your friends on this." We reached our floor and the elevator door dinged open. "That's not changing," she ended and walked out.

It was a weird conversation for me. It seemed random at the time, and the topic jumped around a lot. But it felt like that was the kind of conversation Leah had all the time with people around her. Yet it was reassuring enough that I left the elevator with a smile.

The elevator led out into a large auditorium-designed control room. The bright, industrial strength white lights on the ceiling turned on automatically. With four levels downward, the room was about ten meters in height and stretched at what seemed to be a hundred meters in width. Each levels had two rows of computers, and each desk faced forward to a giant screen made of hundreds of televisions joint together on the large, empty wall in front. Like the rest of the building though, the interior design could use work, with boring, grey concrete floors and neon blue walls that made me think of the most boring aquarium ever.

"Wow..." my voice echoed for a solid three seconds in the empty room. "Big room. We should have a party here."

Leah headed for the computer nearest to our right and booted it up. "We tried that once."

"And?"

"Half of the guys got suspended. They got too drunk and started using the stairs and chairs as slides and surfboards. Broke about a dozen computers." She took out her ID pass and swiped it through a card reader on the table. "Could you hand me your pass? We need two to authorise clearance."

I did as I was told, recalling G telling me during our last meeting that I had a pretty high security clearance. Leah swiped my card and the

71

screen immediately switched to a desktop interface. The professor clicked a few buttons and the screens on the wall all flared up to show the same desktop, each separated by their respective monitors. She pressed another button and the images merged into a single, massive one.

I asked her, "So what did you want to show me?"

"This." She clicked one of the executable icons on the desktop, bringing up a video of an empty, Mist-covered sky. "This is a live feed of what it looks like outside right now. The Mist is at two thousand meters above ground level and practically covers the entire world."

"But the Sun Domes and underground roads projects are in the works right?" I asked of the status of the Mist protection project Joan was spearheading.

"It's actually functional. We've been using the system for the past six months and it's been showing good results. We're just finishing up the underground infrastructures and railroads. But that's not what I want you to see." She moved the mouse cursor over to a scrollbar on the right that ran the height of the screen. She adjusted the tiny bar till it was in the middle, and the feed of the Mist turned to a screen of red. "This is the Mist reading of the area right now."

"Okay. Mist covered skies being bright red on Mist reading machine. Nothing out of the ordinary." I realised how loosely I used the word 'ordinary', given that the Mist wasn't as thick 15 years ago.

"Yes, that is until you adjust the variables for density." She clicked a small button in the lower left corner of the player. Instantly, the red in the video was replaced by a light teal that covered the screen. All except for one, small, thumb-sized area near the upper left corner of the feed which continued to glow bright red. "This setting has the lowest computer statistics for measuring density of Mist. It's quite lenient in its readings. But even then, that small corner over there is still registering as high density Mist congregation."

Stunned, I managed a, "So what the hell is that thing?"

"That's an incredibly dense vortex of Mist. The Mist swirls out of there like water through a drain. The run-offs gets spread out into the atmosphere. Until recently, it has been in the stratosphere, hiding in the clouds and Mist. Because how clouds mixed with Mists messed with readings, even satellites didn't detect it until it hit the troposphere."

"How much Mist is there?"

"We can only estimate. Definitely more than one thousand times its

72

surrounding density."

I walked up to the monitor from which Leah worked from. On the smaller projection, the red blot made up barely one percent of the screen, resembling more of a bug that was squashed on the monitor.

I asked, "How big is it? In real life that is."

"About two meters. Too small for us to send something permanent up there to research it. We can't stabilise with such a small work area. And the electronics of everything we did send fizzles out before we even reach it." Our eyes met as she said so. "It's really dense Mist up there Milton. If humans get exposed directly, we would probably die instantly."

Something else bugged at me, "You said until recently it was in the stratosphere." As a geography teacher, the term was not unfamiliar to me and caught my attention more than any of the other information. "And it's in the troposphere now. Does that mean the thing is moving?"

She nodded, smiling at my deduction. "Just like your grandfather there. Yeah, it's moving downward at a constant rate."

I knew the answer but asked my question anyway. "How long until it gets to ground level?"

"Approximately one hundred and twenty years. Or, if you want to be exact, a hundred and twenty-four."

Looking up to the red dot on the giant screen, I was faced with the nemesis of my century long journey. I muttered grimly, "End of the world."

The Healer, Part Two

Back in high school, I dated Matilda Vines. She wasn't a cheerleader or anything, but when it came to looks, she was one of the 'it-girls' of our school. Smart, charming, and overall nice. I won't lie here, she was terrific in bed as well. If she had not transferred to Hillbury, I would have in all likelihood married her instead of Joan. Which made the first time I ran into my ex all the more awkward. It did not help my peace of mind that I was also on a date with Joan at the same time. But what I experienced all those years ago was nothing compared to all the feelings that bombarded me in the car with Joan as she drove us to our daughter's graduation.

I sat in the passenger's seat while she navigated the underground tunnels of Roagnark. With flame yellow incandescent lights and pipes that redirected through the walls, the underground roadway looked more like an alternate steampunk world than anything I recognised as part of the city.

"I know it looks rickety," Joan explained, "But the construction is one hundred percent safe. The only corners we cut were making it look good."

My head turned and followed a road marker made of scrap metal with a plastic sign stuck onto it. I replied, "I have no doubt it's safe. But this really looks like the hobos' highway. Couldn't you have spent maybe a year making it look neat?"

Joan laughed, "It's good to see you again Milton."

We sat in mutual silence for awhile, an array of thoughts bombarded my head even as I admired the impressive tunnel system built.

Are you still with G? Are you happy? How's Leila? What are you working on now? Do you still love me?

That last question was not something I would ask. I felt confident enough that despite all these years, I would know Joan enough to guess the answer from her actions and words.

We took an exit that came up, leaving what Joan called the 'downway' and into a narrower stretch of road that apparently functioned as streets.

I spoke first. "How are you?"

"Fine," she replied and I watched as a small smile formed on her face. In the yellow light, I saw more clearly the small bags that had defined her eyes. Fatigue was not something she carried with her. Sleeping early, eating healthy, regular exercise. That was Joan. If she was tired in any way, it was due to worry.

"You haven't slept much."

"You can tell?" She sounded slightly surprised, but happy all the same.

"I can always tell."

She chuckled. After a beat of contemplation, she replied, "I've been worried about seeing you again. Physically, we haven't met in eight years. I didn't know what you were like now. And if you would still be okay with..." she slowed down, gathering her thoughts. "With me and G."

I simply asked, "Are you happy?"

"What?"

"Are you happy?" I repeated. "And I want the truth. No sugar-coating it for my sake."

She nodded to herself, lips pursed as she readied her answer. Then, a small grin that broke my heart and made my day at the same time. "Yes."

"If that's the case, I'm fine with it." I smiled at her—No, I beamed at her, I dare say. Though inside, my heart felt torn, despite knowing it was physically impossible. I was, for once, happy that I could no longer shed tears as that would make me look way less cool than I was projecting to be.

75

We pulled up at a tunnel that led to the multi-story underground car parks for Leila's school. Filled with other families, some just parents, others with siblings, few alone, we found a lot marked 'RESERVED' and parked in. However, Joan did not switch off the engine and instead leaned back into her seat, closing her eyes and letting out a sigh. I never found out if it was a sigh of relief or strain.

Through her darkened sight, she said, "I still love you. You know that?" Answering the question that I would not ask.

I took her hand in mine, rubbing the creases in her knuckles gently. "I know."

"Am I selfish? Is this wrong?" I sat with her in silence without an answer. "I have two husbands. And I love both of you. Is this right?"

"You're never selfish. If anyone's selfish, it'd be me."

"We went through this, Mil." She sat back straight to look me in the eye. "You being frozen is the best choice to make."

"I'm not talking about that. It's more that I'm actually happy that you're so conflicted over me," I gave a cheeky grin. "Now that's selfish. Not you. No. You, you're just being human."

She looked to her ring fingers. Our wedding ring was on her left hand and G's on her right. "But still..."

I clasped her hands together, palm-to-palm. The rings touching each other. "You deserve this. Not the stress, but the happiness of having two men who love you. And you deserve to have a beautiful daughter who is graduating, and all the ponies and butterflies in the world."

Her smile came back. "Ponies are extinct, Milton."

"Really? Okay, just butterflies then. Maybe we can replace ponies with zebras or some poodles."

The laughter that followed from her was magical, and I completely forgot about all the grim bodes in life. The Mist Portal, my daughter's feelings towards me, her marriage with G. Everything washed away upon hearing her symphonic laughter.

I urged, "Now, let's go be proud of our daughter."

She nodded and turned off the engine. After exiting the car, we made our way towards the elevator that would take us up to Leila's graduation hall.

"How did you get a 'reserved' spot?" I asked.

Even under the lighting, I could see her cheeks flush with modest embarrassment. "They're calling me 'The Heroine of the Mist' now. For my work with the Sun Domes."

Stopping her in our tracks, I stepped in front of her and kissed her forehead. "I don't know who I'm more proud of. Our daughter for graduating or you for saving the world."

"You'll save the world one day too."

"But only because you made a world that can last long enough for me to save."

At that point, I looked over her shoulder and crossed gaze with a man leaning against a corner wall, away from the crowd the elevator. Then I realised how silent the world had become. The sound of the traffic from outside the lots had stopped, as were the chatters of eager families. Around me, everyone else had froze in their tracks. Children paused in mid-air from an eager hop, a couple stopped in a swearing contest far in the corner. Even Joan was frozen in time, her face locked in the smile that my last words to her had left.

The stillness in the air was deafening.

With a suave gait, the man who I had locked eyes with approached me, his voice a sword that pierced through the moment in time. "Milton Jones."

"And who are you?" I replied, calmer than I had expected to be. Though I was worried about what was happening, especially for Joan, my gut told me the situation was not of life and death. Maybe.

"I think you can call me, Pausa."

"And what do you want with me?"

He stood right opposite me and behind Joan. Though his face looked young, skin without wrinkle, with the smooth contours of a male model, the man had a look in the eyes that seemed to surpass age. And I felt that if anyone knew anything about age, it would be me. When you jump large gaps in time, every little change about a person will scream at your attention. The eyes were one of the most jarring, the age seemingly etched within their veins.

He swept aside the bangs of his short, styled-up hair, strands of black protruding through an otherwise deep brown. Taking a deep breath, he smiled at me. A Confident, curious, excited smile. "You're the judge of mankind."

I blinked. He disappeared. And like a wave splashing against the shore, the sounds around me slammed back to my ears and I jolted from the shock of the world unfreezing from time. The arguing couples swearing caught my attention first, giving me half the mind to tell them to shut the hell up. My head swirled and I felt throwing up was an option to make.

"Milton?" Joan asked, probably noticing how pale I had become. "Are you okay?"

"Yeah," I replied in pauses, still shocked and confused at the event that transpired. "Just...peachy."

The Healer, Part Three

I wondered if elevators as large as some of ours were the norm in the past. The circular platform stretching at ten meters in diameters with cushioned seats built into the walls held half a dozen families and was lit by a ring of fluorescent lights on the ceiling. It was commodious enough that the groups could stand in their own cliques with space left between. However, the normal looking crowd made Joan's constant inquiry about my experience in the parking lot all the more strange a topic that drew stares from gatherings nearby.

"I told you," I said for the seventh time. "Nothing happened."

Joan glared at me suspiciously, "You're *so* lying. You know you can't lie to me."

"What could possibly have happened!" I raised my arms in exaggeration of the deal she's making. "You were beside me the whole time. If anything happened, don't you think you would have known."

She considered my logic, which was pretty much flawless, helping in the lie. "If you lie to me..."

I held her shoulders reassuringly. "I swear on my life," I said, hoping she wouldn't realise I considered myself a dead man.

Her affirmative nod told me she didn't. "Alright. If you say so."

We reached the rooftop garden of the school building and the elevator's large double metal door retracted and opened. We let the other families flood out first, leaving us a clear path onto the artificial yard.

Exiting onto the rooftop, I found myself under the light-violet, Mist filled sky. Surrounded by a glass dome, the level was high enough above ground that I could see the Mist cutting off at the horizon, the purple coloured sky and the lighter brown lower atmosphere separated cleanly at the edge of the world.

The garden itself was of a simple layout. Bushes of flowers lined the perimeter, with a few sparse shrubs scattered around the rest of the area, giving life to the place with their colours of the rainbow. In the centre of it all was a round stage encircled by a dozen neat rows of chairs. Empty paths crossed each rows, dividing the seating cleanly into four segments. Around us, families stood excitedly in groups, almost matching the patches of bushes in numbers and colours. I counted nearly a thousand people in the large garden.

Joan explained, "Every building has one of these gardens at their highest points now." Sure enough, as I looked across the cityscape at the other skyscrapers surrounding us, multiple style of greenhouses capped their tips like hats. "Helps increase the oxygen cycling the city."

"All this in fifteen years," I said in wonder. "You amaze me, even now." I placed my arm around her and kissed her forehead, staring at my surrounding in wonder.

"She is amazing," a voice said from behind. I turned to see G step out of the second elevator, his classic dressing of a suit perfectly fitting the occasion. He looked around the air of New Roagnark, taking in the scene of skyscrapers with their bright domes shining under the violet sky. He turned back to me and reached out his hand. "Just like you."

I took his hand in mine, "Good to see you again, my friend."

"So um...no hard feelings, right?" He gestured with his eyes towards Joan. It wasn't a question of condescension either, but a legitimate, friendly, 'Are we good?', which made it all the more painful for me to reply.

"So long as you keep her safe and out of trouble." I put a reassuring hand on his shoulder. "We're good." I gave as sincere a smile as I could muster, hiding the jealousy within.

From the stage, the MC, a female student dressed in a gold tasselled cap and blue gown – announced in an annoyingly high pitched – her voice screeching through the speakers. "The ceremony is about to commence. Will all families please take a seat around the stage. Thank you."

The crowd began congregating towards the stage and we agreed that we should head to our seats less we be blocked out like a latecomer in a movie theatre. Maybe not in those exact words, I'll admit, but that's the idea.

We managed to find our seats at the edge of the seventh row, which made the whole theatre metaphor moot. I took the innermost seat beside Joan, and G sat next to the aisle. I relit the conversation with the agent.

"What have you been up to?" I asked. I tried to swipe a strand of hair away from my sights, only to realise that I had accidentally sat on my hands. I quickly shifted over to let my unfeeling limb free.

"Well," G began, shifting over as a family of three squeezed through the narrow walkway. "I've been asked to assist Leah in studying the Mist portal."

"The thing that's pouring poisoning gas into the sky?" I asked to clarify, which he nodded. "Why do you call it a portal?"

Joan answered, "It isn't just a dense concentration of Mist. It's also creating the substance. Though the amount it makes a year is less than a cannister. But the production rate is increasing"

G continued, "And it's in an empty region of the atmosphere. As far as we know, there's nothing there. In fact, there doesn't seem to be anything in it either." G looked to the direction of the portal in the sky, having studied it for such a long time that he knew exactly where it was even without any machines or sensors pointing to it. "Empty. Just slowly puffing out Mist from nothing."

"The portal is Leah's theory," Joan added. "We haven't been able to replicate, produce, or control Mist in any lab conditions, and there's no known natural source of it."

"So that thing in the sky is the source," I said, drawing the conclusion.

G took off his horn-rimmed glasses and a wipe to clean it, while elaborating, "But it's empty space. All our sensors and tests says so. Nothing should be up there producing the gas, so our theory is that the space itself is creating it."

"Like a portal," I finished.

The chattering of the crowd died down and I looked forward to find the source. The girl from before had been replaced by a male in the similar fashioned cap and gown. However, he had a small, but noticeable golden pin on his chest that glinted in the light.

There was no podium or microphone visible, so I could only assume that when they spoke, it was due to some new, unseen technology that I had yet to have the opportunity to witness. The fact that Joan and G displayed zero surprise at the phenomenon meant that I was probably the only person in the crowd who had any interest in something that mundane to them. And suddenly, I felt old. Really, really, old.

"Ladies and gentlemen," the male greeted. "Families and friends of our school. I am the student president, Gordon Walker, and I welcome you to the graduation ceremony of..."

His voice trailed from me. As if it was speeding quickly into the distance. In the silence that ensued, I could hear my heart pounding, and a ringing in my ears as if their drums were about to burst. I could see the president's lips moving as he spoke, but the sound reached me as mumbled gibberish.

I raised my right hand over my heart, expecting to feel my heartbeat slowing, but instead, felt nothing at all. Reminding myself once again of my inability to physically feel anything, I took a deep breath to calm myself and scanned my surroundings, thinking that the time manipulating man who called himself Pausa had returned. But I found nothing.

Then, for a split second, I felt my heart beat against my chest and to the palm of my hands. For a split second, I felt breeze on my skin and an ache in my knee. As suddenly as it lowered, the volume of the world returned to my ears like air bursting into vacuum. Something had happened to me, physically.

"And without further adieu," the graduate on the stage announced, completely ignoring – or more precisely, not noticing – about the shocked look on my face. "I present to you, our graduates!"

I snapped back to the situation as everyone around got to their feet. I did the same, and with a gentle nudge from a smiling Joan, turned to face the entrance to the oversize elevator we came out of. From within, in neat rows of fives, the graduates started walking out to the claps, cheers and shouts of joy from their families.

My daughter was graduating. My physical problems can wait.

I started clapping.

The Healer, Part Four

"They say time heals all wounds," the principal, in her navy blue dress said from the stage. Her long red hair and freckled face standing out brightly. Her auburn eyes scanning the crowd. I wondered if when Leila was older, would she look as outstanding as the woman on stage. "And in your years here, you have likely done as much harm as you did good."

It was a sombre speech that glared in contrast to the happy occasion. But I found it strangely fitting. I looked down to see Joan holding G's hand in her lap. I swallowed my pride and looked back to the speaker.

"In time, all our achievements here will be forgotten. But so will all our errors. You are graduating, not just from this school, but from your past selves." From the sound of the principal, she was a realist who knew the hard rough path ahead in life. "It is a fresh start. A chance given by time itself to be better than who we are now."

From the corner of my eyes, I saw my shoulder shift. Looking down, Joan had placed her free hand over mine. I turned my palm over and squeezed gently.

"Graduates. This is not your time. This is the time of the world. It is not the world's job to provide a moment for you to shine. It is your job, from now on, to find your place in the world and make it shine." She finished her opening speech to confused applauses and some looks of

83

disorder. It was without a doubt, a weird speech. Then, in a turn to a tone of excitement, the principal announced, "Now, without further adieu, I present to you, your graduates!"

The crowd immediately turned the haphazard mood into one of celebratory joy, cheering as the graduates waved from their ranks of fives, four groups of them standing at the boundaries of the four pathways that led to the stage. A blond male in a suit, most likely the vice-principal, stepped onto the stage to replace the previous speaker in the centre. Three other teachers followed. The floor of the stage spiralled open, forming a doughnut shaped hole in the ground around the teachers. From its depth, a round table raised from it, hundreds of scrolls arranged neatly in a circle.

The high-pitched female MC from before took to the stage with paper in hand. "Ladies and gentlemen, from the twentieth graduating classes of Barber Siblings University. Our graduates. Aaron, Smith."

From the west entrance of where we sat, a male graduate stepped out from the file and walked up to his side of the platform, where the vice-principal presented him with his degree. After a bow, he looked to his left and waved to the crowd, where two set of hands can be seen waving back.

"Abbett, Howard," the MC announced in succession. Clockwise from Aaron, another male stepped out of his file and proceeded the same way up. This time, he looked left and towards my segment of seats, where his parents waved from the second row.

"Bentley, Lisa."

Again, in a clockwise direction. The school had positioned each family to their graduates' left. It was efficient, and allowed them to continuously present the degrees without holding up a long line. I turned to the group of graduates directly behind us and scanned the rows for my daughter.

Probably sensing my anxiety, Joan whispered, "We're Jones. She's probably buried in the middle of everyone." Gently, she directed me to face back the front. "Patience. Her time will come."

"Creedie, Patricia. Damon, Hewer. Damon, Jonathan..."

I thought back to the opening speech given by the principal. Time heals all wounds, she had said. The last I had saw of my daughter was, for me, just two days ago. For her, and as far as I knew, she had been angry with me for maybe fifteen long years. She had the rights to be angry. I did, after-all, left her and Joan to fend for themselves in what I still considered a selfish decision to save my own life.

"Etkins, Louise. Farfort, Franklin. Fetch, Abigail..."

In the past fifteen years, she had only seen me once. And the last time I saw her, she was just a teen no taller than my chin. And she screamed at me with enough anger to seer pain even into my nerve-damaged skin.

You were gone! Just like that! You climbed into that stupid machine and you were gone for seven damn years, just like that!

Her words rang within my head like a record on repeat. Not that I have ever seen a record player. But the phrase had kept itself strong through the ages.

"Gilmore, Stacy. Gordon, Trey. Hartnell, William..."

I counted the alphabets in my head. J is in two letters. If I turned around now, I would probably be able to see Leila in the queue. My heart started pounding again, harder than before. So much so that I could audibly hear it smashing into my chest. Fear. Pride. Guilt. Excitement. I felt myself drowned by the overwhelming emotions.

"Illias, Zethro. Jameson, Johnson. Jebson, Peter..."

A part of me screamed to run. My mind yelled back, *No!* I needed to face the consequences of my choices. Even if it meant the broken relationship of father and daughter. A outcome I would have to face. And hopefully, will have a chance to fix.

"Jennings, Russell..."

The 'Js' were lasting way too long.

"Joachim, Joseph..."

I wanted to cry. To shout. To show my frustration and regret and guilt and throw it all into the wind which I could not feel.

"Jones, Leila..."

I shot up from my seat, knocking over the chair in the process. I had to have been quite a racket and spectacle as everyone within the garden instantly dove headlong into the town of silence. The only sound was my heavy, erratic breathing. The kind one took when crying heavily. Of course, I had no tears, so as far as I knew, I was a madman playing his part.

From behind me, I heard a hushed, "Dad..."

Two days. For me, that was the number of days since I last heard her call me dad. Yet, it was carried with such a foreign tone that it actually felt like the years it was for her. I turned in my spot and faced my daughter. And she was beautiful.

Her face was bright and without blemishes, like the surface of water on a calm day. Her auburn hair, kept short and still, a sway in the wind, was tucked neatly under her cap. Her gaze steely, her chin sharp, she looked light enough to flutter away on a breeze, even under the oversize gown. Yet, I could feel her strength and determination emanate from her person like the glow of the sun.

Joan and G instinctively moved their seats back to clear a path for me and I stepped out onto the aisle. Whispers started filling the crowd around us. Words like "saviour" and "hero" reached my ears.

You're the judge of mankind. Echoed in my head. Yet none of that mattered to me then.

Leila started walking towards me, as if she was hallucinating and was determining if the sight before her was real. And then she ran, straight into my arms in an embrace that knocked all sense of worry out of me. Crying into my tailored suit, her cap left floating through the air behind her.

"I'm sorry!" she wept. I wrapped my arms around her and hugged her as tight as my weakened body would allow. "I'm sorry! I'm sorry! Dad! I'm so sorry!"

"I love you," I whispered through tearless sobs. I held her head against my chest. "I love you so much."

Time heals all wounds. But that's not exactly true, is it? We just become different people. Sometimes it takes four days, and others, fifteen years. Our cuts and grazes fades, and some becomes scars. Then we carry the weight of our injuries through the years and days into an uncertain future as we leave the past behind us.

86

Goes in Threes, Part One

Everyone was there. For one shining moment, it felt like everything was going to turn out okay. I stood at the entrance to the Cryo-Tube, my family and friends around me. With the main thought going through my mind amids the laughter and joyous chatter was that everything will be okay. Happy endings.

"Oh! Oh!" Leila jumped excitedly, still in her graduation cap and gown, "Mom, take a picture!"

She ran up and hugged me from my side, with Joan readying her camera phone as G, Leah and Doctor Parker stood watching beside us.

"Say, "Freeze!"" Joan punned at my situation.

My daughter and I just laughed it off and Joan took our genuine smile as a cue to snap her picture.

"Randy! You too!" Leila said excitedly, running off to G. Apparently, her nickname for the agent was Randy, which I was secretly glad for instead of being 'dad'.

Under Leila's ecstatic urging, we were pushed to go for a few more rounds of picture taking, ending with a group photo in front of the Cryo-Tube, taken by one of the lab hands. With the elevated mood, the events that had transpired in the past few days for me felt like a joke. A memory even. A tough 'boot camp' that I had just returned from. At any time now, I would get in a car with my wife and daughter and we would return home to have dinner, watch TV, and wake up tomorrow to go to work.

"Milton." Professor Leah came up to me solemnly. "Your day's almost up."

And suddenly, reality was back clawing at my back. I was reminded that I was still a dying man, and that the time I could spend with the people I love was drawing ever closer to a close.

"You can quit now, you know?" the professor told me.

"What do you mean?"

Leila had managed to drag Joan and G into another round of picture taking, this time with random members of the room. I watched as the girl dragged her parents around, chatting and laughing with the team of scientists and engineers that had gotten close with my family over the past few years.

Leah continued, "You're almost at the point where tomorrow with your family will never come."

I contemplated her words. My daughter waved to me from the opposite side of the room and I waved back.

"I know." My physical body was stuck in time. Growing at a rate slower than anyone else. No. It was more than that. I was suspended in time. Stepping from period to period the same man, while the world changed around me. Even if I only had ten days left to live, at least half of it would be spent with strangers from a different age.

"Just say the word, Milton..." She did not finish her sentence, but I knew what she implied.

There would be no hard feelings between anyone if I decided to step out of the program now and spend the rest of my short life with the people I love. It would be a logical move to make. I get to make the most out of my remaining days at the expense of the fate of a world neither I nor the people around me would live to see. I would lose nothing, gaining precious days in the process.

I replied, "Don't worry. I'm going to see this through." I was unsure where my sudden conviction came from.

The festive mood slowly waned as my time to return to deep freeze drew to the doorstep. Doctor Parker prepared me for the freeze, doing a final check on my physical conditions before patting my shoulder affirmatively.

"Good to go," he said.

G and Joan, holding hands, came up to me just as Parker walked off to further the preparations.

Not giving them the chance to speak, I told G, "Thank you."

"What for?" he replied, genuinely surprised. I wondered if he had ever felt guilt for inserting himself into my family. I'm sure he did. He was a good guy. But by taking over my life, he had given me something I could never do, something which I would be eternally grateful.

"For being there for the important parts."

Speechless, he could only smile and extend his hand in friendship. I shook it without hesitation.

"My two boys," Joan said with a grin. "All chummy now."

She dragged G towards me and grabbed us both for an embrace. Caught in an awkward grip, I could only exchange gawky glances with the agent, to which he ended up laughing. From behind Joan, Leila walked into view. I gently parted from the group-hug and stepped towards my daughter.

"Dad..." she mouthed softly.

I placed my arms around her shoulder and pulled her to me. "I'm so proud of you."

She hugged back.

From beside the Cryo-Tube, Leah called out, "Milton. It's time."

With a curt nod to her, I slowly pushed Leila apart from me. She was crying, beads of liquid crystals streaming down her cheeks, dripping from her chin like the droplets from a stalactite. I kissed her on the forehead, long and deep, with all the feelings of love I could muster, trying to mark my emotions over the years into her mind for the days to come.

"Love you, dad," she whispered just loud enough for me to hear.

"I love you too."

We parted and I made my way to the professor who waited patiently by the opened Cryo-Tube. I smiled to her to signal I was ready before stepping into the machine. She began hooking me up to all the equipments and sensors.

From the outside, Joan, said, "Next time, we're going on a vacation!"

"I look forward to it!" I replied.

"To Hillbury!" Leila added enthusiastically, punching her fists in the air.

There was no helping the smile that formed on my face, "Your favourite-test place ever," I mumbled to myself.

With the set-up complete, Leah stepped back from the machine and gave a smile for a farewell. The glass door closed on me and I could barely make out Leila's lips forming the word, "Favorite-test."

The liquid filled up the chamber and this time, I closed my eyes early for a rest. It had been a long day, and with plenty of joy and good times to look forward to. The darkness of the back of my eyelids were soothing. I felt calm, happy, and incredible pain.

I screamed, loud enough that I thought I would end up tearing my throat. My entire body felt like it had been dipped in lava. The searing sensation was almost foreign, having not physically felt anything for weeks. Though I would have given anything to regain my nerve damage if it meant the hurting would stop. Even then, there were no doubts the pain was intense, bad enough that my ears were ringing loud enough to drown out my shriek.

Get him out! Get him out now!

The sensation of a thousand needles piercing my skin sent my arms flailing wildly, trying to tear away the very fabric of my body. The world danced red as I was dragged out of the Cryo-Tube, the warmer air of the room outside only sought to make the stinging even more noticeable.

Hold him down! Anaesthetics!

Impossibly, my right arm felt hotter than the rest of my body, a sun attached to a torso of magma. It was as if fire ants had crawled into its veins while shitting acid as they went around biting everything in sight. I swung my arm out, tearing lose from a grip and striking hard steel. I wanted it gone. I wanted to saw it away. To stick it in dry ice. To burn it with gasoline and have a truck run it over until it was severed from my mind. I wanted to die.

Dad! Hold on!

I couldn't move. I felt straps tightening around my arms, legs, waist, and shoulders. I felt my left shoulder dislocate as I frantically fought to scratch the full-body itch that I could only describe as laying my entire body on a grinder made of salt and pouring a Molotov cocktail over me. And then lighting it aflame. Let's not forget the fire.

Goes in Threes, Part Two

G told me that for the single day that I knew Agent Matthews, my decision to enter cryo-sleep changed the man's life. In that same day, Matthews also said that I had a sharp wit, which I explained was due to my inherited inability to infer a bad time to make jokes and dish out insults. A part of me was incredibly happy that at least one thing about me had stayed the same, even if it was my worst trait.

"You look like shit, dude," I said to G.

He replied with a scoff, "You're one to talk."

In a scene reminiscence of the first time I met Matthews, I found myself back in a bleach-white hospital room, the dizzying stench of alcohol disinfectant managed to irritate even me. Sitting beside me was the agent, dressed in his classic suit and horn-rimmed glasses which I was sure had gone out of style at least a decade ago. My theory was that he wore them more as a point to prove his job than anything else. The man had gotten exponentially older since I last saw him. His hair was full but slightly greyed, with a set of wrinkles that stretched his skin.

I looked around the otherwise empty room. A vase of flowers with a 'get well soon' card was placed on the bedside table.

Solemnly, I asked, "How many years has it been?"

"Before I tell you, you need to know something happened."

"I know something happened," I snapped back, fiercer than I thought

91

I would. "I want to know what I've missed."

He sighed, taking off his glasses to clean them. "Six months after you went into your last sleep, we had a situation. Parker noticed a drop in some science mumbo jumbo. I don't really remember what he said," he admitted to his lack of knowledge in the medical sciences. "We took a look and...the Mist Poisoning managed to jump a few nerves and spread into your right arm."

Slowly, I slid the blanket away from me. Part of me knew what I would see. A sleek, thin, silver robotic limb had replaced the entirety of what used to be my right arm, ending at a cleanly bandaged shoulder. I held the contraption up to the light where it glinted and glowed. My new fingers opened and closed easily, likely due to the practice with my legs, but it still would not turn into a full fist. However, the rest of the prosthetic moved without any visible jerks.

G continued, "We had to amputate. The nerves in your arm were too damaged. The moment you woke up, it caused unbearable pain. It took a while since we did not have the medical capabilities to halt the poisonings' growth."

"How many years?" I asked again, deducing where the conversation was going.

"The freezing process was the only thing that slowed down the poisoning—"

"How many years?" I demanded.

The agent stopped his explanation, slowly putting on his glasses again. It was now spotless and shining in the light after the lengthy cleaning. "Fifteen years Milton. It took fifteen years for us to get the medical sciences well enough to stabilise you."

My arm dropped to the side with a loud clang as it hit the rail of the bed. "Fifteen years. One-five?" I repeated in disbelief.

"Yeah," G confirmed grimly. "And even then, we didn't really want to bring you out yet."

My gut was spinning. It was the feeling you get when you stared over the edge of a tall building and the body reacts to the idea of plummeting to your death with a somersault in the abdomen. That kind of feeling. Though something else about the grimness of the whole situation had thrown me off. Had it just been a damaged arm, the successful surgery should have been an occasion for celebration. Instead, the foreboding mood told me something else was at play.

Sensing more bad news, I asked, "Why didn't you want to bring me out?"

G paused, taking a couple of breaths, opening his mouth as if about the speak, only to close them again. I watched patiently as the man tried to form the sentence he needed to tell me. "Our surgery procedure didn't improve enough with the times."

Without him saying it, I figured the situation out. There was no one here to greet me but the agent. It could have only meant one thing. He was waiting for me, not knowing when I would wake up. "How long have I been here? In the hospital."

"Three days. Two and a half, if you want to be precise about it."

The information hit me harder than I thought it would. I shot up from my bed and sudden heavy breathing took my respiration like a freak storm. G stood up and approached me, putting a worried hand on my back.

"Hey man, you okay?"

"I'm...I've...lost two days."

He apparently had not thought the news would hit me as hard as that either, for he could only stare at me in stunned silence.

I stared down at my new arm. "I have only a week left to live now." My fingers finally managed to ball itself into a fist, the steel creaking as it did so.

In frustration, I swung my robot arm against the railing of my bed and G jumped back in shock. The metal handlebar broke clean off its hinges, flew across the room and clattered against the floor. Red started to seep through my bandaged shoulder.

Anxiously, G pressed the call button on the wall for a doctor. "You can't move so fast yet! You're not fully recovered and the surgery just ended. You could rip your arm off."

"Fifteen years, G. Leila is...she's...she's thirty-seven now." I looked to him. "I missed half her life again."

"Hey!" He held me steadily at the shoulder, turning me to stare straight into his deep brown eyes, one of the few things of him to still hold colour. "She doesn't blame you. Not once. Not one day."

Still in shock, I managed to ask, "And Joan?"

Suddenly, his stare was no longer at me, but through me, and I knew then that there were more bad news to come. After all, good things come in threes. Why not the bad stuff as well?

"Randolf. How is she?" I asked again.

He swallowed hard. Enough that I could hear the saliva gulped down. "She's sixty-one this year," he paused.

Forcefully, I pushed, "And...?"

"Milton, she's old. I'm old."

Somehow, for the first time that day, I heard the ageing creak in his voice and saw the thin bones of his hands. The once young man – smooth and charismatic – now looked like my teacher from junior high, the latter who must have been dead by now. G's hairline had receded, and the slight greying I saw earlier was actually the undergrowth of his hair, where the only brown remaining were the canopy, where they would also soon disappear.

I muttered, "You're old..."

Sarcastically, he replied, "Thanks for reminding."

I clambered out of bed, sweeping the blanket to the floor. Without any hitch, I got back onto my robot feet just as a much older Doctor Parker knocked and entered the room.

"He's awake?" he asked G, before seeing me head for the window, his question answered.

With both hands, I drew back the curtains to the city of Roagnark. The familiar skyline was doused Mist blue. Like a thin fog that had moved in, the Mist had overtaken the entire lower atmosphere. The roads were emptied and abandoned and the faint lights that came from the buildings looked like ghostly lamps in the distant sea. I placed my left hand on the window pane, expecting to feel the cold for some reason. However, my nerve damage had returned, and none of my physical sensations were working again.

Doctor Parker said, "It's been like this for ten years. The underground road is working. The cities are thriving. We even have trains and ports that connects all five cities. We can't fly anymore, but we're alive."

I was entranced by the sight. Before, I had thought that a couple of years had brought about a large change to the world. Then, a decade later, standing at that window, I realised just how small scale a change the years before had been. And that on the scale of the time of the world, how much impact fifteen years had.

"They did a good job," Parker continued. "Leah. Joan. G. Without them, none of this would have happened. Everyone's alive."

I turned away from the window to face the two men. Strictly, I asked, "Where is Joan."

"She—" G started, but couldn't get the words out. "She's—"

"Milton," Parker cut in for the man. "You just got up. You need to rest."

"I'm rested," I said sternly, a low growl in my voice. "Now I'm gonna ask one last time. Where. Is. My. Wife?"

Goes in Threes, Part Three

People used to say that good things always comes in threes. I've always wondered if there was a physical law that prevented bad things from happening in that succession as well. Turns out, there wasn't. Bad things happen all the time. But sometimes, the combination in which these events unfolds are just too perfect in its destruction that 'unfortunate' becomes a tame word in comparison. Sometimes, the world just isn't fair.

"Dad," Leila greeted me once I stepped out of the elevator and into the hallway of the highest floor, nearly tripping over as she hugged me. I hugged back, careful not to use my new arm.

At thirty-seven years old, she was no longer the young girl I once knew. She had her auburn hair straightened into a ponytail, which flayed slightly at the end. Dressed in classy, onyx black-pleated skirt and a long sleeved, white-collared tip, I could barely recognise her were it not for her hazel eyes behind her silver rimmed, light temple glasses.

But I could not bring myself to rejoice at seeing her again. Gently, I pushed her away to an arms' length. With a sombre stare, I asked, "How's your mother."

She took a hold of my one good arm. "Follow me," she said, her eyes glistening on the verge of tears.

I followed my daughter through the corridor. In contrast to the lower

96

levels where I was from, the floor smelled of faint lavender. The ground was a smooth quartz white and the walls were painted bleach instead of wallpapered, with meticulous waves etched into them. It felt more like a hotel corridor than a hospital.

I remarked on the emptiness of the level. "It's really quiet here."

"It's the V.I.P level," she explained. "Other than a few staffed nurses and doctors, hardly anyone ever comes here."

In all the commotion of the past few days of my life, I had forgotten that Joan was considered a hero, and would of course, be given privileges befitting such a status. Though she never lorded privilege and had always treated the people around her as friends. Her humble, friendly personality meant she was never consumed by the fame or power that came with her status.

"Here we are." Leila stopped outside ward 13-G, standing aside to let me enter.

"Aren't you coming with me?" I asked.

She gave a shaky smile, replying, "I think she would like to talk to you alone for this." I nodded uncertainly at her before opening the door and crossing the threshold.

Right before the door closed behind me however, Leila voiced out, "Dad." I turned back to face her. "It'll be okay."

I was sure I gave a smile back. Not as a gesture of reassurance, but of fatherly pride. I had nearly forgotten that at that point in time, she was older than I was. No longer a kid, but an adult fully capable of supporting herself. And apparently, me as well.

With a soft click as the door locked in place, I was blocked off from my daughter. Turning forward, I was treated to a ward that seemed more like a hotel room. Continuing from the design of the corridor outside, the carvings of waves on the wall spread in, expanding into a tapestry of swirled flowers and out into the room. The floors were softly carpeted, and even from my angle, I could see the large screen television embedded into the wall, though it was not on. Beyond the sill, the window was covered by silver embroidered beige curtains. The lightings were a smooth yellow instead of the glaring white common to hospitals, though a knob beside the door showed the option to change the colour tone.

Stepping forward, I looked into the bathroom. The floor was marbled as was the sink. There was a bathtub and a standing shower, with the toilet a comfortable size in contrast to the smaller ones downstairs.

But I wasn't there to admire the view. I was there to visit a person, as reminded to me by the constant beeping of the ECG. The admiration was just my way of stalling from facing the inevitable reality. I stepped around the corner.

Blaring at me was the sight of a hospital bed. A sore thumb in the otherwise luxurious room. An ECG stood beside it, along with a drip that was attached to the patient. Her hair, short and dark grey, wore over pained wrinkles that marked her face. Her skin stretched tightly around her facial bone. The woman named after a saint rested with eyes closed.

As nervous as I was when we went on our first date, I walked up to Joan's bedside. Pulling up one of the visitors' chair, I settled down beside her. Seeing the blanket that covered her was slightly wrinkled, I gently readjusted it.

She was still a light sleeper, her eyes fluttering open upon the light disturbance. When her gaze rested on me, a wide grin beamed across her face and I saw the woman I fell in love with again. "Hey you," she greeted.

"Hey yourself," I echoed back.

I could see her visibly straining as she moved her hand out. I saved her the effort, bringing mine to hers' instead. Holding it in my only real hand, I massaged the lines that ran the back of the tiny palm.

She watched my actions intently before saying, "Mist Poisoning."

I nodded half heartedly. I was hearing the words, but my mind denied the reality.

"There was a ventilation fault in one of the greenhouses. At my age, not long now before it takes me completely."

"We can freeze you."

"Don't be ridiculous," she chided like a grandmother. "I'm an old woman now. The government won't put out money just to preserve me."

Not having it, I insisted, "They will if I talk to them. Or you can have my place. I don't need it."

She chuckled, "Such a gentleman." I looked up to her, her face wore the expression of patience for a child. At that point, I comprehended just how young I was compared to the people around me. "Listen to me, love. I've lived a full life. I have loving friends. A large, loving family. I was even given the chance to save countless lives."

Tears filled her eyes, glistening golden in the light. I moved closer to her, bringing her hand up to my head and taking in her scent, one of the last things I could physically feel from her.

She continued, "I have a beautiful daughter. I have Randolf. I have you. Two men that loves me. And just when I thought you were going to leave me, I was blessed with the chance to grow old with you."

With a cracking voice, I replied, "But I didn't get to grow old with you." I leaned further into her hand. Even at death's door, she was still supporting me. My pillar of strength. One of the reasons why I even chose to go into cryo-sleep.

"I'm sorry," she apologised genuinely.

"For what?"

"For being so selfish."

I kissed the back of her hand. "I'm selfish too. I did all this for my own happiness." I looked to her and smiled, hoping to lighten any guilt she had with my own shortcomings.

With a grin, she said, "I guess we're both terrible people then."

"I guess we are."

After a chuckle, she leaned back into her pillow, staring at the ceiling. "Milton?"

"Yes, my love?"

"I can't feel anything."

Mist poisoning. She had reached the point where her nerves had shut down and she could no longer walk. The only thing left to her was her sight.

Without saying anything, I leaned in and kissed her lips. I heard her breathe in deep, taking in my scent, tasting my lips. Slowly, I parted with her.

Face-to-face, she smiled embarrassingly, "That must have been disgusting. Kissing an old woman like me."

Sitting back down, I coolly said, "I only kiss pretty girls."

She laughed again. And I was sure I was beaming. Her laughter was intoxicating, whatever the age. Her happiness was my happiness. Settling back into a peaceful silence, we simply stayed, enjoying each others' presence.

Until Joan said, "No widest sky, nor furthest seas," she recited my wedding vows to me. "Will part neither you nor me."

"No death day due, or life lived lieu," I continued. She often made fun of the poetic phase of my life. "Will change my eternal love for you."

We both sat in another bout of silence, contemplating those words. Mountains I could trek and seas could be swam. Death could be crossed and life continued. But now, we were separated by the walls of time. Something that no matter how much I wanted to, I will never surmount.

"Milton," Joan said softly.

"Yes?"

"You should go" She said that not with any animosity or annoyance. She just knew that my day was running out, and that I had to go back to the quiescentness of time.

"I can stay," I stubbornly replied.

"Go," she insisted. "And I know what you'll try to say. That you have one week left to live and you want to spend it with me."

She wasn't wrong. That was exactly what I was planning. But I also knew what she was thinking. "But I can't, can I? You all put so much effort into this project. Into me. You want me to see it through."

She smiled, "We can't be selfish all the time." She turned to look at the curtained window, as if seeing through the cloth and watching over the whole world. "You don't know this yet. But you've given hope to a lot of people. A shining beacon in these dark times."

I hesitated, staying in my seat, twiddling the thumb of my metal finger. Then, just as she turned back to face me, I got to my feet. "Okay," I agreed, leaning in to kiss her forehead.

Joan gave a smile that belied both sadness and joy, shining beads rolling down her face. "Goodbye, Milton."

I gently wiped the tears from her cheeks. There were no doubts in my mind that if I still could, I would have blinded myself with my own waterworks. "See you later." Though not completely willing, I turned to leave, determined not to look back.

"Mil," she called out, stopping me in my tracks.

But I did not turn. For a few seconds, I stood staring at the floor, not willing to look up. I knew what she wanted to tell me and I, truly, with all of my being, did not want to hear it. Taking a deep breath to compose myself, I finally looked back to her.

For a second, her smile was so bright, so full of joy, that I saw past her age and wrinkles. The image of the love of my life burned brilliantly into my mind, shining greater than any star.

And she said, "Goodbye."

I croaked out, "Goodbye."

The Winter Train, Part One

Solemn air hung in the chamber. The humming of the Cryo-Tube being the only song that sang from the echoes of the room. I stood in front of the newly upgraded Cryo-Tube. Smaller than even the one before, the machine was now just a pod, slightly larger than my height and width. A single human-sized tank of freezing liquid was stuck to its back with pipes connected to larger tanks at the sides. As with the previous model, this one had a curved glass cover for the entrance, though it did not have any of the cumbersome medical equipments and wires dangling on the inside, making it look neater and more 'household' in atmosphere.

I noted the obvious. "You changed it again."

Professor Leah stepped up beside me, looking up and down the machine herself. "Yeah. We had to get with the times. Things are changing," she said. "Need to upgrade. Everything is different now."

I replied, "But you look the same." Despite the years, her appearance looked exactly as it was when I last saw her. Golden haired with barely a trace of grey. It was as if time had left her behind.

"Being cryogenically frozen does that to us. Exterior overcompensating while the interior moves forward. Don't let my looks fool you, I am pretty old. Eternal youth may be real now, but eternal life? Not so much." She looked to me with a smile. "If you live long enough,

101

you'll be young forever too."

"That's a big 'if'," I replied, turning to face the rest of the room. For the first time, I saw the smudges on the wall, the greying of the once marble-white paint and the grime that had stuck itself to the corners.

My daughter and G were discussing the workings of the new machine with the engineers while Parker prepared the medical instruments with his assistants.

"G. Joan. Parker. Myself," Leah continued, "We might not all be here the next time you wake up. And really. I know I look young, but I am an old woman now."

"Don't say that," I replied, trying to comfort her, even though I was sure she did not need it. "I'm sure you'll all still be well and good when I get back."

"There's no need to lie. It's the truth. Everybody dies some day. I wished someone had said that to me when I went to sleep." She recounted her experience being the first cryogenically frozen human. "I woke up and...so many people I knew were gone. I wasn't prepared for it."

"Well, I'm prepared for it now."

"Are you?" she asked with a questioning look which borderlines worry. "You do know that, for you, Joan is dead. Right?" she said without hesitation or ill-intent.

I didn't reply her. I just stood in silence, subconsciously rubbing my new metal arm. Logically, I would never see Joan again. But a part of me wanted, hoped, pleaded, that she would make it just another year. If I woke up earlier I would be able to see her at least once more. She wasn't suppose to die before I did. That thought had never really settled inside of me. I closed my eyes, the image of her burnt into my memories. I wondered for how long I would be able to retain it, if I would be able to carry her smile with me to my grave.

Leila ran away from her conversation and up to me. On the way over, she looked just like the child that was running into my arms from yesteryears.

"Alright dad, we're ready for you," she said. Upon noticing the grim look on my face, she rubbed my shoulder affectionately, even though I could not feel it. "And remember. I'm still here."

I smiled back, attempting to assure her. I wasn't sure if it worked, for her smile back was less a smile than a forced pull of a muscle. Then, for the first time that day, I noticed the silver ring on her ring finger. "You're married?"

She smiled gawkily, holding out her hand for me to see ring clearly. "Ten years."

"Who is this man?" I asked. "Where is he now? I want to meet him. Is G okay with this? Is your mom?"

"Dad." She held my hand in hers. "In order, his name is Leonard. He's an engineer mom hired on the project. He's on an emergency work trip now. G's fine with it. So is mom. And yes, before you ask, as soon as possible, I'll introduce him to you."

For a moment, I had forgotten that because of the spread of the Mist Poisoning, I was asleep for 15 years to preserve my life, and only came back because medicine had caught up enough to halt the poison and Joan had requested for me. I could not have expected my daughter to wait that long to gain my approval for a man

She waved Parker over. The doctor joined our motley group with a clipboard in hand. "Alright, Milton. This new Cryo-Tube has state of the art medical sensors, so there's no preparation required." He gestured to the machine. Indeed, the cylindrical, hospital-white internal chamber had various black glass pads that, even to a layperson like myself, looked like sensors. Parker passed me a transparent rubber mask. "This thing will help cycle the air bubbles in the liquid into oxygen. Basically a gas mask. So you just have to step in, put it on, and we're good to go."

I nodded to the doctor just as G walked over to bid his goodbye. "Ready?"

I nodded back. I reached out my biological hand to shake his. Instead, he stepped forward and, in a move so caused Leila to gasp, hugged me.

"Come back safe," he said.

Stunned, I could only nod blankly back. I was sure he felt my motion for he pulled away. He smiled, turned, and walked off to the main control panel to oversee the remainder of the process.

Leah came up and kissed me on the cheek. In her usual wispy tone, she asked me to — "Say hi to the end of the world for me." With that, she followed G away.

Parker merely slapped a hand on my shoulder in support before heading off to his medical station. Now, alone with my daughter, I climbed into the Cryo-Tube and she moved to stand just outside the

103

machine's entrance.

"Take care of your mother for me, will you?" I told her. She nodded back. "And make sure your...husband knows about me. And don't forget...don't forget to..." I didn't know what else to say. The words would not form. My mind had finally shut down from the emotional turmoil of the day but I continued trying anyway. "Don't forget to...to—"

She jumped into the machine. In the small, confined space, she somehow managed to wrap her arms around and hugged me like a mother would a child. "Come back to me safe, dad," she said over my shoulder.

My breathing slowed down as my body jerked awkwardly from the physical motion of crying, though my nose and eyes stayed dry of tears. "Okay."

"I love you," she sobbed.

"Love you too."

She stepped back out of the Cryo-Tube, keeping her eyes on me the whole time. Despite her tears, despite her mother's terminal illness, despite everything that should have brought her to her knees in depression, she managed to give me a toothy grin as the glass door closed between us. I put on the oxygen mask and the chamber quickly started filling up with the freezing liquid.

Tired from the emotional roller coaster that had been the entire day, I shut my eyes and waited for the dreamless sleep to take me. I remembered the first time I went on vacation with Joan. A trip to Tikika, where we spent a whole day traversing their countryside on a steam powered trains, one of the few locomotives left in the world. Her laughter filled my mind, so did the chugging of the train. It was then that I asked her if we got married one day, would she move in with me, or I with her.

If I had to choose, I would move in with you.

Why?

I want to make sure you don't go anywhere.

The chugging of the train continue, even as the memory played out its scene, like a hypnotic lullaby trying to drag me off to slumber. And then, it got louder and louder, until I realised the sloshing of the freezing liquid had long since stopped and that I was actually hearing the chug.

My eyes flew opened to the interior of a dimly lit train cabin. Luggage bags were the first thing visible through the grates that held them above head. Sleekly lacquered walls surrounded me, with a single glass window to my right that looked out to dark tunnel walls illuminated by the light that came from my room, giving it some semblance of passing gravelly form.

A voice sounded, "You're awake?" I turned my head to see a middle-aged man on an inbuilt sofa to my left, staring at me in wide eyed wonder.

"Yes," I replied, sitting up from the bed, the blanket falling off me and onto the floor. "I guess I am."

He was in his mid forties with ruffled, rock brown hair that bounced slightly with the motion of the train. In a dark dirt trench coat that covered a white shirt, blue jeans and greyed steel toe shoes, he looked just as ready to become a homeless man as he was about to join a citizen militia.

Getting to his feet, the man hurried to the door behind me and shouted into the corridor without care or regards to any other possible passengers. "He's awake! Lei! Father is awake!"

The Winter Train, Part Two

Growing up, trains were considered a luxury. With the world disconnected, all the cross continental transportations were cut off from each other, with them only being recently re-established. Even then, most people could not afford them. Suitable fuel sources dwindled with each passing day. The fact that we were on one meant either government subsidies or some other methods of heavy funding, which sat uncomfortably with me. The stranger in my cabin did not help make the situation any less out of the ordinary. Or at least, as ordinary as it got with me.

"So, who are you? What are we doing here? Where's the Cryo-Tube?" I bombarded the man in the cabin.

He stopped me with raised hands, "Hold your horses. I'm just part-time here. We should wait for the big shots to come explain this."

"Big shots?"

From the door, a familiar voice replied, "That would be me."

I turned and, to none of my surprise, a familiar older man in black jeans and a grey shirt stood at the door, leaning on a cane in his right hand. The sight of him out of his usual work clothes was such a foreign display that it took me a few seconds to fully recognise him.

"Parker," I greeted the doctor.

The stranger replied sarcastically to Parker, "I was actually talking

106

about my wife."

"Sure you are. She can't hear you by the way." He stepped away from the door to make way for the man. "She's at the front cabin. You should go get her."

"Right." The man got to his feet, nodding at me in recognition before leaving, closing the cabin door behind him. Parker limped over to take the now empty seat opposite me, grunting in discomfort as he sat.

I asked, "What happened to your leg?"

"This? Injury and age doesn't mix," he replied, tapping his right knee. I noticed the greying of his once blonde hair and the dryness of his skin.

"But you're a doctor? Can't you just, I don't know, heal it."

He laughed. Once, a long time ago, I believed that same laughter would have been derisive. Now, with the wisdom of age, it was more of an understanding chuckle with added tolerance.

"That's the ironic part isn't it? I'm the man who heals others, but can't even do the same for himself." He looked out to the cave walls blurring by, as if it was a canvas to paint his memories on. After a moment of contemplation, he sighed and said, "I'm sure you have a lot of question. I'll do the exposition until your daughter gets here."

It was true that I had questions. Most of them were about our location and situation. However, something more personal stood sore and needed answering. "That man just now, is he..."

"Your son-in-law," he answered. "Newton Smith."

"Ah...so uh...what does he do?"

"Really? That's your question?" he asked, raising a brow in curiosity at my lack-thereof. "You just woke up from your sleep in an underground train. Don't you have anything else to ask?" A slight condescension echoed from his tone. Despite his age, the doctor still had a semblance of the same contemptuous pride that had coloured his personality since the first day I met him, albeit just a pick of it was left.

"Of course I do," I replied, slightly annoyed. "But forgive me if I worry about my daughter every now and then."

"Well, I think the couple should answer those questions instead of me. It is a family thing, after all."

Resigning with a sigh, I said, "Fine. So, what are we doing here and not at the lab?"

He leaned back in his seat, making himself comfortable. Twirling his

107

cane on its pivot against the floor, he replied, "You've been asleep for five years now. A few years ago, the East and West Forum Administration came under new...administration. A new head reworked the organisation. They're just called The Forum now."

"Okay, but what does that have to do with us?"

"Patience, I'm getting there." For a moment, he sounded almost wise, if not, sagely. "The Forum funds our project. Apparently the new head, Luviet, has a problem with us. Well, specifically, for some reason, you."

"Me?" I replied in genuine surprise. "Why me? I don't even know the guy.

"But he knows you. Everyone does."

I recalled the whispers of 'hero' and 'saviour' from Leila's graduation, and it occurred to me that it might have been common knowledge that the husband of the woman who protected the world from the Mist had a story of his own.

"I don't know why Luviet did it, but he cut off funding to us. We managed to get one last push for cash and used it to finance a new Cryo-Tube," Parker explained. I listened intently but a part of me was still hung on the idea that the government that once commissioned my preservation would want for the same project to end. The doctor continued, "We're moving you to a hideout where we can keep you alive until the end of the world."

For the most part, I understood what he was saying. But I could not grasp the reasoning behind it. "Why are they doing this?

"Like I said, Milton. We don't know," Parker replied. He stopped twirling his cane, setting it aside and putting his hands together in thought. "The world's been in turmoil for the past few years. There's a likelihood that there'll be a violent uprising against The Forum soon. They're not exactly the most welcomed people right now."

"They must have a reason," I reinforced, trying to absorb years of events and history and make at least an illusion of a coherent picture. "From what you say, it sounds like the people are angry. What are they doing that's pissing them off?"

Parker looked at me earnestly. I had never seen a man stare with such conviction without proposing right after. "You, Milton. They're pissing people off because of what they're doing to you."

"What?"

"Joan may have managed to halt the spread of Mist, but people still have hope that one day, they would be able to walk under the sun again," he explained, a glint in his eyes as he recounted the history. "For some reason, you saving us from the end of the world had turned into the idea that you would be able to somehow free us from the Mist. Close the portal that's poisoning our air or something."

"I-I don't even know what I'm doing. I don't even know what to expect."

"But your story is giving people hope. A lot of people are willing to help you for that glimmer. A lot more would do anything to hold onto it."

It was an overwhelming tale. I was a school teacher just a few months ago. And now, I was apparently transformed into some mythical figure. A saviour. "I... I didn't ask for this, Parker. And I don't... I don't want people risking their lives for me in some revolution or whatever."

"I know." Parker nodded in understanding. "But I don't think you have a say in it now. The people have made their choices."

A sense of dark forebode overcame me with those words. Hesitantly, I asked, "What do you mean '*made*'?"

"The fighting has already started. Small riots here and there." He stared back with weary eyes. "People have died, Milton."

People have died. The inevitability of death was something known all to well to me. Closer than a brother was the feeling. But the idea that others would willingly give up their lives in order to preserve mine stabbed at my heart. The worst of it was that it was not even to save my life, but to protect the story of hope that had been built around it. And there was nothing I could apparently do but wait it out.

The news of death however, triggered my memory, and I asked, "Joan?"

He replied solemnly, "She passed away a week after you went under last." He did not continue, instead choosing to stare at his feet to examine what I could only assume was the much more interesting laces of his shoes.

I swallowed at the news. Though I had expected it and braced for it, I was still left stunned and numbed by the revelation. Blankly, I asked, "And G? Leah?"

Before he could reply, the door to the cabin slid opened. Standing at the doorway was my daughter, holding hands with the man from before, her husband, Newton Smith.

"They're all gone, dad," she said to me. "It's just me and Parker now."

The Winter Train, Part Three

The Cryo-Tube sat silently in solitude in the otherwise empty train carriage. Maybe not completely alone, since I was there as well. But the two of us had been together for so long, the machine felt more like an extension of my body than anything. I listened to the clicks and clacks of the train and the hum of the engine from the opposite of the line. The sound was hypnotising, letting me get lost in my train of thoughts. Hah. *Train* of thoughts.

The carriage door slid opened, letting in broken rays of light separated by the elongated shadow of my daughter. "Dad?" she asked. I did not turn to her. "Are you coming backin?"

"Maybe later," I replied blankly.

For a minute after, I sat in silence, staring at the dim outline of the machine in front of me, Leila's shadow stretched out over me, unmoving from where she stood.

I asked her, "How did your mom die?"

From the corner of my eyes, I watched as her shade shifted, crossing the threshold that separated the cabins and closing the door behind her, once again cutting off light from the room.

Her faint form took a seat beside me. Even in the darkness, I could see she wore a brown hooded jacket and long jeans. I guessed my eyes had adjusted itself for pitch black after having slept for as long as I did.

111

She began, "A few days after you left, she just fell asleep and never woke up. Doctor Parker said she died of old age long before the poisoning could cause her too much pain. Graceful death, he said. As she deserved."

I nodded, satisfied and glad that Joan had passed in peace, and not screaming unceremoniously to the end. It was a suitable way to remember her. "And Leah and G?"

She was quick to reply, as if she had been preparing the story to tell me from the moment I woke. Maybe even earlier. Maybe she had stood in front of me while I slept and poured out the confessions.

"The professor was found beside the Cryo-Tube last year. Just slumped against the machine with a smile on her face. I think she worked on you till the very end."

"What was she working on?"

"Don't know. She didn't leave a note or anything. We couldn't find any modification to the machine either. Sad to say, I don't think she managed to finish whatever it was she wanted to do." She paused a moment, thinking of something to add. "But she looked young as hell though."

"Heh," I chuckled, remembering her telling me that I too might be youthful for life. Though with a robot arm and legs as a difference. "What about G?"

Leila didn't reply. She just sat silently, her breathing the only sound that was produced. I realised how insensitive a topic it must have been. G had been her father after all. More so than I had been.

"Sorry," I added awkwardly. "I didn't mean to, you know, make you sad about it or anything."

She reacted with a surprisingly defencive tone, "I'm not sad."

"It's okay. I know he's your father, and that he's cared for you all your life. It's normal to feel sad."

I couldn't feel it, but I saw the outline of the Cryo-Tube moved slightly as she wrapped her arms around my shoulder, pulling me in close so she could lean into me, lying into my arms as her mother once did.

Tenderly, she replied, "You're my dad too."

Though I was slightly reluctant to return her hug as I was afraid my artificial arm might do it too tightly, I made the effort to do so anyway. And for the first time in a long, long week, I felt like a father again. Or maybe, a little more like the son in a family. Being comforted by my own

112

daughter made me realised just how much an adult she was now. In terms of life experience, she had a decade more than I did. Yet, I felt old, as if the age I've spent asleep translated to an experience in wisdom that came with the elders.

We rocked back and forth, finding comfort in the rhythm of each others' heartbeat and the sound of the train on tracks.

She then said, "He was killed. Randy, I mean. There was a riot one day and a bunch looters took the opportunity to try and rob some of the stores at gun point. He was there just trying to talk everyone out of it. He managed to stop the gunmen. All of them. But he got shot. Lost his life."

I had not expected such a story. It was a shocking reminder of his partner, Agent Matthews. They both died for a good deed. "Lei, I'm sorry."

"Don't be," she sternly replied, though not with reprimand, but a tune of pride. "He was a hero. Saved a lot of lives. Something we seem to be doing a lot. You know, this family of ours."

I laughed, recalling what I told the agent once about us only accepting people into our family after stopping a falling plane. "It's in our blood." I continued to stare at the Cryo-Tube. Then, a solemn question hit me. Without considering, I asked, "Do you regret it? Me doing this."

Without pause, she said, "Wait." Looking at her watch, the glow of the needles pointed the time as slightly past noon. She said, "I want to show you something."

"What is it?" I asked.

"Look to the right," she instructed.

I did as I was told and found that she had gotten to her feet. She moved to the carriage door and pulled it apart. The chug of the train blasted through the now opened container, the tunnels' brown wall flying by us in a dark blur. Wind rustled my hair and hers flailed wildly.

"Careful!" I shouted with worry. "What are you doing?"

"They call this The Winter Train," she explained with raised voice over the rush of the wind, ignoring my cries. "Because it travels through a tunnel that leads out into a mountain basin. The only one of its kind in the whole word."

Just as I began to wonder how a there could be only one basin in the world – since as a geography teacher, I knew otherwise – a glow formed against the tunnel walls, shining in from the front of the train. Slowly, it grew brighter and brighter until I could see the shade of nature. Green moss, weeds and vines grew along it. The first sight of natural plants I had seen in a long, long time. Suddenly, the tunnel ended, and I immediately got to my feet at the sight that followed the blazing brightness of white.

Before me, blocked out by a glass tunnel, was a snowing plain, with rock walls in the distant as high as the tallest of skyscrapers I had ever seen, backgrounded by mountains shrouded in purple Mist. Pine trees with their cone leafs littered the landscape, with hats of white that they wore over like giant ice creams on a stick. The wind outside was gentle, the trees seemingly dancing in the breeze. Snow continued to fall all around, a glistening frozen lake the centre masterpiece of it all.

Leila started explaining, "It's basically a hole in the mountain. The height of the surrounding landscape blocks out the Mist, and cycling winds around the perimeter prevents them from passing by a certain point of the hills beyond. It's the only place we know of in the world that is still free from Mist. Sadly, the soil's not good for crops and it snows almost year round so no one has been able to settle here."

Subconsciously, I said, "It's beautiful."

"It's hope," Leila said and turned to look at me. "Hope that the world would return to its once peaceful landscape."

"You still haven't answered me though." I somewhat insensitively redirected the conversation back on track. "Do you regret me doing all this?"

"Dad," Leila knelt down beside me, holding my hand in hers. Her hazel eyes locked onto mine, and despite not having any similar DNA within, she reminded me of Joan. "You're like this plain of snow. A small part of the world that's still going strong, and will continue to do so for a long, long time. You're not regret. You're like this place. Hope."

The Winter Train, Part Four

I wondered if imagination was linked to sight. Even with my eyes closed, my mind can't seem to project anything onto the blank canvas of the back of my eyelids. Yet, I know I've read before that even the blind could imagine sounds, so perhaps my inability to do so was attributed more to the time I've been submerged in darkness rather than the lack of imagination. At any rate, I decided to stop trying and opened my eyes to the darkness of the cabin.

"Lights," I said, and the fluorescent lamp automatically flickered on as I sat up in my bed, throwing the blanket aside and off me.

Unlike real eyes, my camera substitutes don't feel any discomfort when adjusting to brightness. In fact, it does so with surprising ease and I had the fleeting idea of asking Parker if I could install night vision technology into them.

A knock on the door pulled me out of my thoughts and I called out, "Come in."

The cabin door slid opened and my – I can't believe I'm saying this – son-in-law, Newton Smith, stood at the door. He said, "Hey, I was just passing by and saw your lights on. Is everything okay?"

"Yeah, fine. I just can't sleep," I admitted. "Newton, right?"

"Actually, it's Leonard," he replied, and I remembered Leila telling me the name before I went under five years ago. "Newton is my middle

115

name. Parker just calls me that cause he thinks it sounds cooler."

"I'm gonna have to agree with the doctor on this one," I replied, thinking that I should have thought of an awesome middle name for Leila as well. "Do people still say 'cool' these days?"

"Parker does," he watched as I adjusted my seating to lean against the wall. "Can't sleep?"

"Yeah, I guess I've slept for long enough."

Uncannily, he asked, "Or maybe there's something on your mind?"

"I um..." I was unsure of how to reply. "It's um... it's nothing."

"Want to talk about it?"

"You're really blunt, aren't you?" I said matter-of-factly.

"It's part of my charm."

I chuckled at his directness, that personality of his matching the rather stout built.

Deciding it's better to get things off my chest sooner than later, I asked, "How did you meet my daughter anyway?"

He adjusted his standing uncomfortably. "Well..." he looked towards the chair opposite me and I gestured him to sit. Taking the invitation, he closed the door behind him and removed his coat, draped it over the chair, and took the position on the cushion after. "There's not much to the story, really. I was an engineer hired to maintain the Cryo-Tube. She said 'Hi', I said 'Hi', back. G told me to back off. One thing let to another and..."

"You're now porking my daughter."

"Now who's being blunt?"

"Well, I'm her father, so I think I have the right to be blunt."

"You know I'm older than you, right?"

"Still her father."

"Heh," he laughed awkwardly. "Right. Just so you know, we have a kid now."

"I know. She told me. John is it?" I leaned into the wall of the cabin and contemplated on the idea that I was actually a grandfather. It dawned on me that I will likely never see him. "How old is he? Three?"

"Four, actually. We named her after Joan. A little at least." Newton reached around into his coat pocket and retrieved a leather wallet. From within, he took out a small film of photograph and passed it to me. I wondered if anyone else in the world was still old fashioned enough to

116

carry around pocket photographs. "We left him with a friend since we didn't know how dangerous this trip might be."

The picture showed Leila and Newton, with a young boy with a fluff of red hair standing between them. I had no doubt the boy was my grandson for he had the same bubbled chin Leila had when she was younger, an age and image which was no more than a week old in my mind. He was pictured happily blowing out the candle on his third birthday cake, and I could not help but regret not being there to celebrate with them.

Newton said, "I know that face."

"What face?" I asked.

"Your daughter have the same face when she does something wrong."

"You know Leila is adopted, right? We don't really share a face."

"All families share a face. One day, I'll probably share your face too." I stretched out to return the photograph to him, to which he held out his hand in rejection. "Keep it. I can take more pictures with him, but I think that will be the only one I can offer you."

"Thanks." I coupled my reply with a nod of appreciation before pocketing the photograph.

"You know, John's pretty much the only kid in school who doesn't think of you as a hero. He's young, but somehow he knows you're only doing this for family."

"About that." A question came to mind. "What's with all this hero stuff? I've been hearing it since Leila's graduation and I don't really understand it. Leila tried to explain it to me but I couldn't fully grasp the idea."

Newton crossed his legs and leaned into his seat. He stretched and looked up to the ceiling as if searching for a memory. "It might have been harder for Parker or Leila to explain, since they've been on the project since day one." Having quickly found the rhythm of his story, he sat back up straight. "But before I was brought on, I was just some common folk. And there was this interview they did with Joan where she talked a little more about her inspiration to do the work she did. Then something about you came up and people started digging. The story of this project came to light and so did the reasons behind it."

"And people started thinking of me as some saviour..."

"It's not that far-fetched. Take it from my point of view. The entire world is being shrouded by a poisonous Mist that is threatening to kill every single living thing alive. That's some pretty life affecting stuff." He looked at me with the same intrigue as if I had been a different species. "When I first heard about you, I was just a teenager. I thought that you were some brave man who was sacrificing his life to save the world. You were the superhero everyone needed to hear of in a time when everything seems lost."

"And now?"

Newton shrugged, "The same, just with more emphasis on family." He paused slightly before adding, "And maybe a little selfish."

I laughed a little at the jab. It was funny because it was true, in that there was a degree of selfishness in my actions. I wanted to live. "Whatever the reason, I'm here now."

"Yes... that you are."

For a moment after that, we sat in silence. The rumbling churn of the train once again accompanying us.

I began, "Newton—"

He cut me off with, "Please don't call me that. It's a terrible name. I don't know why my parents would even name me that."

I replied sarcastically, "I'm certainly not going to call you Leonard." I paused again to collect the thoughts that had been cut off. "Anyway, thanks for the talk. I really needed it."

"No problem." He stood up, realising the conversation had outlasted the topics. "Try to get some sleep."

"I will," I lied. I then ended with, "Son."

"That's weird," Newton admitted, shaking his head with a grimace. "I don't think it's quite fitting."

"I know," I replied slyly. "But I either call you that or Newt."

He laughed, "Right, Newt. That's worst than Newton I think." He opened the door and looked back to me with a smile. "Fine then, son it is. Night. Father." The door slid shut behind him.

Alone in the room again, I took out the family photo Newton gave me. I stared at the smiles of my daughter, wondering of the life that I had missed with her. Her wedding. Having John. Her first job. Her first home. I knew they had happened and there was nothing I could do to relive those moments of her life with her.

I thought it was unfair, that I had the power to jump forward decades in time but not a single ounce of strength to move it in the direction I wanted. The whole journey, from the first day I entered the Cryo-Tube, had practically been chosen for me by others, and I could only watch as the world flowed by me. Events that are out of my hands. Death that stretched away from me. Life just out of my reach.

The Winter Train, Part Five

With engines still running, the train rumbled gently beside the platform of Tikika. Men twice my size, with muscles bulky enough to break off their bodies and start a new state, loaded the Cryo-Tube from the cargo carriage onto a ridiculously large trolley, something which I found weird. Not the men, but the fact that they were using a manual trolley instead of an autonomous one.

I leaned over to Leila and asked, "Where are the automated cranes?"

"Oh..." she replied hesitantly. "The Forum has cut off electronic trades with this city."

"What? Why would they do that?"

She looked worryingly left and right, "We shouldn't talk about this is in the open." It was a reply which I found eerily similar to something out of an espionage film. "Let's get to the car."

I followed her to the front of the station, noticing just how empty the public place was. At most I saw about two dozen people, even though the time was clearly midday. Even the passengers that exited the train were no more than the number of good fingers and toes I had left.

"I know the situation isn't exactly peaceful in the world right now, but where are all the people?" I asked as we reached the steps of the station. A black van waited for us at the foot of the steps.

Leila ignored my question. Or more accurately, refused to answer.

She lead me down to the vehicle while I hastily followed behind her. The door opened from the inside with Doctor Parker greeting me. We got into the six-seater, with me and Leila taking the middle passenger seats. Parker moved to the front, and Newton waved to me as the driver.

Once the door slid shut, Leila began, "We haven't told you everything, dad. We didn't want you to worry."

"Wait, Lei," Newton said, "Are we really doing this? I thought we discussed that there's no point."

"That's right," Parker added. "He won't even be here for everything."

Angered, I exclaimed, "Can you guys stop talking about things as if I'm not here? And what's this situation that you all don't want me to know?"

Leila sighed and said, "Look around you dad."

"What do you—"

"Just... look around."

I did as she asked, staring out the tinted window to the underground road. I did not see the futuristic world I had expected. Surrounding the station entrance were just a handful of citizens, cycling along on bicycles and horse drawn carriages. The ones on their feet ogled at our van as if it was a monster from another dimension.

I could hear Newton letting out a surrendering breath as he started the engine, the sound of which drew even more wilting stares. As he drove off, I heard the deafening quiet of the city as our tire screech rang louder than blasting rock music into headphones.

Almost breathless at the archaic looking streets, I asked, "What happened?"

"Like I said," Leila continued. " The Forum cut off electronics trade to Tikika. That means anything with a chip or anything else metallic in it has been embargoed here. Even cars. You're sitting in one of the last thousand vehicles left still working in the city."

"Why would The Forum do that?"

Parker said, "It's a long story Milton." Then to Leila, he reprimanded, "One that he does not need to know."

"He has a right to," she replied.

"But there is nothing he can do!"

Agitated by being ignored again, I raised, "But she's right! I have a right to know what's happening to the world that I'm supposed to save!"

Newton, apparently ignoring the conflict between his wife and the doctor, immediately explained, "In the past few years, The Forum has been using the Five Cities to heavily mine ores through the expensive underground networks Joan had created. They practically monopolised the metal industry."

"Newton!" Parker exclaimed.

I said, "Look, doctor. I have to know this."

"Why? Not to sound insensitive, but you won't even be here when all the things go down. All we're giving you is one extra thing to worry about."

I hailed back, "You're a logical guy. Maybe something happens in the next few years. Something that I can help fix when I wake up!"

"He's right," Newton said. "We can't live forever. But Milton here is as close as we can get. If anything happens in the future, he's the only one that can take care of it. And to do that, he needs to know what happened."

Parker laid back into his seat in defeat, letting out a long, drawn out breath. "Fine. But you guys do the explaining."

Leila put a caring hand on my shoulder. "It's gonna be a long explanation."

"I can't believe I'm saying this," I replied to her. "But I have all the time in the world right now."

"Okay. As Leonard said, The Forum embargoed metal trade with Tikika," she explained as she settled back into her seat. "That's because before the embargo, Tikika decided to rebel against The Forum."

"Why?" I asked. Of the all the cities, Tikika was considered the most peaceful and cooperative.

She continued, "'Cause The Forum had successfully created basic artificial intelligence and had started to manufacture automated fighting machines. Basically, robots of war that can fight intelligently and kill without morale."

"What?" I exclaimed in absolute surprise. I felt I had just dived headlong into a pool of science fiction. But after a look at the serious face given by my daughter, I realised, "You're not joking."

"Of course not!" Parker voice out. "That's why they cut off funding to you. They moved all of it to produce those damn machines." He outed his previous lie about not knowing the reason for the funding cut.

Still in partial disbelief, I questioned, "What is the point of this? The world is being overtaken by Mist and The Forum has time to prepare for

122

a war?"

Newton added, "This was all happening even before Joan passed away. We've been trying for a peaceful solution, but The Forum over the decade gradually moved to a totalitarian stance. A lot of people weren't happy with it. Including my parents." He grimly paused, and I knew what he would say before he even continued. "So they threw all of them into prison. For life. A lot of things like that was happening around the world. So, when news spread that they've decided to cut off funding to your project, the husband of Joan the Hero and future saviour, it became the last straw."

It then dawned on me. The reason for the secretive nature of this move and why I woke up in the train instead of the lab. They needed to move me quickly, and waking me up earlier would have caused too much trouble, given that the post awakened me would have been disoriented and unable to move efficiently.

My son-in-law continued, "The Forum's changed a lot in the past few years. They've become a group for giving power to selected few while putting the rest in the palm of their hands. If this discord continues and the rest of the Five Cities join in the rebellion, we might have an all out war, and not just the isolated rioting that's been happening."

Remembering that Roagnark was the capitol for The Forum, I deduced, "You guys are fugitives." I looked to my daughter who could only stare at the back of the seat in front of her. "You didn't just move me, you broke me out of Roagnark."

Parker stated, "Told you he'd figure it out."

"Shut up," I shushed.

"Now that's just rude," Parker countered.

"Shut up!" My voice got louder that second time. "Shut up! Shut up! Shut up!"

It was the first time since going under that my mind had the chance to synchronise with the happenings around me. Having had a full day to rest and catch up on events, I finally started putting the pieces together. Of why I was so far away from home. Of the effects of the new world had on my safety. But most disturbingly, how I ended up where I was and why Parker did not want me to know more of the situation at present.

I asked, "How many?"

Confused, Leila asked, "What are you talking about, dad?"

"How many?!" Thinking faster and clearer than I had in days, I said,

"You needed to get me here. Here! To Tikika! Which means that whatever you're doing is not only off the book, it is completely against the wishes of The Forum, since they are not exactly best friends right now."

"Shit," Parker mumbled. "He's *really* figuring it out."

"Then there should only be one way to get me here! You needed to take me by force. And you had the means to do it, since so many people were supporting me," I pushed on, gesturing in frustration. "There's only one reason why you wouldn't want me to know what's happening. And that is if I'll start questioning the worth of keeping me alive. And there's only one thing that can make me do that. One thing drastic enough to make me question myself. So I will ask again, how many?"

Leila looked at me, tears beginning to cloud her eyes. Her voice breaking slightly as she said, "A lot, dad. A lot of people died to get you here."

The Winter Train, Part Six

We left the common highway almost two hours ago, meandering through the twisting side streets of the underground network, getting farther and farther away from civilisation. By the time I woke up from my nap, Parker had switched places with Newton, carrying out the last few minutes of our drive to the location. We had turned off the concrete tunnel and into a smaller dirt cave.

"This road leads through a mountainside," Leila explained to me. "The new site for the Cryo-Tube is just near the exit."

The road was lit by small electric lamps that brightened automatically as we neared. But otherwise, we went at a slow speed to avoid bumping into things in the dark. Slowly, a soft blue glow appeared at the end of the tunnel and grew larger as we approached. The rumbling of the wheels on dirt suddenly stopped as we travelled over a new patch of smooth, concrete road. The vehicle then burst out into the light of an open cavern.

A wall of falling water formed the west wall of the cave, bright teal light shining through the gaps with splash-back from the falls reaching even the windscreen of the van. A large truck was already there, with the same burly men from the station unloading the Cryo-Tube from the vehicle.

Leila slid her door opened and Parker and Newton followed suit,

125

getting out of the van. Realising we've arrived at out destination, I unbuckled and proceeded after them.

"Where are we?" I asked generally, staring in wide-eyed wonder at the cave as I stepped out of the vehicle onto the makeshift concrete road.

I noticed a few concrete pillars, artificially built around structural points of the cavern. Water dripped from stalactites on the ceiling onto moss filled mounts on the ground. The cave walls glittered with specks of water that had made their way from the waterfall wall.

Parker came up to me and led me by my elbow. "We're on the outskirts of Tikika. Somewhere near the border to The Wilds. It's far out enough from the safety of the city that The Forum won't think to look for you here."

"And what are we doing here?" I asked, starting to follow without his lead. He let go of my arm as we joined up with Newton and Leila.

"This is going to be where you sleep for the coming years," Newton answered. "We're using the power of the waterfalls to power the Cryo-Tube. There's a generator built into the mountain and will be hooked up to the machine. The entire room we'll house you in is made of stainless steel alloy. My design, naturally. It'll last for quite a long time," he finished rather proudly.

Together, we headed towards a large double steel door embedded into the wall of the cavern, following behind the muscle men and Cyro-Tube. The group in front stopped just short of the door and Leila ran up to the left of the monolith.

Sliding open a hidden panel, she revealed a number pad embedded into the arch of the gate. She typed in a series of six numbers, distinguished by the beeps – which, to this day, I have no idea what they do aside from making an annoying noise – and the large metal door rumbled open, sliding aside and showing the darkness within like an opening into a new universe or a threshold to outer space.

Leila directed the workers, "Move it in and hook it up to the generator." The men nodded and moved to work, followed by Parker and Newton going in to help, though I was not sure what a limping doctor could do in that situation.

I walked up to her, "This is where I'll be?" I stared into the dim room, lit only by the slowly fading light outside.

She replied, "We're out of the boundaries of the cities. This is just one of the places in nature we found that still blocks out the mist, thanks

126

to the waterfall." She turned to me with a hopeful smile, "This cavern is actually at the edge of the mountain basin that we passed by on The Winter Train. The water of the falls comes from the snow that melts there. Poetic, I think."

"Yeah." I looked down to my prosthetic legs, thinking of all the things that were lost in my journey there. "But isn't it a long drive? How are you guys going to wake me up again."

A downcast look covered her face as I said that and I immediately knew the answer.

I continued grimly, "I'm not waking up again. Am I?"

"No." She shook her head, tearing up. "Not to see us again at least," She sighed deeply, wiping away the tears that swelled in her sights. "You still have five days left in your life. It should be enough to get you back to the portal if you could find some sort of transport. Even a bicycle would do."

I was dumbfounded. I stared at her and she tried to evade my gaze. But after trying to hold back, she broke and began to cry uncontrollably. I held out my good hand, gently wrapped it around her head, and brought her into my chest, where she cried into without holding back.

Between sobs, she muttered, "I don't want you to go."

"I know." I nodded into her. Yet, I replied, "But I don't have a choice any more."

Her head bobbed up and down in agreement, and I knew she understood my position then. "I'm so sorry, dad. I made you choose this."

"You don't have to apologise to me. Ever. Not ever in your lifetime." My voice creaked as my body attempted to cry. Yet, the cyborg part of me prevented me from doing such a simple action of life.

Newton walked up to us and his eyes shone with the understanding that the news had been broken. "We're ready for you," he told me. "Whenever you are."

Slowly and extremely gently, I tried to pull my daughter away from me, but she refused to budge as her cries turned into pained sobs. Seeing the struggle, Newton came up and lend a hand, managing to tug us apart.

I looked him in the eye, "You take care of her."

And without missing a beat, he replied, "To the end of her days." Leila turned to cry into his arms.

Not knowing what else to say, I could only turn away from the couple and step into the darkness, the glow of the Cryo-Tube's interior lighting the only thing guiding my path forward.

Standing beside the machine, Doctor Parker, awaited me.

"Doctor," I greeted again.

The man with the limp and cane replied with a wise tone, "You can still walk away from this, Milton." It was a reminder of the choice Leah Hullway gave me just a short two days before.

Dejectedly, I replied, "I can't now. People have died for me now. If I walk away, I would be stepping on everything they stood for." I laughed and could hear my mechanical fist clenching in self hatred. "Which is a bit screwed up if you ask me. Since if there was ever a time when I wanted to quit, today would be that day."

"I know. And I'll say again, you can still walk away from this."

I smiled at the old man and hugged him. "You're the good friend I never asked for or wanted." I patted his back approvingly. Our silence was my answer to him and he seemed to have understood. I stepped back and asked, "You know, I never knew your full name."

He smiled back. "Greene. Greene Parker."

"Good. Good name," I replied. With a heavy heart, I turned away from him and slowly, I climbed into the machine which hummed in anticipation of me. "Well, Doctor Greene Parker, I will never forget you."

"Yeah. You'd better not," he said with a cheeky grin. Turning away from the machine, he headed off to the light of the outside, his silhouette like a hero walking off into a sunset.

From the door, Leila ran in, her steps clacking behind her. And for a moment, the image of the little girl running up to me for a hug flashed across my mind, right before her auburn hair flew into the Cryo-Tube behind her as she embraced me within the confined space.

She croaked through tears, "I love you. Dad. I love you so much."

I hugged back. "I love you too." I cursed my eyes internally, for at that moment, I wished I was blind again. Since at least then, I could still cry. How many times over the past few days have I wished to be able to cry?

"Remember Hillbury?" I ended as she unwillingly backed out of the machine.

"Yeah," she replied with a sad smile, her face illuminated by the glow of the Cryo-Tube. "Favourite-test place. Ever."

With that, the glass door closed quickly and silently between us and the preservation liquid began filling up the Cryo-Tube. The sloshing of the water as it entered were louder and more prominent than I've ever heard them before, as if the machine was crying on my behalf. The world darkened around me as the anaesthetic took its effect.

I thought of all the people I've lost and was about to, the image of their faces burnt sharply into my mind. My wife and daughter. My father and mother. Golph and Matthews. Leah and Parker. My son-in-law, who I've only met once. My grandson, John, who I will never meet. And all the nameless, faceless strangers that gave their lives to get me there. For a moment, right before darkness took me, I thought I felt a tear rolling down me cheeks. But of course, that was not possible. I can't cry. Nor can I feel. Without my prosthetics, I would not be able to walk, write, or even see. I was as much of a nothing as the darkness before me.

Then light burst into my eyes. Gunshots and explosions blasted and echoed off the walls around me as the glass door of the Cryo-Tube shattered. I was washed face first out the machine with the gush of blue liquid, falling like a rag doll to the ground.

My head spun from the sudden awakening as I watched blood from my nose mixed with the pooling liquid. I tried to push myself onto my feet but my left arm, still asleep, gave way. My robotic right though, pushed full force and I was spiralled onto my back.

"Get up!" I could hear a female voice shouting for me. I turned my head left to see rubbles of steel and stones scattered around the chamber floor while light from the outside drew jagged shadows across the ground. "Get up, old man!

I turned onto and over my limped left arm, knuckling my right to push myself awkwardly up. I grunted as my muscles strained from the act, not out of pain but simply a reaction of the body from the twisted position. My entire weight leaned into the mechanical arm and my head pivoted on the ground. But being disoriented and without the ability to feel, I could not gauge my physical position and was left stuck halfway between a worm and a snail.

"Oh for fuck's sakes," the female cursed.

A shadow covered my left side as the woman raised my sleeping arm over her shoulders, lifting me to my feet.

"I got him!" she yelled. "Let's get out of here!"

I looked up to the entrance. The once thick steel doors were blasted wide open, with half a dozen men and women dressed in brown dirt camouflage garbs and wearing gas masks standing to the sides of the entrance, both inside and out of the chamber. From an assortment of guns, they fired brightly lit tracer rounds towards the six-legged metal robot spiders.

Last of the Wars, Part One

She wore a gas mask that covered the whole of her head, hair included. The rubber of the accessory stretched all the way down and around her neck and her clothes were all tightly sealed and lengthily sleeved. The combined ensemble, gloves, boots and all, were enough to completely cover my 'rescuer' from head to toe with not a lick of skin visible. Two pistols were holstered on both her thighs, with her main firearm, an assault rifle, strung over her left shoulder.

"Stop gawking!" she commanded, dragging me to my feet. My prosthetic legs, not needing any form of rebooting like my physical body does, found their steps almost instantaneously.

"What's...going on?" I asked groggily, pushing myself away from her.

I stumbled towards the wall where I took cover, out of the line of sights of the attacking machines and clear of the line of fire from the humans who kept up their shooting.

"What does it look like?" She ran up to me while shouting through her mask. "We need to get you out of here before you get skinned by those damn machines!" It was then that I noticed a name tag dangling from one of the many carabiners hanging around her waist.

I read aloud, "Amelia?"

"Con-fucking-gradulations. You figured out my name. Now can we

131

get a move on?"

Needless to say, I was reluctant to follow. But between mysterious humans with guns and alien-like robots clawing their way into a mountainside, I had to go with humanity on that.

Unsure of what to say, I simply nodded to her, to which she signalled to her – I guess – squad, "Back to the tunnels!" Turning to me, she commanded, "Stick close to me!"

She rushed forward towards the cover of the walls of the blasted opening and I followed after, sliding behind the steel between her and another soldier. She pulled her rifle up to ready in her left hand, preparing herself to shoot if necessary.

The soldier behind me, wielding a inconsistently small sub-machine gun said through his muffled breath, "Name's Borris sir. It's a real honour to meet you!"

"I guess I'm likewise then!" I yelled back a greeting as another round of suppression fire took place.

Annoyed, Amelia scolded him, "Save your bootlicking for after we get out of this!" She turned to the Cryo-Tube and I saw a figure working on the machine that I had missed before. A man, padded at the joints from shoulders to knees and carrying a backpack almost the size of his body, stood at the machines' side, pulling open panes after panels. "Brother! You found the data?"

On cue, the brother pulled out a hard-drive from the bottom of the machine. Raising it above his head, he shouted back, "Got it!" He made a beeline for the opposite wall where he took cover with two others.

"Alright," Amelia said and turned to Borris. "EMP those bastards!"

Borris circled around me with a politely out-of-situation—"Excuse me."

From one of his many belt pouches, he pulled out an egged-shaped device which, by the orders given by Amelia, I would assume was an electromagnetic pulse bomb. He squeezed the side of it gently and the device's edge glowed with a blue light.

"Fire in the hole!" he shouted as he got to his feet to toss the grenade.

The grenade left his hand, flying out of sight towards the hulking spider bots. A metal spike was returned in kind, slashing through the air before me, piercing clean through Borris's chest, taking him off his feet and flinging him backward from the sheer momentum. The spike clang into the Cryo-Tube, embedding deep into the metal.

I heard myself called out, "No!" I sounded as if I was an outsider listening to a recording of my own voice.

I jumped out from hiding, with Amelia's futile attempt to stop me being swatted away. I ran towards the downed man, popping out of cover just as the EMP wave blasted through the air. My prosthetic legs and arm gave way and I fell forward towards him. The last image I saw before my camera-eyes frizzled out was of my good hand wrapping around Borris's wrist.

"Milton!" Amelia's brother yelled. "Amelia! Get him to the tunnels!"

"No!" I shouted back. I couldn't feel what I was doing or see where I was. I could not even move most of my body. All I could do was will my body to keep a grip on Borris. Even that I was not sure I was actually doing. "We're not leaving him!"

Amelia's voice came close to me and I could hearing her screaming into my ear. "He's gone! He's gone! The EMP won't last! We've got to get you out!"

"We've got to save him!" I pleaded back to the group, but was ignored.

I could hear myself being dragged away, the rocks crunching under me as I sobbed in protest. But with just one working limb, I could only hear the failing flails of my arm slapping against the ground.

The brother gently said, "Stop swinging. You're going to hurt yourself." And with reluctance, I stopped fighting. I heard my hand gave the ground one final thud as it went limp in resignation.

My mind blanked out. As the sound of the waterfalls muffled, I could only think of how someone else had given their life for mine. How somehow, I once again became the princess that needed to be rescued. I lamented and could hear my teeth cracking as I gritted in anger and frustration. A small explosion rocked the area followed by the sound of collapsing rocks. The cacophony of splashing water muted almost instantaneously as the tunnel got barricaded.

"We're safe for now," I could hear Amelia say. "Put him down and go scout ahead. Make sure the path is still clear."

With that, the sound of two distinct sets of footsteps retreated into the distance, echoing off the tunnel walls for a full minute before finally fading away.

Numbed and still in shock, I asked, "Why? Why did you save me?"

And the only reply I received was the shallow breathing of my companions. "I'm no hero. I can't save the world. There's no use risking your lives for mine."

"Stop whining," Amelia replied coldly. "Just be glad you're still alive."

Her brother muttered futilely to stop her, "Milly..."

"At what cost?" I asked. My eyes began to reboot, but slowly. I could see a patch of grey and hear the lens of the cameras zooming in and out as it calibrated itself. "Borris is dead."

Even colder, she said, "He knew what he was getting into."

Something in me snapped and I yelled, "How could you say that! Don't you even care about other people?!"

She screamed back, "Of course I do! But what's the point of dwelling on it! Our goal was to save you!"

"Why!?" I shouted. "Why can't you just leave me to die and save yourself?"

"You fucking idiot!" she let out, banging her fist against the wall. Colours returned to my vision but the image was still too blurry to make out anything beyond blobbed figures. "Was mom trying to say something when she named me after a dumb fuck like you?"

Her sentence stunned me as I caught the one word that stuck out. "Mom?"

"Yeah! Amelia. Milly. Milly-fucking-Smith!" she punctuated violently. "You want to know why we saved you? Because we're fucking family you retarded fuck shit! Argh!" In my shock, I could only sit and listen as she stomped off, cursing colourfully under her breath.

Scuffling up beside me, my vision finally fully returned as I took a look at the man that was her brother. Older than the photo I had of him by at least two decades, he treated my bleeding arm that was scratched up in my fit and struggle. I looked down to my hand and in it was a blood covered, brown, plastic analogue watch. Borris's watch.

The brother replied, "Sorry about Milly. She's a little straightforward at times. And short tempered. And violent. But she means well. Mostly."

I looked to the young man with his mask off. With a straight scar across his lips angling rightward down his chin and crossing a ragged stubble of beard, he looked as worn as the stretched glazed look in his eyes suggested, but somehow still managed to maintain an air of calm and patience with his gentle smile. His auburn hair, the colour of his

134

mother's, was kept in a short crew cut.

With a croaking voice, I whimpered, "John?"

His smile widened as he finished cleaning my wounds, wrapping a bandage around the cuts of my arm. "Alright, grandpa. Let's get going."

Last of the Wars, Part Two

John and I hiked through the long tunnel. Though just wide enough for two humans to fit through, my grandson told me that it was the same tunnel I travelled through in a van 23 years ago, just squashed under the tectonic shifts from earthquakes. Burnt out electric lamps still hung on the walls, but the only source of light came from our torches, showing the way with cones of white. Our feet crunched the damp earth beneath us, the air cold from the frosted misty breaths I breathed. The dripping of water played in the background.

I asked him, "So, you're what? Twenty six?"

"Twenty seven," John replied. "Why do you ask?"

"Just wondering, you know."

"Why?"

"Why are you asking why?"

"Just curious," he replied matter-of-factly, which was the same answer I would have given. "My mom says I got it from you, curiosity."

I wanted to remind him that that was not physically possible, but remembered what Newt said about families sharing faces after a time, even if we aren't related by blood. "And I got it from my grandfather," I instead said. "Runs in the family."

"Yup. Skipped Milly though." We continued walking a distance with no sight of Amelia or any of the other soldiers. "She just charges through."

I held up the watch that I had pulled off Borris's corpse. I wondered if I would be able to feel nausea at his death, now that my mind and gag reflexes had been somewhat severed. And if not, does the fact that I did not vomit on the spot show a sign of some sort of sociopathic apathy? "So what are you guys? Tikika soldiers?"

John remained silent and continued walking and I knew I had hit a rusted nail. It should have been the point where any normal person under normal circumstances would back away. But I can confidently say that not only was I not a normal person – being a cyborg – and the conditions we were in were even further from any semblance of sanity. At least it was for me. Not to mention that I was his grandfather.

"You're definitely not from The Forum. Hillbury? Roagnark? Lucinda? Penstine?" I pushed.

With a sigh, he replied, "Milton. There aren't any cities left."

Stunned, I said, "You don't mean..."

From further down the tunnel, Amelia shouted rather casually, "Everything is gone!"

And following immediately after with incredible synch, John added, "The Forum and us are the only ones left. As far as we know anyway."

I slowed down my pace and John slowly slipped out of my sight as I pondered the implication of the sentence. I could still see the light from his torch and I followed it diligently. "Who's us?" I asked.

"Bunch of small groups. Wanderers. Rovers. Small villages in other Mist free natural formations. Most of which are just areas smaller than a basketball court. It's been like this for about five years now," he replied grimly. I could only listen lamentably that everything Joan had did for the world had been buried under within the past decade. "At the start, The Forum just used the machines to sort of barricade themselves away from the rest of the cities. Self sufficiency. Then suddenly, the robots started attacking."

I managed to catch up with him, sighting his back. "What happened after that? You're saying all the rest of the cities fell to robots from one place? What about the armies?"

"Sure, we put up a fight at first," he continued, not turning around to face me. "But they are robots. When we destroy one of them, they'd just pick up the pieces and put themselves back together. We didn't stand a chance against them. Immune to Mist and able to resurrect themselves. It was insanity. An endless army."

From there though, I could not think of anything to ask further. It was a pretty clear-cut situation. The world had a war. And we, the humans, lost.

From the front of the line, Amelia shouted, "John! Mask on! We're near the exit."

Listening to his sister, he put his mask back on before turning to me to offer his spare.

I accepted it, but not without asking, "Is this necessary? I already have Mist poisoning."

She must have heard me for Amelia yelled, "It's a precaution, you idiot!" Her angry voice echoed down far behind and onward. "We don't have many doctors left to treat your condition so we've got to take as much care as we can!"

I huffed somewhat childishly, and wore the mask. "Fine..."

Though it was a simple rubber cap mask, I had some trouble with feeling its position on my head and had to slow down to manually adjust it. It was then I was reminded how all these small simple actions are hindered by my physical numbness.

I asked John, "Is she always like this? I don't remember anyone in the family as hot headed as her."

"Yeah, well again, sorry about that. She was four years after me. Born just right at the end of the year after you were brought here." As we continued our way to the exit, he reminiscence, "Unlike me, she wasn't around your Cryo-Tube at all. Didn't really see your existence. To her, the stories of you were mostly just that. Stories. She has a lot to live up to with very little motivation to do so. Imagine growing up in a hopeless world surrounded by people with stories of hope. It can drive you up the wall sometimes."

"Huh..." was all I replied and wondered how much difference not being around me could actually make a person.

He swung his pack front and rummaged through it, pulling out a black ball of cloth. "Here."

He tossed it to me. Reflexively, I caught it. Unfolding the bundle revealed a black canvas hoodie.

"Zip up. There's a pair of glove in the sleeves. Wear the jacket into the glove. Let's try to reduce the amount of Mist exposure you get."

I did as I was told, but again, somewhat rebelliously replied, "Couldn't you have just gotten me one of those suits of yours?"

"Yeah, well, these things are kind of hard to come by. What you see is what we have," he explained. A glow appeared from the end of the tunnel and the surrounding was slowly lit up with a faint teal. We turned our torches off. "Don't worry though. We're not travelling far. We have a vehicle just outside the cave waiting for us."

"Cave?" I wondered, remembering that right outside the path was just one of the side road of the underground highway. How was it possible that we will walk through a cave if the other end was equally beneath the earth?

As the light grew brighter and brighter, I could hear the lenses of my camera eyes adjusting their irises to compensate for the change in brightness. I could see the edge of the tunnels ending as John stepped into the light. As I felt the answer to my question dawn on me, I followed out into the Mist covered sun before a conclusion was drawn, and could only stand breathless, shoulders slumped at the sight that appeared instead.

To my left and right were the remains of the underground highway. Dark and emptied, debris filled the roads. The painted lines had long since been rubbed away by time. But right in front of me, where a wall and ceiling should have been, was instead a hole the size of a...well, I don't know. I had nothing in my life to compare it to. Perhaps the entire length and height of the original chamber that housed the Cryo-Tube. That was how large the hole was. Blown inward, the remains of the walls were crunched as rubble on the road before us. A smooth, curved, half-pipe dirt incline, about a hundred meters in length, stretched up and out to the ground world above, revealing the faint sun behind the thick Mist. A glowing glob in the sky.

"What the hell happened here?" I asked, stunned at what laid before me.

"War," Amelia said as we caught up to her. "War happened. Beyond here is the battlefield of Tikika. And this crater was part of the last desperate bombardment attempted to put a stop to the Forum."

I felt out of my depth. More so than all the other times before. I was in the aftermath of a war zone, fought nearly half a century from the point in my life where all the madness started. In a foreign world with people I only knew for a few hours, I suddenly felt inexplicably alone.

139

"Not just any war," John continued. "It's the Last War. The last of the wars that we will ever fight as the human race."

Last of the Wars, Part Three

I don't know if the rumbling of the chassis was from the rickety build of the old RV or the unevenness of the road. Though equipped with a bed and chair – the latter which I sat on – the cushions and mattresses had long since been torn bare, leaving a makeshift wooden plank in their places as seats. The electric motor whirred seamlessly in the background while the oxygen regulator hummed as it filtered out the Mist from the outside with breathable air within.

With all their equipments removed, one of the male soldiers threw a bottle of pills to John from the front seat where his companion acted as driver. Without hesitation, John took off his mask and swallowed a pill from the bottle before passing the drugs on to his sister, who sat beside him on the bed.

Curious, I asked, "What's that?"

"Sintrinolamine," he replied. Amelia remaining quiet as she struggled to get her mask off. "Medication for preventing Mist Poisoning."

Suddenly hopeful, I excitedly asked, "Like a cure?"

"Donef bif stupif," Amelia muffled from behind her mask, halfway to removal but with the strap still stuck on her chin.

To his sister, John said, "I told you not to tighten it so much."

"Sat tup!" she scolded back.

141

Returning his attention to me, he continued, "It's not a cure. It's...more like an immunity booster for low level exposure. Before any symptoms sets in. But once you've started..." He stared at me with pitied eyes. "There's still no going back. The medication's in limited supplies too, since there are no longer any pharmacies."

"Oh..." I looked down ay my legs and to my metal arm. Inside me, I wondered how much further medical science could have progressed had the war not happened.

"Stop sulking!" Amelia finally managed to pull off her mask, taking in a large breath of fresh air. "You're almost ninety years old. That's a pretty long life for someone with Mist Poisoning."

Aside from her short, mud brown hair, she had the splitting image of her mother during the latter's graduation. A gaze as sharp as her personality. A face as smooth and calm as the clearest sky. Despite her ferociousness and frustrated furrows, she held the looks of a kind nanny, albeit having a bad day.

"Milly," John tried to stop her, "That's a little rude, don't you think?"

"Oh you've known me our whole life. Do you really think I care?"

"No," he sat back dejectedly. "Can't blame me for trying though."

However, I could not focus on their conversation. Lost in thoughts, I blurted out, "You look just like your mother."

To which she replied quickly and sharply, "Don't be such a fucking cliché." That immediately broke my mood of reminiscence.

"But your personality is..."

"Shit?" she answered without hesitation, taking one of the pills after.

"I was gonna say 'hard', but shit works too, I guess."

John added, "You two aren't going to get along, are you?"

"What are you saying?" Amelia replied sarcastically. "Me and Milton here are like best friends right now."

"You know," I said with some uncertainty. "You can call me grandfather."

"How about I call you 'old man'?"

Slightly annoyed, I replied, "I'm thirty years old."

"No, you're eighty-eight," she corrected with a smirk. "Old man."

I sighed in resignation. Not wanting to put up with her childish behaviour, I instead asked John, "Where are we headed?" I looked out towards the front of the vehicle. Beyond the windscreen laid a vast expense of empty, barren landscape littered with broken tanks and destroyed machines, covered by a thick layer of Mist. However, visible dots of white littered the scene as snow fell from the heavens. "Where could we possibly go?"

"To the Winter Basin. You should know of it. It's the place that the Winter Train passes through on its way to Tikika," he explained. I remembered the scene of pure white snow-scape, unhindered by Mist. "There's a small rebel camp there. That's where we'll be going."

"Why?" I asked the simple question. The looks on my grandchildren's faces as they exchanged glances told me everything I needed to know. "It's nothing good, is it? Why did you wake me up?"

Sighing, John state, "We received information that The Forum found out where you were. Since we didn't have any resources for the journey, we had to make a deal with some people to get to you."

Worried now, I asked, "What's the deal?"

To which Amelia said, "You don't have to answer that, brother."

Leaning over to her, I finally saw the caring sibling relationship between them as he placed a gentle hand on hers without her reacting. "He's going to find out anyway. Besides. This is what mom and dad would do."

"Why do you always have to do things like mom and dad?" she replied with a slight anger. "You're not mom or dad. You're you."

Finally agreeing with her, I said, "She's right. You're you." Suddenly, after a long few days, I felt like a father again. Having a chance to take care of people instead of being taken care of. To raise. To teach. "You don't have to tell me. You're not obligated to do anything. Like you said, I'll find out myself anyway."

"It's not good news," he added. "You'll probably punch me when you find out."

"Nah," I reassured him. "You're family. Said so yourself. If I can't trust family, then who can I trust?"

Amelia nodded blankly to my statement, starring at me with a look that reminded me a lot of Joan when she tried to process something stupid I said. "Not bad, old man. You were almost parent-ly for a moment."

"Grandfather," I requested again.

"Old man," she insisted.

John gave a smile as we conversed. Thinking through, he finally

143

said, "The Forum is currently home to cyborgs. Human-machine hybrids. We made a deal with the rebel leaders in order to save you. But you'll have to help them get into Roagnark."

I looked down on my robotic arm in understanding. "Cyborgs you say? So I'm like a Trojan horse?"

"Yes," Amelia added, "It may seem kind of meaningless to risk your life now, since your Cryo-Tube is destroyed—" a statement which I had not considered or even passed my thoughts, given everything that had happened.

To which her brother continued, "—but don't worry. The old models are still kept in the old chamber that used to house you." His voice lowered to a tone where the drivers could not hear. "We're going to use the rebels, just as they are using us. We get you in, but before they destroy the city or whatever it is they want to do, we'll hook you up to one of the old models to sit through the next few decades."

I ran through the entire plot point, contemplating on whether or not to accept it. I was still dying, with less than a week of life left. Not valuable enough, I felt, to risk life and limbs for. Especially for my two grandchildren who had full lives left to live. Yet, the barren land in front of me was not the optimal world I wanted to leave to them. I was torn between a risk for a better future for them, or safety for a darker one. From my pocket, I retrieved Borris's watch. A man who, for my sake, gave up his remaining time.

"No," I told them. "No more. No more dying for me. Especially not you two."

Amelia sharply replied, "Don't be fucking sentimental, old man. Doesn't suit you."

"What?"

"I grew up thinking you a selfish person,"

"Milly..." her brother tried to stop her again.

But she continued unwaveringly, "All those stories of you, sacrificing your days to give mom and grandma a better future with you. Bullshit."

Shocked at her directness, I could only ask, "What are you saying?"

"You heard me," she replied, getting to her feet as her soliloquy reached its crescendo. "You're a selfish asshole. You don't get a say in what we do. You saved your life for your own happiness. I'm right, aren't I?"

144

She was. Every word. I only accepted Matthews' offer all those years ago because I wanted to have a future with my family.

"So listen closely, old man. We're not saving you for you this time. We're doing it for ourselves. For the people that we care and will care about. We are going to save you, and you are going to fulfil that prophecy of your grandfather and save the world, so that our grandchildren will have happy endings."

John could only stare at her solemnly, and I could tell there was much justified suffering and backstory behind her ferocity.

"No more stories of you being some hero in the future. We are the future. And you are going to be a hero. Now."

Last of the Wars, Part Four

I was a geography teacher. I taught kids what the shapes of landmasses on the planet were, where each city was located, and where all the big mountains could be found. The closest I've ever gotten into a fight was when I was drunk for the first time at eighteen and punched a lamppost for insulting my honour. It may come as a surprise that I lost that bout, swore vengeance, and passed out. Make no mistake, violence isn't in my nature. In fact, even confrontations makes me nervous. John and Amelia's combined aura of distaste though, nearly brought me to my knees.

With a coat around me to protect my desensitised body from the cold, the three of us stood with our backs to the RV, surrounded by a group of rebels armed to the teeth with guns. In the snowing basin, the Misty sky hung overhead, enveloping us in a giant bubble of poisonous gas. Leafs and branches on the pine trees around us remained still, showing no wind within the area. Yet, the air seemed to rage through the scene.

Impossibly angrier than usual, Amelia bited, "We've brought him, Jason. Now you hold up your end of the bargain."

The leader of the rebel, a buzzcut, red headed man stepped forward out of line. His face was rough, scarred across the lips, chin, cheeks and forehead. His skin wrinkled and held in a constant unpleasant scrunch,

146

Jason looked to be in his late 40s. Unlike all his men, he wore a black short sleeved shirt, not caring one bit about the cold. A pistol was holstered to the belt of his jeans. His eyes – a steely grey – almost distracted from the commanding grimness he wore.

"Of course, Miss Smith. If nothing, we keep our promises."

"Promises?" she spat back. "What are we? Five?"

John cut in before things escalated. "If our deal still stands, Colonel Jason, why are your men pointing their guns at us?"

"We have to make sure," the Colonel replied. "Milton Jones may be the 'Hero of the Mist', but he is a Roagnarkian cyborg."

Amelia replied, "From over fifty years ago."

Jason studied their reply, staring up and down and measuring us with his eyes. With a wave, he silently ordered his men to stand down. The rebel soldiers then turned and walked back to the campsite behind them.

The Colonel then requested, "If you two will excuse me, I would like to speak with Mister Jones in private."

John replied, "There's no need for a briefing Colonel. We've already told him about the arrangement."

"Yeah," his sister added. "And Milton's not one of your lackey soldiers."

The man moved his hand over the grip of his pistol and the siblings tensed themselves.

Though calm, Jason had a stinging, commanding tone when he said, "It's not really a request. Remember, so long as you are here, you are under my jurisdiction. And if you want my continued protection to get your precious 'Hero' to Roagnark, you're going to do as I say."

Sensing a potentially violent confrontation coming up between the well armed rebels and my feisty granddaughter, I stepped forward. "Okay. Fine. I'll go." Turning to the siblings, I told them, "I'll find you two later."

The pair looked at me worryingly, before exchanging looks with each other followed by a nod and a synchronised, "Fine"

"Okay, guys, that was freaky as hell."

I parted with Amelia and John and followed Jason through the camp. Though they called it a camp, it looked much more like a small settlement. There were tents set up at random intervals, with a countable three small wooden houses scattered around the basin. As far as I can see, there were more than just rebel soldiers there, with a few men and women, children included, going about their day in casual, civilian winter clothes. Conversing, doing laundry, preparing meals. Normal, everyday activities. Then, there was the firing range where soldiers shot BBs at cardboard cutouts of robots.

We headed for the sole large, military-grade, rapidly deployable shelter, which is basically a fancy name for a big ass green tent. Entering, I was not surprised to find myself in a war room, complete with military fold-able tables and benches, maps of surrounding areas pinned onto boards, and boxes upon boxes of equipments kept stored from prying eyes.

The colonel gestured to one of the benches, offering me a seat as he took one opposite me.

"No thanks," I replied. "Robot legs. Don't get tired." Of course, I couldn't feel tired even if I tried. But from my grandchildrens' reaction to the man, I was not quick to trust and thought being on my feet would be more commanding against a commanding officer. "What did you want to talk about?"

"The Smith kids told you about what we're doing?"

"Yeah. You're going to use me to infiltrate the city. Open it from the inside."

He closed his fingers together, seemingly impressed by my foreknowledge. "Correct. But there's something else we need you to do after that."

Immediately, I replied, "No."

"You haven't even heard what I'm asking of yet."

"That's not part of the agreement I know. I get you into the city. What you do after that is your business."

Jason got to his feet to stared me eye-to-eye. "I don't think you understand what's at stake here. The entire human race is on the brink of extinction and you are just going to sit by?"

I kept silence for a moment, staring at some blank spot on the table in contemplation before replying, "Fine. Let's hear what you have to say."

Appeased, the Colonel returned to his seat. "My intelligence has gathered that there's an E.M.P bomb stored at the warehouse for old Forum projects. And also, apparently, your credentials are still stored within The Forum's system, seeing as you never officially left the

148

organisation. Apparently, dying slowly and boringly has a way of making people forget about you."

I remembered days and years ago when Leah told me that my security clearance was one of the highest in the organisation. "So you want me to get you into the warehouse?"

"That's right. If we can get our hands on that E.M.P bomb and get it working again, we can cripple the entire city and take it overnight. No casualties," he emphasised the last point.

"No casualties?" I asked, surprised. I remembered Borris using the same technology on a smaller scale. The E.M.P grenade disabled my implants, but otherwise, I'm still fine. "Sounds too good to be true. So why are you telling this to me and not John and Amelia?"

"Those two and I have contradicting views on the world," he leaned back as he said so, as if to distance himself from me. "I would rather we keep this to ourselves."

"And what if I don't?"

He pulled out his pistol and laid it across the table. "We'll kill them before they can even step out."

Everything grew darker all of a sudden. I was faced with a firearm, threatened in my direction. Did I mention I'm not good with confrontations? Not least with a trained military professional armed with a deadly gun.

I swallowed hard. "What do you want with us?"

"Just you," the colonel said. "All you have to do is help us get the E.M.P bomb, and I'll let your family walk away. Unharmed."

"No casualties?"

"No casualties," he confirmed. He got his feet, kept his gun, and walked towards the exit. "We'll be leaving camp for Roagnark tonight. You have until then to make up your mind. In the mean time, you and your...grandchildren are welcome to wander around our camp. But if me or my men sees any of you trying to leave, we'll put a bullet through your brain. And if you tell them, I'll hold them hostage," he threatened with a disturbing calmness before leaving the tent.

I stood alone, listening to my heart which I just realised was pounding harder than it had ever done before. A part of me wanted to run away, to grab Amelia and John and just make a beeline for the world outside. But there was no place to go. The entire continent was covered with Mist. Just leaving the basin would kill us. A rock and a hard place was not an adequate description for the position I felt we were in.

From my pocket, I took out Borris's watch, the time stopped at the moment of his death. I needed a plan. I needed information. I needed to know my enemy. And I can't believe I have an enemy now.

Last of the Wars, Part Five

A large tarp tent was pitched into the side of the quarry walls. Fading torches at the entrance made its presence known to the camp. Otherwise, the structure would have gone unnoticed in the mass of them. After my talk with Colonel Jason, I asked around for the tent's location. Once I found out, I headed straight for it, forgoing to even update my grandchildren.

It was an open tent, large enough for a table and two crude beds to be placed underneath. I wondered, with all the snow around, how the people kept themselves warm.

I walked up to the tent where a woman slept at the table, her head buried in her arms.

I called out, "Lindsey Gardner?"

She jerked her head up, starring blankly in my direction. "Hello?" she said, blinking to regain focus before reaching for her glasses. Her brunette hair long and dishevelled, her eyes green sitting on black bags, face heavily freckled, the bridge and right hinge of the glasses taped back together, a worn brown coat covering her. Lindsey Gardner was as everyone has said, a simple survivor.

Once she squinted and got sight of me, she greeted, "Hello. Yes, that's me, can I help you?"

Taking the greeting as an invitation, I stepped into the shelter. "I'm

151

here about Borris."

"Ah, my idiot brother. He's back, I take it?" She stood to her feet, rubbing her eyes from underneath her glasses. "Told him the Hero of the Mist is just another fairytale. But would he believe me? No. Went on some stupid adventure to—" She caught sight of my prosthetic arm, shining silver in the snow.

"I..." I could not find the words to continue, nor the strength to look her in the eyes as I slowly raised Borris's watch in my hand. "I'm sorry."

I could hear her swallow hard when she saw the watch. Slinking back into her chair, she stared at the watch while I tried my best to raise my eyes above the table. I failed quite miserably. She did not protest when I took a step forward, setting the watch down on the table.

Have I ever said I was a teacher? I must have repeated that quite a few times by then. I was a teacher. Dealing with death by war was not something we had to teach in school. It was as far from my job as you could possibly get. Sure, I had to council a few students with bad family history, but none ever had people they love shot dead by a robot tentacle.

"I... should go." Thinking she might want to be alone and she might hate the man who got her brother killed, I turned to leave.

Just as I stepped back out into the snow, she said, "My brother never really liked fighting. He was a good shot, but never had the anger for it. Too much of a daydreamer." I turned back around. She looked up to me and smiled through tearing eyes. She gestured to the chair beside her. She was holding the watch in her hands now, rubbing the face of it with her thumb. "He never really liked the Colonel either. Said the old man was too obsessed with fighting the robots. But he always believed in the story of the Hero of the Mist. The man who will one day bring the world back to normal. Whatever normal is. We don't have funerals anymore. But we can still mourn the dead. Sorry but, I don't have any thing to offer a guest."

I nodded in agreement. Surprised at how calm she was, I sat asking, "You're not... angry?"

She sighed, and I could see her frosted breath. "With how the world is right now, we're lucky to be able to die for something more than sickness and injuries." Despite her attempts at hiding it, her lips trembled as she held back her emotions. She took off her glasses to wipe the tears that had built up on the inner rim. "If you don't mind me asking, what were his last words?"

Fire in the hole. Those were his last words. But I felt that at this point, a little lie would do more than the truth. "Excuse me," I lied. Just a little. His second last phrase. "His last words were 'Excuse me.'"

"That's just like him," she let out a chuckle, and the dam that held back her tears broke as she cried into her hands.

The emotions I felt were as confusing as the whirl of white around us. Sadness. Pity. Regret. Guilt. I wished I could cry, so I would not look as emotionless as I did. I wondered if I was allowed to comfort her, but without processing the thought, my hand was on her shoulder.

We sat that way for awhile. Her crying while I gently rubbed her back. The only sound louder than her sob was a howl of wind that did not manage to pierce as much as her wails.

Somehow, she managed to regain her composure. Though her tears did not stop, Lindsey got her sobs under control. "Thank you. For coming to tell me."

"I don't... deserve it," I said truthfully. "I got him killed."

"No. He got himself killed. To save you. It's not your fault." Her brows furrowed as anger took her. "If it's anyone's fault, it's that Colonel Jason."

Confused, I asked, "Why? Isn't he here to help protect you?"

She gave a snort of derision. "Protect us? Him and his band of 'rebels' just decided to set up camp here one day. Put all sorts of nonsense in people's head. Getting us killed for his stupid war." Her hands balled into fists. "The robots don't care about us stragglers. We had a good life here. We had scavengers using The Winter Train tracks to find supplies from Tikika. We even managed to get some food planted."

I looked around the desolate snow-scape. "Here?" I asked.

"Yeah! Do you know how hard it is to grow stuff here?" She got angrier by the minute. And it seemed she knew that. Taking a deep breath, she calmed herself down. Looking at Borris's watch, she continued, "Then one day, Jason and his men rolled into camp. "Commandeering the place," he says. Took our food. Our resources. Our people. All for his 'fight for freedom'. "All great wars needs sacrifices," he says."

I heard the whirring of gears. I looked down to see my robotic arm scrunched up as well. Focusing, I relaxed it, less I damage the hardware by accident. "Is that how Borris got talked into this?"

"No. Borris volunteered. Said he wanted to do something to help us.

Thought you, the Hero of the Mist could make life better somehow. Believed all the stories about you right till the time he left." Her tears came back, but she gave up on trying to wipe them away. "He wasn't like the others that went. He wasn't one of Jason's men or convert. Never bought into that crap about sacrifice or war or peace. He's about as straight as they come. Just wanting to do good."

I finally managed to meet her eyes and I noticed her own set of pity for me. "He sounds like a good man."

"He was. He would have liked to know you more. I'm sure you'd have given him a reality check, Mister Hero."

"I'm sorry Miss Gardner. But I'm not a hero," I truthfully confided.

"I know," she admitted. "Milton Jones exist. Right here. In the flesh. But the Hero of the Mist is just a story about you. A fairytale. Predicting the future and all that bullshit. But stories are powerful things, Mister Jones. One good story can change the world. Inspire millions." She looked back down to the watch. "That's what my mother always said."

I felt my stay reaching its end. "I should go," I said, standing up. She did not object, focusing on the watch in remembrance. But just as I was about to leave, not knowing what came over me, I asked, "The Colonel told me to do a mission for him. Threatened my family for it. What do you think I should do?"

She looked at me with a dead seriousness in her eyes. For a moment, I thought she was going to scream at me to leave. Instead, she warned, "Just go with it for now. The Colonel always make good on his threat." Her words shook me. A sense of dread and fear now crept up within. But she continued, "But don't, not even for a moment, trust what he says. If there's one thing I learnt surviving out here, is that family's about the only thing you can believe in these days."

Last of the Wars, Part Six

With the sun far below the horizon and the blanket of night thick, the camp was lit faintly with parted torches. Gathered around an open tunnel, the men heaved, all thirty of them, carrying the contraption onto the long abandoned tracks of The Winter Train. As wheel and rail lined into place, the men dropped the handcar unceremoniously onto the track. The steel clanked together like a pair of cymbals, ringing throughout the snowing camp.

While I watched the rebels worked to attach the makeshift wagon behind, Amelia and John came up to me, rifle and SMG slung around their shoulders, backpack on their backs, masks hanging onto their belts, ready to leave at a moment's notice.

I turned my head and followed as they walked up beside me, inspecting the scene before them. "You don't have to come with me," I told them. "You two have no obligations to me."

"Don't be stupid," Amelia reminded me. "If you die here, how are we going to face our parents later?" She turned and walked away, leaving me with her brother.

John added, "Don't take it to heart. The scolding that is. She calls everyone an idiot."

"Yeah," I replied, matter-of-factly. "I can see that."

"But she's right. We're not going anywhere." He slapped me on my

155

metal arm, drawing his hand back immediately in slight pain. "Get use to us." He walked off after his sister, fanning the sting of his palm.

I stared at their backs as they disappeared one-by-one into the armoury tents. I wondered what kind of life they had before me. If they had a family of their own. Children to love and care for. I made a mental note to ask them later.

"I'm guessing those are your grandkids?" I spun around to the voice.

Behind me stood Lindsey Gardner, Borris's sister. She wore a hooded grey camouflage patterned coat over long sleeved black shirt, jeans, and a leather chest piece. A gas mask dangled from the bandoleer around her chest with a bag to her back. The woman looked as ready for war as everyone around us.

She continued, "I thought they'd be younger. But they look almost your age."

"Time traveller." I pointed to myself. "Eighty-eight this year."

"Right...Hero of the Mist."

"What are you doing here?" I asked, confounded. "And dressed like that?"

"I'm coming with you."

"What?" I was genuinely surprised. "No. No! You can't come with us. I'm not gonna have even more people risk their lives for me!"

"I'm sorry," she replied sarcastically, "But when did I ask for your permission?"

"I—"

"No," she cut in curtly. "I'm not going to let my brother's life be sacrificed in vain. If anything happens to you, I will never be able to make it up to him. Look over there." She pointed to Jason's group of men who lifted a second wagon into place. "Every one of them is Jason's people. And as far as I know, you can't tell your grandkids about that asshole's plan. So I'm the only one who can watch your back. What are you going to do if Jason stabs your family in the back because you couldn't see behind you?"

I opened my mouth to argue, but my brain was set on stun. Blankly staring back at her, desperately trying to think of something to say with my hand stuck in mid motion, I stammered out, "Um..."

"Yeah, I thought so."

Like Amelia and John before her, Lindsey headed for the armoury to gear up. My gut clenched uncomfortably. Don't get me wrong, I couldn't

156

feel my gut. But from the way it grumbled and churned, I would say it was uncomfortable about something.

Then it occurred to me that I was likely hungry. Like everything else, I couldn't feel hunger either. Before that day, I had been guided by Doctor Parker for all my meals and other health issues, as I can no longer trust my body's ability to warn me. The sun had set hours ago, and I had not had anything to eat since I woke up.

Approaching one of the rebel groups loading the wagon, I asked, "Hey guys, you know where I can get something to eat around here?"

The closest one, a muscular man in his early twenties, took a look at my arm and laughed. "Yeah. The garage is at the end of the camp. I'm sure there's some oil cans lying around."

Confused, I replied, "What?"

With a smirk, he replied, "Robots don't need to eat. You just oil up. Maybe a little lube?"

Offended, I stepped forward to confront him. But before a word even escape my lips, he pushed me hard in the chest and I stumbled back.

"What the hell?" I shouted.

The group just laughed. What I assumed now was the leader – the man who I had been dealing with – took a large step forward, covering the gap between us. With just one arm, he wrapped his hand around my collar and lifted me off my feet, as light as if I was a piece of paper.

"Don't forget your place, robot. You may be a legendary hero, but if you don't want your family to get hurt, you're going to be our bitch."

Stubborn as I was, I instinctively brought my metal arm up to his, grabbing his wrist firmly. His eyes grew wide in terror as I clenched his wrist tightly. The whir of gears in my hand sounded more threatening than any angry growl.

"Let go of me, or I'll show you just how robot I am." The rest of the rebels behind him pulled out a variety of handguns from belts and coats, wordlessly aiming them at me, but backing up with a fear that I could not understand.

From beside us, running in, Amelia, John and Lindsey approached, weapons raised in my defence.

"Drop 'em, fart-kuckles," my granddaughter ordered, her command of colourful vocabulary continued to amaze me. "Or you'll be eating lead out of each others asses for the rest of your lives."

"Wow, Milly," John commented. His calm demeanour was now more

157

of a terrifying chill. "I've never heard 'fart-knuckles' before. You must be pissed."

Lindsey added, "You two are weird."

From the command tent, Colonel Jason walked over to us and at the top of his voice commanded his men to— "Stand down!"

The rebels lowered their gun and I mutually released the man holding me. Though once we were free of each other, he hastily began rubbing his pained wrist from my steel grasp.

Approaching me, the Colonel said, "I'm sorry, Mister Jones. My men are not the military trained soldiers I would have preferred. They are not above outburst of gang-type violence." The man was eloquent and sounded almost sincere. But behind his tone was a veiled threat. If I refused to follow his orders, he would set his men loose on us. "But at troubled times like these, we take what we can get."

My throat, still slightly coarse from the vice grip, caused me to croak when I spoke. "Yeah. What you can get. Just make sure they stay the hell away from us."

"I'll do that," the Colonel agreed. Though whether or not he would keep his words remained to be seen. He waved for the rebels to follow and the men trailed after their leader as they returned to the command tent. He shouted back to us, "Get yourselves ready. We leave in an hour."

"You alright, old man?" Amelia asked, the three of them approaching me.

I replied, "I'm fine." John lifted up my chin with no resistance from me, checking for any injuries that I could otherwise not feel. "Just a little rattled."

He gave a nod of clearance once he was sure the bruise was just a bruise.

"Don't be," Lindsey said, keeping her pistol. "We can't afford to be unhinged by that man. We don't know what exactly it is he's planning."

I turned to watch the rebels entering the tent, Jason following in last. Before he disappeared behind the canvas, our eyes met, and he nodded to me with a smile that, though not sinister, sent my heart racing with worry.

"Let's go get something to eat," I said, not taking my eyes of the Colonel until he vanished completely into structure.

Once, a long, distant time ago, I read fantasy books of groups of unlikely characters, brought together by coincidence of one form or another, to be thrown into an adventure of a lifetime to stop some evil being from taking over the world.

My foul-mouthed granddaughter. Her queerly calm brother. The sister of the deceased man who saved my life. A racist rebel group. And a morally questionable officer. What an adventuring company we made. But instead of a possibly evil overlord, the most dangerous element could be right in front of our eyes.

Interlude, Evening Tea Party

The clicks-and-clacks of the handcar being driven over the tracks reminded me of The Winter Train. But instead of a comfortable passenger cabin, we were stuck inside a cart that was dragged behind two other much more spacious wagons. Apparently, the cramp travelling arrangement was "all they could find", the rebels told us, as they and their leader travelled peacefully in the wagon.

Though the cart was large enough for all four of us to have leg rooms, Amelia, John, and Lindsey still slept sitting, each of their heads against a corner, hugging their rifles like bolsters. Even though I could not feel physical discomfort, just the sight of their bodies, twisted stiffly in their sleep, had me adjusting my own sitting. I wondered how many nights they had spent like that, in awkward, ill-fitting positions as they travelled the desolate wastelands.

A soft screech came from the front as the handcar stopped its acceleration, the makeshift train slowing down as it did so. Carefully, I got up and leaned over the edge of the cart just as we came to a complete stop.

I watched as two men got off the handcar extension. One simply climbed straight into the wagon behind them while the other stepped closer to me, signalling to us the change in shift before following his companion in.

160

According to John's watch, dawn was still two hours away, and we were expected to reach Roagnark by nightfall. The siblings had agreed to take the first shift together, but their peaceful sleeping faces had me climbing out of the cart in their state.

As I passed the second wagon, Colonel Jason, sitting against the inner walls opposite the entrance, stirred awake and asked, "Just you?"

"Robot arm," I replied, showing him my metal prosthetic. "And I don't sleep much these days."

He nodded seemingly in approval before closing his eyes as he went back to sleep. I wondered how much of our exchange was just him reacting naturally to his surrounding, and how much of his words were said while fully conscious.

The handcar was as classic as it got. Steel framed and wooden planked for a flooring while paint peeled and chipped from the faded red base. The walking beam meant to be operated by two people was positioned steeled in the middle. At each of the seesaw ends were a chair, both wooden, but of different makes and design, installed after for the comfort of whoever was operating the machine.

I climbed onto the contraption and took a seat facing the tracks. Almost gingerly, I placed my robotic hand on the handle of the walking beam and solely with my elbow, pulled the bar down.

To my surprise, the machine moved smoothly, and I could not tell that my body had exerted any kind of strain from the action. It seemed that the entire work of moving the handcar had fallen to the gears in my arm.

With equal ease, I brought the bar up. Back down. And up again. The rhythm continued and before I knew it, we were up to speed on the tracks, moving faster than we had been able to in the past six hours.

I chuckled. "I should have done this in the first place," I said to myself, wind rustling through my hair.

"You probably should have."

I jumped in my seat. I was sure there were no one else on the platform with me. Releasing the bar in shock, I stared, mouth agape at the new presence that sat opposite me.

"Oops," the man said as the beam slowed itself. He waved one hand over the contraption. Even though I expected the handcar to decelerate and stop, it continued to move, the beam continuing its ups-and-downs without any force on my part. "There. No need to overwork that arm of yours."

"What did you do?" I asked, only to immediately realise I had only about a dozen other questions that were significantly more essential than that.

He ruffled his deep brown hair, strands of white dancing as he did. A proud grin stretched his face as he explained, "Oh! I just wrapped this entire um... train in a time bubble. It's looping the few seconds that it was at its maximum speed. And we are travelling around two times the speed of the world outside." His grin grew wider as he gave me two thumbs up. "Heard you were in a rush. We should get there before noon. You're welcome."

The man looked familiar to me, his sharp face and smooth features stuck out, though not as much as his eyes, a setting dirt black. Then, something he said jumped at me. "Time bubble?"

"Yes!" he exclaimed, clapping his hands together in delight. "I'm a time traveller, just like you!"

"Pausa..." I said the name, and the memory of the man I met at Leila's graduation flooded back to me. And I noticed, just as it was before, that the world around us was infinitely silent. The wind that blew past me before had gone still. Our little square, separated from the world.

"You remembered my name! That's so nice of you!"

I stated, "It's only been five days." I was both surprised and relief at how casually I was able to say days instead of years. My instincts knew that whoever this Pausa was, he was not just a kindred spirit, but telling the truth. A traveller of time.

"Really?" he replied in surprise. "It's been a month for me. But then again, I've been around. Stuff to do. Things to see. You understand?"

Strangely I nodded as if I understood. At the very least, I seemed to have imagined that I understood. "But what are you doing? Why are you doing this?"

"Look, Milton," Pausa began, rubbing at the bridge of his nose to relax. "I knew your grandfather when he was a kid when the whole *Day of the Mist* thing happened. I was there and I couldn't do much for him, even though I had power over all of time," he sighed, elbows sinking into his knees in genuine regret. "One wrong step in any direction and my entire time-stream collapses in on itself from the paradox. Billions of billions of people will die. There are so little things I can do to help these days. This here though, I can help. Getting you to Roagnark earlier. That

162

much I can do."

"I don't get it," I replied, getting increasingly confused by the second. Every word he said made less sense than before.

"You don't have to get it," he said, his energetic persona seemingly having ran dry. He was sombre, sincere, and, if I was not mistaken, tired. "Just know that there were people close to your grandfather that I could not help save. And that I owe him a great debt. Making sure you reach the end of the world is my way of making it up to him."

Sadly, I no longer have headaches, but I was still getting dizzy. "You're still not making sense." Though the language he spoke was definitely English, the words, when put together, was like reading a sequel to another story that I had skipped. "What exactly did my grandfather do? You're telling me that him being a car mechanic that worked with the government and had the ability to predict the future with songs is not the end of it?"

"Well, when you put it like that, of course it would sound confusing as hell," he replied. "But, you'll find out soon enough, what exactly it was he did." He held out his hand in front of my face and said, "Don't blink." He snapped his finger.

Of course, reflexively, I blinked. And like our last meeting, he disappeared without a trace, the seat as empty as before.

A mixture of surprise, disarray, frustration, and revelation circled my thoughts. I muttered to myself, "I've got to stop hanging out with weird people."

For a split second, I wondered if it was possible that everything I had seen and heard was just a dream until I realised that the only noise in my ears were the ringing of dead silence. The handcar was still moving on its own, the walking beam still rising and falling to the steady breaths of time.

Cyborg People, Part One

The makeshift *train-gon* – that's the name I've decided for this train-wagon hybrid monstrosity – finally came to a stop at the end of the tracks. The tunnel had collapsed before us, just a stone's throw away from the old Roagnark underground train station, which according to my grandchildren, had been defunct since the war started. Black rings around the ceiling showed the explosion used to close off the path, an intentional blockade made by The Forum inside.

I dismounted from the handcar just as the rebels got out of their wagons and my own party climbed out of the cart behind, stretching their aching backs as they did so.

Jason approached me first, asking, "Where are we?"

"Roagnark," I replied.

"Impossible," he looked to his watch. "We're six hours ahead of schedule," he looked at me with shifted eyes.

A time traveller came while everyone was sleeping, put the train-gon into a time bubble, and zoomed us here at twice the speed of time. Was what I wanted to say. It would have been an infinitely more interesting story than me, raising my prosthetic and saying, "Robot arm. Super fast. Doesn't get tired." I realised how badly I wanted to make a masturbation joke with those lines.

"Huh..." He stepped towards me, face coming closer than I was

164

comfortable with. His stare was intense, like that down a barrel of a gun. "Guess you *are* a cyborg," he said the word with the same underlying hatred as a racist would say 'nigger', but never admitting that they were racists. "We'll start digging a way through. Once that's done, you're going in to do what we promised."

"And what's to stop me from running away once I'm inside?"

I already knew the answer even before he looked over to my grandchildren. A part of me was just optimistically hopeful that he would have forgotten. "So long as you do this for us, nothing will happen to them. I guarantee it."

I wondered if I punched him with my metal arm would his head snap off. My first violent thought in over a decade was that of murder. "And how am I supposed to get in?" I asked instead.

From his coat pocket, he took out a metal orb no bigger than an apple, with a base that was grounded and buffed flat. "There's a sensor wall surrounding the entire developed border of the city. There's an old border right at the entrance of this old train station. Just go up there, place this orb down at the centre of the entrance and it'll allow us a two meters gap to move in from. But it has to be placed from the other side for it to work."

"That's it?" I asked, suspicious of how easy the job seemed.

"That's it," he replied. "But of course, I told your grandchildren something different. That the machine needed to be placed near to the generators in the middle district of the sector. That should give you plenty of time to find us the warehouse with the E.M.P bomb."

I took the device from him. It made a low humming noise and I could see my hand vibrating slightly from whatever machinery that was working within it. I wondered how it was powered and for how long it would last. Perhaps it was one of those perpetual motion devices.

"Me and my men are going to dig you a path. Shouldn't take long." He waved the rebels over. A pair of them pulled out a jackhammer-like machine from the wagon, though with infinitely more complex moving parts, wiring strung in and out like veins. "You might want to spend what time you have left with your family."

His back turned to me as he walked away towards his men. I stared as he turned out of sight and behind the wagon, wary of how nice he acted to me with his last sentence despite the threat of having hostages and the possible murder of my family line.

165

Lindsey came up to me. Unlike the siblings who stood relatively relaxed talking amongst themselves behind, she had her hand firmly on the grip of her rifle. Her tension though, was expected, seeing as she was the only other person there who knew what Jason wanted me to do.

She asked, "What did he say?" I showed her the device, to which she immediately identified it as a— "Shield Damper. You're going to going put a hole through the sensory fields?"

"That's the plan."

"But he told us that..." she was probably going to repeat the fake plan that the Colonel had provided. "Of course. So that you could find the bomb."

"Yes," I reaffirmed her with an extra nod. "Should I just do it? He said it's just an E.M.P bomb. No casualties. I've been hit by one and I'm fine."

"I don't know," she replied honestly. I could see her brows scrunching in thought as she ran through the scenario. "Personally, I won't trust anything that Jason says. For all we know, it's some sort of nuke instead."

I let out a sigh loud enough that my grandchildren turned to look. I smiled at them, to which John waved back and Amelia stuck her tongue out. Then the two parted to their own activities.

I said to Lindsey, "I'm going to go in there. See things for myself. But if things even starts to look like it'll go south, get those two out."

"What about you?"

"Once I'm in there," I explained, keeping the Shield Damper into my coat pocket. "I can hook myself up to the old Cryo-Tubes, no problem. And as long as I don't drop this Shield Damper thing down at the border, Jason and his men can't get to me. But you guys..."

"Oh..." she said as she understood. She looked left and right, making sure that the rebels weren't staring. From her back pocket, took out a black walkie-talkie. "Take this with you. It doesn't have much battery left. Batteries are hard to come by these days. But it should last you a few hours. Radio back if you think something might go wrong."

Without hesitation, I took the device from her. My heart was starting to drum as I thought about all the dangers that could happen to these people I leave behind. "I'm sorry for dragging you all into this."

"I told you already. This is me doing this, for my brother. Not for you," she said coldly. Though I could not get angry at her lack of

166

emotion. She patted me on my shoulder and turned away and back to the cart where Amelia was unpacking the rest of their gear.

John waved to me from the wall of the cave where he leaned alone. I went to him, keeping the walkie in my already brimming pockets of tools and gadgets.

"What's up?" I asked once we were within talking distance.

He did not meet my eyes, but instead, stared down at the tip of his boots. "That girl, Lindsey, do you know her well?"

"Not really. She's Borris's sister and she wants to help finish what her brother started."

"Yes, I know that," he replied, a slight frustration in his voice. "But anything else? Where's she from? Hobbies?"

"John, I just met her yesterday. I don't know all these—" and my mind wrapped itself around one word. "Wait, hobbies?" I examined his face which was blushing uncharacteristically. "Oh my lords, you have a crush on her?"

He jumped away from the wall at my exclamation, pulling me in with an arm around my shoulder. Head-to-head, he whispered. "Do not tell Milly, okay? I will never hear the end of it."

"Why?"

"What do you mean why?" His calm demeanour faded as he got flustered. It seemed to me that like his sister, he too lacked certain skills in the emotional department. "She's very protective. The last girl I asked out she stalked us on our date and hooked her up to a polygraph machine."

"Where did she get a polygraph machine in a world like this?"

"I don't know! Apparently something great-grand uncle Oliver passed down to mom. Point is, don't tell Milly."

"But I wasn't asking 'why Amelia?', I was asking 'why Lindsey?'," I corrected him.

"Oh," he stated, surprised. "How do I put this? She seems nice. We had a little chat before we got on the cart and we really hit it off. And she didn't try to shoot us, which is nice in a girl."

"She didn't try to shoot you?" I asked, my tone slightly more condescending than I hoped it. "That's your reason for liking her?"

"Look, Milton, there's not a lot of good people around the world these day," he started, his tone suddenly solemn. "There's a lot of ravagers and hunters around who wouldn't blink an eye at killing two travellers like us. There's even less room for any romantic attraction. It's very rare to find someone you're both attracted to and doesn't want to shoot you between the eyes."

"Then go for it!" I encouraged, slapping him a little too hard on the back as he squirmed in pain. "Sorry. But really, go for it. Not now though. After all this is over. When you guys are all back somewhere safe."

"How? If you haven't noticed, our lives aren't exactly stable enough to settle down." I could see the hesitation in his eyes. The uncertainty. I had felt the same way right before I asked Joan to marry me, though under drastically different situations and reasons. "You know what, forget I said anything. It's a stupid idea anyway."

"John." I grabbed his arm before he could leave, forcing him to halt and stay. "If there's one thing I've learnt in the past fifty odd years, is that life is short and fleeting. And I mean, *really* fleeting. I never got the chance to spend my golden years with your grandmother like I wanted to. I wasn't there for your mother's wedding, not to mentioned all the missed birthdays."

John stopped struggling, his embarrassment and frustration fading as I spoke.

I continued, "Life is never stable. We have wars and famine and disease and death. Not to mention the great grim reaper of time always on our tail. We blink once and decades could fly past without us even flinching. Chances coming and going, fading with each day." I took his hands in mine as my parents did over 60 years ago when I asked them for the same advice about Joan. But this time with my own experience added to pass down. "Bad things will always happen. But chances for good comes ever so rarely. Grab them. Don't let go. Ride the wave. If better things come, good for you. If it ends, hold on to those happy days and drown your memories in them."

I did not realised how much I needed it, but apparently John did. Just like his namesake, he saw right through me and embraced me with a hug.

"Hold onto them," I choked out. "Hold onto those happy days and never let go."

Cyborg People, Part Two

When I was a kid, my parents would take me to ride the trains for the simple joy of riding it. I would run up and down the cabin for reasons that only my younger mind could comprehend. Though if I had to guess, I would say the bliss of having fun without borders were as welcoming as ice cream on a hot day. The tracks were empty now. With the tunnels cleared, I was pushed into the station alone. With only a flashlight to guide my way, I climbed onto the station platform. A thick layer of dust had coagulated into a black smirk on my hands and I wiped them against my pants.

The walls of the station were filled with graffiti. Apparently, despite the dystopian world outside, the sensory field borders, or the passage of time, teenagers were still teenagers. Sprayed over every single available space were words like 'SILK' and 'GOOSE' and other phrases that were nonsensical to me, most of which I took as the equivalent of 'cool'. A single graffiti however, was plastered over every other, but split separately so they covered all three major walls. The number '139'. Probably a sign for a gang or something similar.

I headed towards the exit where the once automated access gates were now defunct, rusting slowly with time. I had to manually push the rotary bars which proved little challenge, despite the spine shrivelling screech from the rust.

169

"Oh..." I let out as I neared the closed shutters of the main hall. Even though I had not physically felt anything in weeks, I could sort of sense a tingle, perhaps psychological, down the length of my arm, and I knew that the sensory field was marked by the same shutters.

I approached the gates and saw one had bright white light shining through the bottom, likely unlocked and served as the entrance for the aspiring graffiti artists. Using my robot arm, I easily lifted the shutter over my head and stepped out into a brightly lit—

Park?" I said out loud, the shutter crashing shut behind me as I let go of my grip.

Park goers turned to the sound of the crash, which meant that all eyes were now on me. *So much for stealth.*

There was a clear blue sky, with a few fluffs of clouds and the bright white light of the sun shining down on me. Lush green trees populated the grounds with not a building in sight, even after the horizon. There was a playground to the far east where children swung on swings and slid down slides. Families had picnics on small mounts of hills and joggers ran the paved tracks. In the middle of everything was a pond where elderly threw crumbs of bread to feed the fishes.

"What?" I voiced in confusion. I had expected to be in one of the underground tunnels. The world overhead, flooded with Mist, was supposed to be uninhabitable. "I must be dreaming." I wished I could pinch myself to test it.

"Excuse me, sir!" I turned to two officers dressed in police-blue uniforms, walking towards me with hands on the tasers at their hips. Immediately, I could tell that both their left eyes were cybernetic implants, the crystal clear darkness and shifting lenses giving them away.

"What were you doing in there?" they asked. That's right. '*They*'. I am addressing them as a single being, because I can.

"I'm uh..." I turned back to look at the shutters where the sign 'SENSORY BORDER: NO TRESPASSING' was plastered across it. "I was... doing... the..." I tried to think on my feet but the otherworldly sight of a park had broken my concentration.

"I'm sorry sir, but we will have to take you in for questioning."

I could hear my heart beating against my chest. Getting caught at that point would be detrimental, not just for me, but for the people who followed me here. Amelia, John, Lindsey, all of them would be put at risk. Yet, the more I thought about it, the less my mind wanted to work.

"He's with me." I turned to the voice. A woman, dressed in a long sleeved dark green shirt, blue jeans, brown work boots with medium length, frilly blonde hair, walked up to us. Her face was lean and sharp, her maroon eyes rugged and steeled.

"And who might you be?" the officer asked.

From her pocket, she pulled out a laminated card. "Chief engineer of the F.R.C. This man was helping gather some fault data from the underground tunnels." The officers took the card and a red light flashed from their mechanical eyes as they scanned the credentials.

They passed the card back. "My apologies madam." They turned to me and nodded in approval. "You two have a lovely day." They proceeded with their patrol, leaving me with the mystery woman.

I turned to her and though wary, I uttered, "Thanks. Whoever you are."

She ignored me, looking at our surroundings and back towards the officers, making sure they were a distance away before saying, "Walk with me." She headed to the west.

Mostly out of my own curiosity and partially because of my lack of choices, I followed. Before I could ask a question however, she fired the first shot.

"What are you doing here?" she questioned with an annoyed tone. Instantly, I felt a certain familiar antagonism with her.

"I don't..." I tried to wrap my mind around the situation but decided to just play by ear when my thoughts went nowhere. "I don't think I should answer that. Who are you anyway?"

She ignored my question and continued, "I've been tracking you all morning. The moment you crossed the border into Roagnark territory, pings were going crazy on my system. You're lucky no one else knows who you are, Milton Jones."

"How did you know my name?"

I was getting increasingly irritated when she again skipped my question and said, "I'm taking you to a safe place until I can find a way to get you to the Cryo-Tube."

"Wait? What? No! You can't do that?"

And for the first time, she directly replied, "Why not?"

"My grandchildren are being held hostage right now. I can't abandon them." I did not think it was smart for me to have revealed my situation there and then, but something inside me slipped, and my gut was also

171

yelling at me to trust her, despite her being slightly irritating in my honest opinion.

She stopped in her tracks and turned to me. "Milly and John are here?" I stopped walking as well.

"You know them?"

Again, she went back to ignoring me, instead thinking out loud, "If they are being held hostages, there must be some sort of demand. What's the demand?"

"Wait!" I finally exclaimed, my frustration with being ignored having hit its peak. "You are going to tell me who you are and how do you know them, right now!"

She looked crossed, her brows furrowed. She turned away from me and continued walking. In the distance, I saw the 'sky' cutting away at the edge of the park and a glass door that led to a different darker street was cut into it. Apparently, the park was just an artificial simulation. The 'sky' a virtual dome.

She continued, "If you want my help, you're going to have to tell me what are the demands. You're not some pampered hero anymore, Milton. Time to sack up."

I clicked my tongue at her. I could not help but feel that we had met before, for her attitude was annoyingly familiar. I gave the proposal some thought, and concluded that I was indeed a cornered rat between Jason and The Forum. I needed all the help I could get. "Fine. The rebels have Amelia and John and a girl called Lindsey. They demand that I help them sneak into the city and lead them to an E.M.P bomb."

The engineer stopped walking again, this time though, her eyes were wide with what I could only say was shock. Maybe even fear. "E.M.P bomb?"

"Yeah. Sneak in, use the bomb to disable the city. No casualties."

"No casualties?!" she exclaimed, stepping up and grabbing me by my collar. "I cannot allow you to do that! Do you even know what an E.M.P bomb will do to us?"

I pushed her hand away, her allegiance now even murkier to me than before. "Nothing happens, alright? I got hit with one of them and it shut down my implants for a few minutes. That's all. Everyone will be fine. But if I don't do this for them, my grandchildren will end up dead!"

She grabbed a hold of her own shirt collar and I noticed that her left and right index fingers were shining metallic. She pulled her shirt down, revealing a metal plate grafted over her left breast, right over where the heart would be.

Her teeth was gritted as she spoke, trying to get me to see how dire the situation really was. "Yours are just attached to muscles. But half of the city has cybernetics connected to vital organs to keep them alive!" My eyes stretched wide with shock. "If an E.M.P bomb goes off near us, it will kill over a million people!"

I stood speechless. My brain ran through the scenario and scanned her face. Was she lying? She did not looked to be lying. "Who are you?" I asked again, knowing that her answer would decide our next move. "How can I trust you?"

The woman pulled her shirt back up and with a sarcastic tone that I had only heard from one other before, she replied, "Who else?" She took out the laminated card again and handed it to me. On it were her name and information on her next of kin. "I'm Clover Parker. Doctor Greene Parker's granddaughter."

Cyborg People, Part Three

The base of every building in Roagnark had been replaced with holographic domes that simulated artificial sunlight. Within them were parks and walkways, complete with water fountains and benches, street lamps and trash cans, even trees and bushes. But even without my sense of touch, I could tell not a single breeze blew through and the air was simply air-conditioned. The leafs of the trees did not sway and water condensed on metal surfaces.

Sitting on the bench at the base of The Forum Technological Warehouse building, I watched as blue-collared workers walked in and out of the 'tower', the metallic front gate awkwardly placed in the middle of the dome, the building extending upwards and disappearing into the fake sky at the ring of the fifth floor.

In front of me, at the top of a spiral fountain was the Cryo-Tube. Mark One. The old tin can with its bulky build and malfunctioning doors, chromed, shined, and waxed. The fat rice cooker from over a half a century ago. A plaque at the edge of the fountain read:

THE BEGINNING OF SCIENCE
Spurred on by the revolutionary feats of
engineering and sciences made during
Project Dawn, this prototype Cryo-Tube,

174

**which kept the Hero of the Mist alive for
the first part of his journey, now serves as a
reminder of all the miraculous inventions
based off it used in our daily lives today.**

"Hey, mister!" I turned to see a little girl, no taller than my stomach, standing beside me. Wearing a sky-blue, red flowered dress, dainty little white shoes and a slightly oversized sun hat, she was the poster girl of the purity of children. "Mind if I sit here?" She pointed to the empty seat beside mine.

Clover Parker had specifically instructed me not to interact with any 'man or woman' while she searched for the E.M.P bomb's location within the warehouse. So naturally, I told the little girl, "Sure thing!" —with a stupid grin across my face.

The girl smiled back, teeth shining in the light. Taking off her hat, she placed the large accessory over her lap as she took the seat. Her hair, a short, smooth auburn that leaned towards red, reminded me of my daughter. I thought of Leila on the day I first got into the Cryo-Tube. Small enough to hug, young enough to be untouched by the troubles of the world. Then I looked down and saw the girl swinging her legs. Her skin-coloured, matte painted, robotic legs.

"Your arms are cool, mister!" she exclaimed. Apparently, she was eyeing my prosthetics as much as I did hers. "It's all shiny and silver, like the Mist Hero!" she spoke of me with the same reverence that kids of my time had for Santa Claus.

Kindly, I asked her, "Where are you parents?"

She pointed back towards the warehouse. "My dad forgot his bag. He's a dunderhead sometimes."

I laughed. "He sounds like a dunderhead to me."

Somehow, I had managed to strike up a conversation with the girl, for she replied, "What's your name, mister? I'm Sally!" she gave me her name, beaming with pride.

The girl was overwhelmingly trusting with a stranger like me and I worried for her a little. But something told me that her judge of character and her intellect was far beyond her years. "Sally? My grandmother was named Sally."

"Really?" she grinned. "Was she also named after the Hero's grandmother?" Somehow, my family background, down to the name of

175

my grandparents, had become common knowledge.

I smiled at her and whispered, "Do you want to know a secret?" She looked at me quizzically, before curiously nodding. "Okay, but you must promise to never tell anyone." She nodded again. Covering my mouth in faked hushed tones, I said, "I *am* the Hero of the Mist."

Her eyes widened in wonder and I could see a glitter of hope in them. "You're lying!" she called on me.

"I would never lie," I lied. "Lying is bad."

"If you really are the Hero, then you must have been to the outside!" I nodded affirmatively. She shifted to face me, her hat nearly dropping off her lap in her excitement. "What's it like outside without the Mist?"

"Well..." I reminiscence on the days when the skies were clearer. Though I was not lucky enough to have been born in a time without Mist, my childhood was still filled with clear skies and sunlight. Smiling, I recalled, "Sometimes, the sky was clear and blue, and you can see birds flying across them like a painting on the largest canvas in the world. Other times, there would be these clouds, white and fluffy as any cotton candy. Wind would blow, strong enough to ruffle your hair and lift your spirit. Colours of the world shone, lit with bright red as the sun sets over the mountains." I took a deep breath as the image of the world of my youth washed over my memories. Before the freezing. Before the war. Before the ravaged wasteland. The beauty that the world had seemingly forgotten.

Sally stared at me, half a smile on her face as she pictured the fantastical world I had just told her. "Wow..." was all she could say.

"Yeah," was all I replied.

From behind us, a man's voice called, "Sally!"

We turned, and a man in an white jumpsuit, his beard a godly ruffle on his chin, waved to us from the gates of the warehouse.

"That's my dad," the girl said, turning to me one last time.

I smiled and held up my hand up for a high-five. She slapped it happily. "Remember," I said. "Secret."

She gave a toothy grin before hopping off her seat. Rushing to her father, her mechanical legs pushing her at full speed, she leapt into his opened arms for a twirling hug. They exchanged a few words and the man turned to look at me before waving. I waved back and the father-daughter pair walked off towards the exit.

Clover Parker plopped down in the spot that Sally had left. "I had no idea you were so good with kids," she noted.

"Yeah...well, I used to be a teacher." Despite my resignation being less than half a year in my mind, I replied with such a foreign tone that I might as well have been talking about a previous lifetime ago. "Did you find it?" I asked, referring to the E.M.P bomb.

"My grandfather brought me here when I was a kid. I had a terminal illness that would have killed me before I even reached puberty." Once again, she completely ignored my question and I am reminded of how irritated I was with Doctor Parker's personality when we first met. But nonetheless, I listened intently. "Once we got here, he begged The Forum to let us in. In return for immunity boosters and cybernetic implants, he promised to spend the last of his life working for them." She looked around the dome at all the workers and civilians that bustled through. "A lot of people here are like me. We had some issues with our bodies that couldn't heal otherwise. Diseases, accidents, blindness..."

"Amputations," I added, thinking back to Sally and her mechanical legs.

Clover continued without even an acknowledgement of me. "The Forum isn't what I would call 'the best'. Their war with non-modified humans are all but kept a secret from us, with only trickles of news here and there from back alley sources and down the grapevines. And I can't say the world would be worst if they were taken down. But an E.M.P bomb in the city... that's not the way."

I realised that she was trying to convince me to not go through with leading Jason to the weapon. It also meant that—

"You found the bomb," I asked, and she nodded in reply.

I stared at the plaque in front of the antique Cryo-Tube and I wondered if all of our efforts to help the world counted for anything. It seemed that at every turn, with every happy day, there were ten more bad ones waiting to run us over.

Clover must have caught my stare. She explained, "We got a lot out of Project Dawn. Cyber-prosthetics, Mist Immunity Boosters..." She tapped the metal plate on her chest. "Life preservers, hard-light holograms, virtual reality simulation, renewable energy, the dome system, and so much more." She immediately changed the subject. "I hope you have a plan. My granddad always said your family always had some sort of plan up your sleeves."

I could visualise the cogs in my head turning, a puzzle on the verge

177

of falling into place as an idea took root. From my pocket, I pulled out the walkie-talkie that Lindsey had given me. Turning it on, I spoke softly into it, "Lindsey?"

After a moment, a tone crackled in, and in an equally quiet voice Lindsey replied, "Milton? I hear you. What's going on?"

"I'm on my way back." Now that I had all the information I needed, it was time to get control of the situation. "And there's something I need you to do."

Cyborg People, Part Four

There was a trashcan right beside the shutters that closed off the station. With a quick look around me, I turned on the shield dampener and placed it behind the bin. My original decision to put the gadget inside was overwritten by Clover, who berated me with, "The bins leads to an incinerator, you dumbass."

Annoyed, I replied, "Hey, I'm new here, alright? No need to get you panties in a twist."

Skipping past me again, she instead asked, "You remember the plan?"

"Of course I do. It's *my* plan!"

She simply nodded and I wondered if she actually heard me. It's entirely possible that in her 'ignore everyone' mentality, she just saw my mouth move and thought it was an appropriate response.

She continued, "I'm going to head back to the warehouse and wait for you there. Remember, you only have one charge. Any more and your arm will burn out, so make sure you only use it when you are sure it will work."

"Yes, mom..." I replied sarcastically, "Just make sure you get the room ready by the time we get there. I'll stall for as long as I can." I waved her away. Childishly out of character, she stuck her tongue out at me before heading off to the warehouse.

I watched her back grow smaller in the distance before ducking out of the dome. I did one final check of my surroundings and after making sure no eyes were on me, I gently lifted open the station shutters and slid under it, quietly lowering the shutter to a close once I was inside.

Standing within the still empty and abandoned station, I stood planted to allow my eyes to adjust to the darkness. I no longer felt the tingling sensation that I had in my arm when I first neared the border, which I could only assume was the work of the shield dampener or a really effective placebo. Either way, I had no idea, nor the necessary knowledge or training to know if the gadget was working. I just had to trust that it was. When my vision finally returned and I got a good look around at my solitude, with the muffled sound of happy park goers behind me, my situation sunk in. I could hear the grinding of my clenched teeth from the stress and try as I might, I could not relax myself enough to ease them.

There were a few up-sides to not being able to physically feel. I don't get tired as easily. There's also that whole situation where I can withstand injuries that should knock a normal person out with the pain. And when things get tense, I don't feel that uncomfortable grip in my stomach.

With deep, hesitant breaths, I headed back to the rebel camp, empty handed and alone. Down the steps into the station, passed the broken gates, and passed the graffiti walls. Onto the train tracks, I tracked the dark cave perimeter to where the dug entrance was. Through the small, cramp, makeshift tunnel, light slowly building up at the end, I stepped out to be surrounded by Jason's men, all with their guns trained on me. Held as human shields on the front line were Amelia, John, and Lindsey, hands bound behind them and a gun to each of their backs.

Jason stepped out of the crowd and onto centre stage, a personal greeting to me. "Sorry, Milton, but I had to make sure that you held up the end of you deal." A twisted grin stretched the man's face. "Did you find the bomb?"

From their lack of reactions, I assumed my grandchildren had already found out about the plan. I asked him, "No casualties. You remember saying that?"

"Yes," he agreed, circling around me. I calmly faced forward, not wanting to give him the satisfaction of thought that I might fear him. From behind, he punctuated, "No human casualties."

"What about cyborgs? What about all the people in Roagnark who needs technology to keep them alive?"

"Those things aren't human." He stepped back into view. "They stopped being human when they let those machines inside them. They're just monstrosities now."

"What about me?" I asked fiercely. "Am I a monster too?"

"No..." He stepped up to face me, a glint of madness in his eyes, a fanatical timbre to his voice. "You're too cowardly to be a monster. Too weak."

"It's not a weak thing to have a heart."

He jabbed a finger at the cage of my heart. "You're a machine, Milton Jones. You just have to do as you're told. Go save the world. Serve your purpose. You don't need a heart. You don't have one."

"No," I coldly replied. "*You* don't have one."

For the first time, the cold, calculating, heartless man seemed taken aback. His eyes widened in shock, his nostrils flared angrily. He raised his right hand in signal and his men pushed John forward onto the ground. John knelt down, a gun to his head, execution style.

Jason threatened, "If you don't bring me to the bomb—"

Without flinching, I replied, "I'll bring you to the bomb."

"What?" He must not have expected to hear that, for again, his eyes popped opened in surprise. His deep brown irises were surrounded by bloodshot white as he strained to make sure sense of what I just said.

"I'll bring you to the bomb."

Amelia shouted, "Don't do it, old man!"

I ignored her. Getting emotional would do nothing to help the situation.

Seeing through me, Jason asked, "What's the catch?"

"There's no catch. I'll bring you to the bomb," I repeated a third time. "But you have to bring the three of them with us. And you can only bring two of your men."

"No deal."

"Don't be stupid, Colonel. This is a fortified city. You can't just walk in there with Platoon Bootlick marching behind your ass." Amelia's dictionary was rubbing off on me. "You'll get us all killed before we can even take a step!"

"And why should I trust you?"

I swung my arms opened and the Colonel jumped back, pulling his pistol out. His men did the same, putting me in their crosshairs.

I exclaimed, "Why shouldn't you? I'm alone. I'm unarmed! Figuratively speaking." I shook my robot hand. "You have hostages, you have guns, you have people! You have every conceivable edge on me! What are you afraid of?"

I could see Jason and his men contemplating the situation, though not for a second did they lower their guns. I hoped the bluff worked, because I do have one hand above theirs. I had a plan.

John grunted, "Don't do this! Those people are innocent! They are not part of your stupid war!"

John's rebel soldier rewarded his outburst with a rifle-butt to the head.

John hunched over to the ground in pain as Amelia screamed, "Leave him alone you shit shot, or I'll rip your eyes out!"

I shouted, "Stop it! Both of you!"

"Shut up, old man! If you think we'll thank you for saving us by committing genocide, you've got screws looser than the old fart knuckle!" Of course, fart knuckle being Colonel Jason.

"SHUT UP!" I yelled back furiously. "If you got nothing smart to add, then shut your trap and let me handle it!" I was starting to see where Amelia would have gotten her foul temper.

Jason watched our exchange intently, as if trying to read my face for any signs of deceit, which was ironic, as he had not a moment ago, said I wasn't human. He cocked his head and I met his stare. We were two grown men with the fate of millions of lives on our hands, reduced to a childish staring contest. Of course, with artificial eyes and physical immunity, I won.

Finally, slowly, the Colonel lowered his arms. "Fine," he grunted, slightly displeased. He turned to his men, "Hamilton! Loyde! You two with me. Small arms only. Bring the prisoners." He turned back to me. "Like you said, we're the ones with the guns. If you take even one step out of line, we will shoot everyone. And not just your little party, but anyone we see."

"Got it," I replied. "I'll take you to the fucking bomb."

With a twisted smile, he said, "Good. Now let's go kill us some cyborg people."

Cyborg People, Part Five

Disappointment could not even describe how I felt after we simply strolled past the front gate of The Forum Warehouse. Conflicted would probably be the closest word I could use. The guard at the reception merely nodded to our group in acknowledgement and the lack of metal detectors in a city where half the population had pieces of metal in their bodies meant that guns got through security checkpoints without much difficulties.

"Disappointed?" Jason asked, as if he could read my mind.

I replied, "Hardly."

I stood at the head of the group with Jason, while our rear flanks were watched by his two men, with John, Amelia, and Lindsey trapped in the middle. Though their limbs were free, the three were still hostages to the situation.

Amelia voiced out in a hushed whisper, "I can't believe you are doing this."

I did not need to turn back to know that was directed at me. I continued walking, ignoring her discontent.

She continued, this time to Jason, "What makes you think we won't just suicide charge you once we get the chance?"

"I'm sure you will do just that, Miss Smith," the Colonel replied. "But despite your foul mouth and questionable attitude, you're not stupid.

183

Or are you?"

John asked, "What are you getting at?"

"You can try to attack now, but failure would mean no one left in the city would be able to stop us. I'm assuming you would wait until the most opportune moment to do so with the least chance of failure," he explained calmly as we entered one of the large elevator platforms. The door closed behind us. "But as long as I do not give you such an opportunity..." He pulled out his gun for a glimpse and his men did the same, hiding the firearms in the larger pockets of their coats, though with their fingers still on the trigger. "There's absolutely nothing you can do."

I glanced back to see the siblings exchange defeated looks. Though Lindsey, who had opted to remain silent through the walk, gave me a slight nod.

We reached the 13th floor and an announcer over the speaker noted that we had reached the "Armoury." We exited the giant elevator in a file. The level was just what one would assume a warehouse to look like. A wide corridor stretched in front of us before cutting a sharp right at the final shutter of the row. The ceiling was nearly 10 meters high and each storage room were marked by large red numbers painted on 5 meters high shutters.

"Storage nine," I said, and Jason led the way.

Realising no one was in the building – or at the very least on the same level – with us, Jason's men fully drew their guns and pushed them into Lindsey and Amelia's back, guiding them forward like a pirate would to someone walking the plank.

Our footsteps reverberated loudly through the empty halls and even the sound of Amelia's grinding teeth was audible. We stopped before gate 9. A smaller, human sized door served as an entrance beside the giant shutter. Embedded in the wall next to the door was a hand scanner.

Jason gestured to it with his gun. "Go on," he egged me on.

Though I did not liked being ordered around, I could only give him a solid, angry stare. I stepped up to the machine and, though unsure of what would happen, placed my flesh and blood palm onto the scanner. A soft green glow flashed beneath my hand, followed by a click as the door unlocked.

A wicked smile was drawn across Jason's face as he heard the door opened. With my free hand, I gently pushed open the barrier that guarded the storage space.

I demanded, "Here you go. I've done what you asked. Now let them go."

The Colonel simply stared stoically at me before walking into the now opened room. I could hear his footsteps echo from within, along with the rare clunk and rasping of metal and wood. It seemed he was examining the place. After what seemed liked hours but really, only minutes passed, Jason stepped back out into the hallway with a smug smile that I wanted to slap off him.

"You did hold up the end of your deal, Mister Jones." He waved his hand in a signal and his henchmen raised their guns at my family and Lindsey. "But I'm afraid we can't have you running around alive and spoiling my plans."

Calmly and slowly, I held up my robot arm, palm outstretched to Jason's face. At first, the old soldier looked at my action quizzically, scanning the inches on my being before settling his gaze at the palm of my hand. His eyes grew wide, a look of fear I had yet to see in the old soldier's eyes.

"You know what this is?" I asked him.

His knuckles let out a reverberating crack as he formed them into fists. "Makeshift grenade," he identified.

Within my hand, tied around my middle finger, was a metal ball filled with gunpowder from bullets, wrapped in sheets of metal salvaged from Lindsey's walkie-talkie. It was no bigger than the size of my palm but I was confident in its abilities to inflict damage.

My anger had to be showing for there was a slight growl when I said, "Smart man. I figured you wouldn't let them go, so I had Lindsey prepare this little surprise for you. Easy to hide, especially since your men were only looking for guns and not explosives." I did not turn to look, but I could have sworn I heard my grandchildren sighing in relief and a snicker from Lindsey.

Somehow, Jason managed some of his confidence back, asking, "How are you going to set it off? I don't see a detonator or anything of the sort."

"Had an engineer friend of mine whip up sparklers in my hand. I just think it and boom, shrapnel in you face." I felt like one of them comic book heroes, throwing out quips at super villains.

"You're bluffing," he called.

"Try," I replied.

185

He stared at me.

I stared at him.

He asked, "What do you want?"

"Simple. You hold up your end of the bargain and let us go and we'll leave you to your bomb."

"And why should I trust you?"

"You probably shouldn't." I smirked. Or at least, I thought I smirked. Can't tell without feelings in facial muscles. "But I think getting blasted in the face right now is probably not that good a thing."

I was calm. I was beyond calm. A part of me was enjoying it. I wasn't sure if I was supposed to like the intensity of holding a possible mass murderer hostage, but the enjoyment felt primal. Instinctual. For some reason, I thought of my grandfather.

Jason asked again, "What do you want? No. Why should I give you what you want?"

"You'll still get your E.M.P bomb and take over the city either way. All I'm asking is that you let us go. Besides, even if I were to tattle on you…" *Tattle*, such a grown up word. "…you would still have the bomb. Nothing lost."

I could see from his squinted eyes that he was seriously considering the deal, looking for a way that such an arrangement could possibly backfire. He knew it was a trap. He must have known. Otherwise, I gave his intellect much more credit than I should have and I should feel ashamed of having been stumped by an idiot.

After the long pause, Jason said, "Fine." He gestured for his men to release the prisoners. "You're all free to go."

The soldiers lowered their guns but Amelia did not move. Instead, she vehemently exclaimed, "I'm not going to let you guys get away with this."

"Wait in the elevator," I said.

Lindsey tried to calm her down, "Come on Amelia, Milton knows what he's—"

Amelia cut, "I won't forgive you for this, old man!"

I punctuated, "Wait. In. The. Elevator!"

She hesitated, shot me an angry look, and stormed off with Lindsey.

John looked at me worryingly and said, "I hope you know what you're doing." He followed them away.

I turned my attention back to Jason, my hand still held up like a cannon attached to my limb. "Get in the room," I ordered.

"What?"

"I'm going to close the door behind you. You'll still have access to your toy. You just won't be able to shoot us in the back."

Again, his calculating eyes scanned me. He knew that as long as he had the E.M.P bomb, whatever deal I made him would end in his favour, and I was counting on that train of thoughts. The idea that he had the upper hand.

Finally, he nodded. "Let's go boys. Rig up the thing and we'll be home for dinner and drinks." His men gave a soft cheer and quick laugh before going into storage space 9. He turned to me one last time. "You're a good family man, Milton Jones. And that softness will be your downfall."

"Keep walking, asshole," I growled back.

He turned, and without another look or word, followed into the room.

I rest my hand on the scanner again and the door closed shut behind them, locking with a click. I placed the makeshift grenade on the machine, activated the electric spark Clover Parker rigged for me.

I closed my eyes.

The machine exploded.

Time to meet the wrath of a furious granddaughter.

Cyborg People, Part Six

Walls that were once marble white were now stained brown. Isolated from the rest of the world, the chamber that had once held the Cryo-Tube continued to stand strong. But the chamber was now emptied, a far cry away from its scientists and researchers filled hay days. The old lightings had long since burnt out, and the only source of illumination were from the torches the group brought along and a lamp that Clover retrieved from her home. Amazingly, the underground river generators still managed to provide power to the facility, as the ventilators continued to whir and the electronics still functioned. According to the siblings, the last group to have worked with their mother – my daughter – spent two years delaying the building of The Forum Warehouse on top of the chamber and reconnected the entrance with sewer lines which we used to enter. The Forum then buried the old building.

The second model of the Cryo-Tube, with its sliding glass doors, was left in the centre of the room. Amelia and Clover was busy hooking up both the power cables and themselves. At least, that was what I got from their conversation.

Angrily, Amelia questioned, "So you just up and left us?"

"It's not like I had a choice," Clover replied. "If you hadn't noticed, the only reason I'm alive today is because of these implants."

Amelia clicked her tongue in frustration. Though she understood the

188

reasoning, her pride did not allow her to swallow it. "We could have gotten you help!"

"And where exactly were you going to get that? There are no cities left with proper medical sciences to treat me. So yeah, my grandpa brought me here, sacrificed the rest of his life to save me. I'm not going to apologise for that."

"You could have at least said goodbye!"

"I did!"

"Saying "I love you Milly" and a kiss isn't a goodbye. It's more like "I think we have a great future together and I want to fuck you" or something."

"Oh, grow up! We were thirteen years old. We weren't going to have sex."

"That's what you got out of that?"

"You're the one who started it!"

"Don't make me E.M.P you."

I was glad they were arguing. For the first time in days, I was not the centre of attention. No doctors or worried families to coddle me. No dying wife who wanted a last goodbye. No crazed mass murderer wanting alone time with the Hero of the Mist. I was Milton Jones, human being. Technically, a cyborg-person, but that was fine too.

Watching hacked footages of Jason and his men trapped within the warehouse, John said, "Hard-light holograms. Very clever."

"Yeah," I replied. On the computer screen, we watched as Jason kicked at the fake, hologram projected bomb parts. The Colonel then ordered his two men to try to pry the door opened. "Clover mentioned it, and I thought if it was anything like the stuff I grew up hearing about and better than the hologram I used, we had a good chance at tricking him."

I was still dumbfounded at how my improvised plan had worked. I had thought for sure that at least one of us would have been shot. My mother once told me that grandfather had a knack for impromptu plans as well, and though they always sounded inane when said out loud, they somehow almost always worked themselves out. I wondered how much of the success of my plan was due to sheer dumb luck, and how much was talent from my grandfather's genes.

John noted, "Big leap of faith though. What if he saw through it?"

"I doubt it. Old fart soldier who hates technology? Couldn't turn on a microwave to save his life I bet, let alone tell the difference between hard-light holograms and reality."

"You think he would get out?"

"Unlikely. The guards will figure out something is wrong soon." I wanted to end by saying that he would likely be killed, just as the robots that attacked us yesterday did to Borris. But I did not want to end that conversation on such a grim note.

"You know, Milton," John said with a smile. "For a moment there, me and Milly really thought you were going to kill the city just to save us. I'm glad that we were wrong."

Despite that, the thought had crossed my mind, should my original plan had failed.

From the opposite station, Lindsey piped out, "Hey! Stop being wishy-washy and get back to work, you two!"

Nodding like a kid who had just got told off by his parents, John replied, "Right. Sorry boss." He turned to me with a grin that I'd like to describe as 'stupid'. "She's so cute when she's angry."

"Did something happen to you two?" I asked, quizzical.

"Well, after you left, I took your advice and asked her out. You know, if we survive that is. And she said yes!"

If we survive. I've heard that line before in old movies and television shows, but it somehow managed to sound even cornier in real life than it did in fiction. Nonetheless, I congratulated him on his small victory in life.

"Thanks," John replied, turning off the video feed and continued working on rebooting the old Cryo-Tube. "You were right though. Good things in life are hard to find and pass us by too quickly. We should take a hold of it while we can."

I turned back to Amelia and Clover, who had gone to working in silence. Intrigued by their relationship, I dug into it from John. "What's up with those two?"

"They used to date. About what? Ten years ago now?" the brother replied. "Then one day, the Parkers just up and disappeared. Without a trace. Gone like a ghost. Poof into oblivion. Swung behind—"

"I get it," I stopped him before his metaphors went too far. "They were gone."

"Well, now we know what happened," John sighed deeply, scratching his chin as an error window popped up on the screen. "Milly's been pretty pissed about the whole thing for years though. They were really into each other, after all."

Sarcastically, I replied, "Yeah, loads of chemistry there."

"There is!" he insisted. "You know how Clover does that thing where she talks as if you're not there? If you ask her questions she'll just continue talking over you?"

"Yeah, what about it?"

"The only people she never did that to were her grandfather and Milly."

"I—" I started to rebut, but quickly realised that he was right. "Huh. That's just fascinating. Do you think I should go talk to her? Give her some grandfatherly advice?"

"Don't you mean 'old man' advice?"

"Hey! Don't you start that too."

"Why are you so insistent on being called grandfather? You know grandfathers are still old men, right?"

Enthusiastically, I started, "Okay, work with me on this. See, if someone gets pregnant at sixteen, and their child gets pregnant at sixteen as well, then that technically makes them grandparents at thirty-two years old. And I'm totally cool with that age." I was sure I was grinning like an idiot for John was chuckling. "But if you call me an old man, then I'm just old, you know? Like fifty plus or something."

Through laughs, he replied, "I never took you as someone who cared about age."

Slightly more sombre than I had intended, I replied, "John, I'm a time travelling, terminally ill man who is going to outlive three generations of his family. Age is all I have left to care about."

"That's not true," he replied with a smile. "You have us to care about. For now at least."

Softly, I muttered, "Thanks."

"And for the record..." I looked up to him and saw the fleeting kind face of my daughter in him. "I think you make a pretty good grandfather."

A loud clunk came from the Cryo-Tube, and I turned, expecting Amelia to have taken a wrench to the machine in frustration. Instead, the machine started to hum gently as the internal lights lid up.

"Woohoo!" Amelia shouted in triumph.

It was a strangely nostalgic sight. Despite having just been in the contraption a few days before, the box-shaped Cryo-Tube felt like a distant relative. For some reason, I yawned, as if the machine was beckoning me to sleep.

"Alright." Lindsey walked up to us. "Time to get you back to bed."

I looked to the group and suddenly, I was at a lost for words. I had one day left to live and I was about to step into the last goodnight. I do not know if it was due to the events of the past day having hardened my nerves, but I felt no fear nor hesitation. No regrets of what-ifs and never-weres. I was ready to face the end of the world. I was ready to die.

Cyborg People, Part Seven

At first, they struggled to hook up the ECG pads and the other medical instruments to me. That was until I told them to forget it, since there would not be any doctors left to watch over my progress.

"Alright," John said. "Just give us a moment then to figure out how this stupid software works."

I stepped back out of the Cryo-Tube. Clover and Amelia stood on opposite ends of the room, minding their own businesses as far from each other as possible.

Lindsey approached me and apparently sensing something bothering me, asked, "What's wrong?"

I nudged my head at Clover and Amelia. "Those two. I don't know. Some sort of tension between them."

"Wow."

"Yeah. Intense. I know."

"No, what I mean is that it's about to be your last few hours alive and you can still think of other people? That's kind of amazing."

"Really?"

"Yeah."

I said, "I'm just weird I guess."

She nodded, though in the darkness, I could not tell if it was as an agreement to my statement, or a nod of approval of my actions.

193

I asked, "Listen, could you go talk to Clover for me? See if you can get her to go easy on Amelia?"

She raised her brow quizzically. "You want me to give life advice? How old do you think I am?"

"Um..." I realised that Lindsey had been such a mature minded woman that I had not thought of her age as anything but that. After all, she was able to forgive me for her brother's death, or at the very least, not blame me for it. "Thirty?" I shot randomly.

"I'm twenty-five!" She waited with bated breaths as I struggled to find a reply that couldn't be interpreted as an insult. When she realised that wasn't happening anytime soon, she shook her head disappointingly. "Fine, I'll go talk to her. You just get yourself ready to go under." She turned away.

"Wait!" I stopped her. From my pocket, I retrieved her brother's watch. "You dropped this on the way down," I said, holding it out.

She stopped in her tracks, bit her lower lips in thought, then held out her hands. Not to take the watch though, but to close my hand around it and pushing the gesture away. "Keep it. Remember where you've been. Remember all those that helped you." Before I could reply, she walked away.

I muttered, "Thanks," under my breath. She was indeed a woman beyond her years.

As if having read my mind, Amelia came walking up to me. Trying to act calm and cool, I leaned my hand against the Cryo-Tube, no doubt looking like a cheesy movie hero, minus the sunglasses, famously toned body, or anything that might give a view of pleasure. So more like a creepy man at the bus station actually, selling candies to kids.

She asked, "You ready?"

"Not yet," I replied. If there's one thing I've learnt over the last two days was that the best way to deal with hard-headed people like my granddaughter was to be as direct as possible. I had Jason and Clover to thank for that epiphany. "Still have to settle this whole thing with you and Clover."

"Settle this whole thing?" she scoffed. "What are you? My father?"

"Grandfather," I corrected.

"Old man," she insisted.

I let out a sigh. "Listen, kid, you're going to lose a lot of people in life. And it's not often you get a second chance with them." I nudged my head over in the direction of Clover, who surprisingly, seemed to be having a calm discussion with Lindsey instead of the heated one I had expected of her. "Don't let her slip out of your grasp just because of pride."

Amelia folded her arms and pouted, "You've had a few second chances over the years."

There was something about Amelia that reminded me of Leila. A mix of her stubbornness, inability to express her feelings, and still be empathic of others.

I told her, "Every one of those days I hold close and dear. Every day I get to spend with all of you is a blessing, followed by years of curses." Leila had grown up without me. Amelia and John had grown up without me. My wife grew old without me. Solemnly, I said, "I missed a lot too. So take it from me, take all that you can, while you can."

She looked to her feet as if in thought. When I tried to continue, she waved me off and went towards Clover. I do not know if I got through to her, but she did not curse or swear at me or anything, so that's a plus.

From the main console, John exclaimed, "Milton!" I turned to him. "We're ready for you."

Somewhere inside me, confidence welled. I did not know where it came from or what it was for, but I fearlessly turned my back from the room and stepped into the old Cryo-Tube and strapped myself in. The group of four gathered around at the main console in front of me. Despite only being lit by a single lamp and their respective torches, the four of them looked clear as day to my eyes.

I smiled at them and shouted happily, "Happy endings!" Before strapping on the oxygen mask.

They looked confused for a moment before breaking into slight chuckles. John gave me a thumbs up. Amelia stuck her tongue out. Lindsey and Clover waved me goodbye. I waved back as John flipped a switch and the glass door closed before me. The familiar blue liquid slowly filled the chamber.

Amelia ran up to me, squishing her nose against the long since misted glass. She shouted, her voice a clear whisper, "See you later, gramps!"

Before the water completely filled me, I strapped Borris's watch onto my wrist. Finally, I smiled, closed my eyes and muttered, "Happy endings..."

195

A beeping noise started next to my ears but sounded distant and muffled, as if I was listening to the beep of a sonar from underwater. Then I realised I couldn't breathe. At first, I was baffled by how I was able to tell that I had no air in my lungs and it was only after a few seconds that I realised that they were burning in pain. The joint which my robotic arm was connected to was also shouting for me cut it off. I was drowning.

Do something! I screamed to my body. Or I'm going to die!

Somehow, through the pain and confusion, I managed to raise my legs to the glass door. I pushed against it, leaning into the back of the liquid filled chamber. Even underwater, I could hear the grinding of the gears in my legs as I pushed the limbs to their limits. But despite my efforts, I was losing consciousness and this time, I feared a more permanent sleep.

Is this it? I travel decades to die by drowning?

Something at my feet gave way. I could feel it. I could physically feel it. The slight jerk as the glass door shifted forward. The cool liquid wrapping my body. The burning ache in my shoulder. The continued ripping of my chest as the last of the oxygen left my body.

The glass door broke and the liquid gushed out of the machine, leaving me dangling by the harness. But I still could not breathe and I struggled to catch my breath. I must have opened my eyes at some point but I could not be sure, for no matter how hard I looked, my vision was completely dark. I couldn't see what was causing my suffocation. I took my hand to the oxygen mask and ripped it away from my face, the pulling of the adhesive felt like the tearing of a band-aid. Air flooded back into my lungs, invading like college boys at a strip club, tearing a path through my already pained oesophagus. The violent inhale forced me to cough uncontrollably and I spat and drooled as-and-how my body wanted for comfort.

As my body got itself back under control, I looked around the room as my camera-eyes adjusted to the darkness. The faint blood-red glow from the Cryo-Tube gave them just enough light to shutter in an image. It was not that I was blinded or my eyes had failed, but the room was shrouded in complete darkness.

I coughed out, "Amelia? John?" To no reply.

Despite the situation, I was more worried about the pain in my shoulder. Though slightly glad to have the sense of touch back, the sudden return and the continued ache was troubling. Good things never came without bad consequences.

I unbuckled myself from the machine, revelling in the stretching of my muscles as I did so. There was an itch on my nose. I scratched it. I groaned with an almost primal pleasure. Then I stopped when I realised how much my voice echoed, how loud the silence was ringing in my ears. I turned to the digital clock embedded on the Cryo-Tube. 61 years had passed, but still 20 years too early for me to wake up.

"This is a joke," I said out loud. "It has to be."

It was not just because I was dangerously early to be spending my final day, but also because I was finally able to feel again, yet there was not a single soul around me to hold.

The main console, where John and gang stood just moments ago, was empty. But a single red light blinked at me. I thought at first my eyes were just malfunctioning, but upon closer inspection, there was indeed a light blinking on the console above a big red button.

Entire body still soaking wet, the room keeping itself at a temperature that cooled, I approached the console and stood with my hand above the button. "Only good things happen when red buttons are pushed," I reasoned against reason and pressed it.

The computer screen embedded next to it flickered alight. Booting, loading, colours slowly filled. The words:

VOICE RECOGNITION

Printed across the screen.

"Milton Jones," I announced.

CONFIRMED

A bar began to load. Once it was filled, a familiar white room flashed into view. It was the chamber as it had been over eighty years ago. From off screen, a figure moved into the camera's line of sight and the face nearly brought me to tears.

I think she worked on you till the very end.

Professor Leah Leslie Hullway, with a her bright smile, signature yellow dress and lab coat, and a slightly greying blonde hair, looked into the camera and greeted, "Hello Milton. If you're hearing this, you're

197

probably at the end of the world." As if reading my mind, she continued, "You're also likely alone right now."

With a bleep, the red light above the big red button turned green.

Leah continued, "I'm hoping that the light is still working by then. There should be a button beside this screen. Just press it and it will download a collection of videos to the internal hard drive of your eyes. It's just a little something we put together to make sure you're not alone at this last stage." Another smile, one that pierced the gloom of the room. "Good luck Milton. We're with you."

The Final Day, Part One

"Initiate video playback," I said out loud, as per Leah's instruction. I also set the new earpiece that popped out of the console into my left ear. I wondered if she got the engineers to build that compartment specifically for me, or if it was just something that had always been part of the set.

My left eye blinked to black before slowly loading up colours. Gradually, after some static, those flashes of colours sharpened into a clear image.

My grandparents once told me there was a time, before even them, that people would make casts of the faces of the deceased as mementos or portraits. As a child, I would have nightmares of the faces of dead people coming alive from these death masks to talk to me. Imaginations were wild back then. In real life however, it hits the heart much harder than the fear of nightmare could, at strings that were not expecting to be tugged.

"John, get the fuck out here!" Amelia screamed into the camera, ruining the heartfelt moment again. Her face settled dead centre on the screen. "Camera's rolling!" She waited for her brother to reply.

"Wait! I'm stuck!" I heard him scream. "Lindsey! Help!"

I heard Lindsey cursed something off-screen along the lines of "Useless idiot" Amelia shook her head disappointingly away from the camera.

199

She turned back to face the screen and I realised she was in the chamber. Not with me now, but in a brightly lit, slightly cleaner chamber from decades ago.

"So um...hey old man. Found mom's diary and she said this video thing would work, so I'm hoping it does." A loud crash came from behind her and she winced in almost physical pain. Recovering after a sigh, she continued, "Anyway, if you're watching this, we're all probably long gone. But we wanted you to know what's been happening with us and some other mushy stuff."

I pulled out the chair behind the control console, probably the same one Amelia sat in as she made that video and realised that as the video continued to play, my other eye continued to adjust its aperture to cope with the darkness. I wondered if it would be able to see fully in the dark after the video was done playing.

"So first thing's first, the bad news." Of course she would start with the bad news. Amelia might be one of the most negative people I've ever met, or at least the most vulgar. "A few years after you left, details of what The Forum had been doing to the people outside Roagnark hit the public. There's been a rebellion and you know, city wide evacuations and stuff." She looked towards the door, as if expecting her words to jinx her. She turned back. "So we're here, one last time, in Roagnark, to get Clover and as many civilians as we can out of the city before shit hits the fan."

Another war. More fighting. A thought crept into the back of my mind. What was the point of my family and friends risking their lives to save the world if everyone just goes back to fighting each other the moment we turned our backs? Joan's effort to stabilise the effect of the Mist was negated by the first war. Our efforts at stopping Jason's E.M.P bomb was overwritten by this new rebellion. I wondered if humanity could only fight.

Amelia continued, "So um... this would probably be the last time we get to see you." She turned the camera to the Cryo-Tube where I floated peacefully within. "We're leaving you stuff and gear, you know, in case of an emergency. I'll uh...let John explain all that." She nodded off screen and got off the chair.

John slotted in, his hair having grown considerably longer since I last saw him, covering his eyes. It was a much rugged look than I remembered and a new scar ran across his nose. "Hey grandfather. So

200

good news first before I tell you about our little gift for you." Of course, the opposite of his sister. Positive John. "Well, me and Lindsey are engaged."

The news brought a grin across my face. It was weird, finally being able to feel the pull of my facial muscle.

John continued, "And I'm sure Milly's too embarrassed to tell you this, but she and Clover are married now. It's been kind of long distance. She's really happy we're getting Clover out of Roagnark today." The grin got wider, and I felt my eyes trying to tear up, but the implants prevented any real crying from taking place.

Amelia shouted, "Hey! I was going to tell him that!"

"No you weren't!" John shouted back. "You were going to stammer and drag and act like a tough little girl."

"Don't make me shoot you!"

He returned his attention to the camera. "Anyway, Clover's doing some maintenance work on the Cryo-Tube right now, but she's afraid the machine might not last, even with her repairs, so we're leaving you a package behind the tube." He turned the camera to the machine again. This time, Clover popped her head out from behind it and waved to me, pointing to a hard cased container behind. John turned the camera back to him. "I told her not to worry, but she just rambled on, as usual. Just in case she's right though, we've got a back-up plan for you in case we can't get to you in time. Or, you know, we're too old or dead," he ended grimly.

Clover jumped into the shot, which was impossibly fast, given her previous position. Talking over John, and seemingly, even me, she said, "Here's the backup. In case anything should happen, we've left tools and wirings inside the emergency box. Just follow the instructions I've included there and wire up the main console to the original Cryo-Tube. You know, the one that's in front of the Forum Warehouse? Apparently, that one is still fully functioning. There's also cryogenic fluids inside the Warehouse itself. It's all in the instruction manual, so seriously, just follow that."

Seeing everyone else gathered, Amelia and Lindsey jumped in, relegating John to a tiny corner at the bottom of the screen. Lindsey exclaimed, "Hey Milton! So as long as nothing happens to that statue Cryo-Tube, it should work fine, since the domes are all sealed."

Amelia noted, "Hey, the camera's running out of battery."

201

John exclaimed, "Didn't you charge it before we left home?"

"I told you, the charger's shot."

"You shot the charger?"

"No! I'm just saying it's not working."

Everyone turned to me, and after looking dumbstruck for a few seconds, all smiled to the camera.

"Don't fucking forget us, old man!"

"Bye, Milton!"

"I'm bidding you farewell."

"Have a good one at the end of the world, grandpa."

The image suddenly blacked out as the battery died on cue. My left eye blinded by the darkened video playback software, I relied solely on the sight of my right to guide me. I followed the instructions of my grandchildren and headed around the Cryo-Tube. Right at the spot where Clover once stood was the supply box. I unclipped the metal strap that had rusted somewhat and opened it. Inside were two wires, coiled half a meter wide and as tall as the box, which was the height of my knuckle to my elbow. Unravelled, they could probably stretch for a mile each.

There were also some supplies. A few cans of food, a flask of water, a toolbox, an instruction manual as Clover had stated, and an industrial crank torch with a shoulder strap.

A loading bar appeared in my left eye and I assumed it was preparing the next video file. I separated all the supplies and with my mechanical arm, began cranking the torch.

Suddenly, a sharp pain shot up my elbow and I let out a curse through gritted teeth. I nearly passed out from the pain, the sting continuing even after the initial jab had subsided.

"Shit..." I was drooling a little from the pain and spat out a mouthful of saliva. "Mist Poisoning...." I deduced.

It had been a while since I had thought of my condition. Mostly because of the lack of physical feelings, I had partially forgotten about it. But my previous worry was validated again when another round of pain erupted from my legs. I crumpled to the ground, bent over and spitting out groans. Then, the pain took a turn and rocketed up my spine.

My wretched screams echoed through the empty chamber for what felt like hours. By the time the pain subsided, I was sweating, my entire body aching in pain, and I once again lost feeling in my left arm. Lying sprawled across the floor, facing the ceiling, I took quick laboured breaths as I tried to calm myself down and to mentally will the suffering away.

Then, colour flooded my left eye as the video began and a different kind of pain, equally gut wrenching, gripped at my heart and pulled with the force of an elephant running from a mouse.

"Hey dad," my daughter, Leila, all grown up, greeted me through the screen. I wondered which point of her life she was talking from until she said, "So um... mom's gone. Yeah..." I noticed her eyes were red from crying. She was recording from the days after Joan passed away.

"The city got quite restless since mom passed away, so I'm not sure if this will be the last time we get to speak. You haven't met my husband yet, have you? Or maybe you will? In the future? Of all people, we should know more than anyone else how uncertain the future is. But yeah, my husband. Leonard Newton Smith. I think you would like him. And um..." She seemed to be trying to find words to say, but started tearing up again, no doubt thinking of her mother. It seemed she was at her limit, grieving for Joan and speaking to a frozen me. "I love you dad. And I miss you. And I hope one day our family can have some sort of happy ending, to make all this worthwhile."

She reached for the camera and with a flick, the image disappeared from view.

"No..." I subconsciously let out, not wanting to lose sight of my beloved daughter.

I sat back up, the pain having subsided tremendously, aided by the soothing experience of hearing from my daughter again. I still could not feel my left arm, though it continued to move fine. I took a deep breath as another loading bar came into view. I looked to the container of wires, got to my feet, and prepared myself for survival. I had to get to the next Cryo-Tube before the day was up or the Mist Poisoning would kill me. After travelling all this way, with all that my family sacrificed, I refused to keel over and die.

The Final Day, Part Two

Strolling through an abandoned sewer in a possibly post apocalyptic world was not on my mind when I first entered the Cryo-Tube. In retrospect, that scenario really should have come up at some point over the past hundred years. The only source of light was from my shoulder torch, and the only living things around me were countable by the glint of their beady eyes. The only other sound beside my steady steps were the jingling of the carabiners that held the coil of wires that dangled from my backpack.

"Oh," I said out loud as a glint of paint shone back at me. "A ladder." I found myself speaking aloud on the way over after I cut off the video playback.

I was watching Doctor Parker's video when I nearly slipped on a patch of moss. Partly because it was hard to watch where you are going with one eye distracted, but also due to the doctor simultaneously boring me with a prolonged lecture on my health.

"Thanks for everything, doc."

Behind me, the coil of wires had been unravelled like breadcrumbs. Attached to them at the end of the line was the underground power generator. According to Clover's notes, the cables were made from high density, extremely conductive metal, allowing them to survive the decades without corroding to time and served their purpose for transferring power from the generator to the old Cryo-Tube.

I tugged on them to make sure they were not caught on anything before beginning my climb up the ladder. At the top of the climb, I pushed against the manhole cover and climbed out into Roagnark's tunnelled streets, right outside the entrance to the Forum Warehouse dome. The pathway was darkened by decades of neglect with a stench of rust in the air. The door was kept shut. With no power going to the gate, I decided to brute force my way in.

With my robot arm, I pushed against one of the door. The gear in my arm whirred as I did with the door slowly creaking open. It was the first time I could physically feel my arm working, and it was a feeling that would no doubt take time to get used to again, but felt good to have nonetheless. The nano-cables attached to the nerves of my arm seemed to tug gently from the inside, as if it was trying to pluck a booger from within my body. When the door was opened just wide enough for me to squeeze through, a loud crack like the snap of a whip blasted at my right ear. Pain jabbed at my right shoulder as my arm snapped back.

"Argh!" I screamed, grabbing at my cybernetic with my flesh and blood, neither arm capable of feeling anything again.

The pain faded almost instantaneously and I made a quick check of my arm. It was still attached, but the elbow no longer responded correctly to my will. It just shook and vibrated when I tried to move it.

"Damn it..." I cursed. The crack must have been caused by a gear that broke apart. Thankfully my hands could still move, rotating, opening, and closing fine.

Not wanting to risk another injury, I squeezed through the small gap instead of trying to widen it. Once through, I removed the cables from their carriers and strung it onto my broken arm, using the malfunctioned million-dollars cybernetic as a hanger.

Abandoned and without life, the dome of the Forum Warehouse was shrouded in darkness. My torchlight ran over the scene, lighting the grey walls like a spotlight unto a stage. What was once a realistic simulation of clear blue skies were now lifeless and cracked, rusted and burnt. In the middle of it all was the original Cryo-Tube, the big metal rice cooker.

I announced, "Initiate video playback."

My left eye stopped transmitting images of my surrounding and quickly loaded up the next video in the playlist. I walked backwards towards the Cryo-Tube, slowly uncoiling the cables behind me. There was still a quarter of the original coil left, and I thought it very Parker-like for Clover to have over-prepared.

As the colour of the video faded into view, I stopped in my tracks. On the screen was none other than my wife, Joan. She looked to be in her late 40s, after Leila's graduation but before the onset of her illness. Shamefully, I had almost forgotten what she looked like. But when her image popped into view, memories of her flooded back to me like a broken dam. How she always smelled of plants. How she always seemed to have some dirt stuck in her black hair. The lovable stains on her shirt after a hard day's work. The ever supporting shoulder that carried me through my life.

Sitting at her kitchen table, a sky-blue nightgown on her, I could immediately tell she had not slept well in her recent time. "Hey Milton," she greeted. My legs nearly buckled when I heard her voice. She paused, gathered her thoughts, and continued, "I'm um... not sure how long this video is going to be. Leah told me not to make them too bloated, since she's not sure how many she can fit into your memory."

She stopped again and yawned, then buried her eyes in her hands as she tried to rub her face awake. Even across the ages, I could tell she needed a moment to herself. So without wasting any more time, I continued my work, pulling the wires towards the Cryo-tube.

Joan found her breath and continued, "It shouldn't be a surprise to you by the time you're watching this but we just found out about your arm."

"Ah..." I let out the half sigh, understanding her trepidation. The sudden spread of Mist Poisoning to my arm was a shock that nearly killed me and had delayed them bringing me out of cryo-sleep for a decade.

She continued, "I don't know if this will be the last time I get to talk to you. I don't even know when we can get the medical sciences up so we can fix this whole mess." I wanted to reach through the screen and hug her tight and was slightly angered that G wasn't there to comfort her. I noticed the living room clock ticked away past 3 A.M. and guessed the man was likely to be asleep. She added, "G's asleep right now."

I dropped what I was doing and broke out in laughter. My voice echoed throughout the empty dome, cackling away like a mad man in the shady parts of a city street. It amazed me, no, overjoyed me, that she could still anticipate what I was thinking despite there being no logical possibility of her being able to do so. I do not think I have ever loved her as much as I did that moment. With death knocking at the door and darkness surrounding me, she continued to be a light in my life, a little flame that burnt longer and brighter than a wildfire.

She smiled to the camera, a gesture that warmed my heart and steadied my soul. "We miss you. I miss you. Leila's so proud of you right now." I could tell she had more to tell me. Things about her life, her feelings. But she set them aside. "I have this strange feeling that, right now, you might be wondering if what we're doing is worth it. Or maybe it's just me."

She was right, I was wondering. Without focusing, I bumped into the Cryo-Tube podium. I turned around to make sure I do not trip with my next step before setting the cables down on the platform and circled around to the plaque. Though weathered away, one of the phrases that could still be read was 'Hero of the Mist'.

Joan followed with another one of her rare sighs and said, "The past few months, The Forum's been cracking down on spending. Even some of our anti-Mist projects got cut. It's all political plays, and it really makes you think. Even in such dark times, people still want to consolidate their power." I looked to the bench that I had once sat on and thought of the little girl named Sally that came with a glitter of hope in her eyes. Even without Joan saying it, I knew where she was headed with her train of thoughts. "But I'd like to think there are still good people left worth fighting for. And if you ever start doubting yourself, I want you to remember that."

I saw two more words through the dusted plaque. Project Dawn. The name of the project. I had hardly heard much of it, mostly since I did not have the time or luxury to ask. I was mostly rushed from one place to another. But I felt that the name was made to inspire renewed hope. Hope like the one that the little girl, Sally, embodied.

Joan reached for the camera to turn it off but stopped in contemplation mid-move. Then, to me, she said, "I love you Milton. Forever. And you are my greatest inspiration. I could never have lived all these years, doing all the good I've done, had you not given me the courage to do so." She smiled again and I melted. "Stay safe. Love from everyone."

The video blipped its end, and I was once again left alone in the post apocalyptic world. I took a deep breath to calm myself before picking up the cables I left and started to rig the old Cryo-Tube.

The Final Day, Part Three

I had forgotten how fatigue felt, but was reminded by my sweat and heavy panting. As I stood in the empty corridor of the Forum Warehouse, exhausted after pushing the large trolley cart of tanks of cryogenics liquid with just one good arm, I had to stop before the reception desk to catch my breath.

Through their own videos, G had announced to me his engagement; Leah rambled on about her theories of my grandfather's prediction; and Matthews had thanked me for inspiring him, just a month before his death. Even my parents gave me their love. Now, in my left eye, Leila, the little girl I had known her for her whole life, just a few weeks after I've left, held out the gleaming trophy of her 2nd place victory in a song writing competition.

She said happily, "And when I got on stage, everyone clapped, and I didn't feel so scared anymore!" Grinning as giddily as she did when I got her a toy, Joan sat beside her, young and proud. "Look at how shiny this is!" She waved her prize again.

"Alright, Lei, time to go," Joan told her, smiling through the camera at me in farewell.

"Aww...but I want to talk to dad more," Leila added, just before the camera turned off.

I meekly croaked, "Don't go."

209

I realised I never got the chance to hear the song she wrote, or ask if she ever learnt to play an instrument. And the knowledge that I would never see them again finally seemed to have sunk in. I felt a roll of water moving down my cheeks. Surprised, I reached for it but could not find the droplet. Since I couldn't physically cry, I wondered if I had just imagined the experience, or perhaps a droplet had gotten on my face somehow.

Finally, I took a seat, back against the cart of tanks. I was no longer tired, but I could no longer find the strength to stand. I sighed, stretched out my feet and rested into the crate.

"What's the point?" I asked myself. "Everyone's gone."

Initiating Video Playback

The words flashed across my eye and I sat straight up. The videos had been playing chronologically backwards. From Amelia and gang, to Leila, Parker, Joan, G, Matthews, my parents, and the last video of my wife and daughter together. There was no one else I expected to reach out to me after all of them.

I got to my feet and found renewed strength in curiosity and started to push the cart again. Even after I've reached the door, the video had only been half loaded, which was much longer than any of the previous videos left to me.

As I waited for the video to load, I managed to push the cart out the door, down the hill, and next to the Cryo-Tube before the loading bar even reached the final 10%. From within the crate, I took out a pair of short polyethylene water pipes. I connected them to opposite ends of the Cryo-Tube and finished the initial installation just as the video came on.

"Hello, Milton," the man said to me.

I dropped what I was doing and stood dumbfounded, half my sight staring at blank space while the other at the man in the video. I remembered him from a distant past. Before the Cryo-Tube. Before Leila. Before even Joan.

With green eyes that shone even to his later age and deep maroon hair that I inherited with pride, my grandfather, Timothy Kleve, greeted me from the other side of the video.

The old man began, "I wonder how many people before me started with, 'If you're watching this...'? Quite a cliché thing to say. But uh...well,

210

you know, if you're watching this, you should be..." He took out his phone and swiped at it. "Twenty years to the end of the world, if my prediction is right." He swiped at the phone again and squinted at the document on it. "Which it is. I'm so smart."

I had forgotten how childish the old man could be. I gave a derisive sigh and went back to work on connecting the tanks of liquid to the machine, wondering if when I'm asleep, the tubes might break. I decided not to think of the things I can't control and carried on.

He continued, "You might be wondering, why you? Why not a trained soldier or someone more experienced or qualified?" I admit that I had thought of that. But at the time when I accepted the offer for the program, I had only a selfish intention of prolonging my life in mind. "Well, truth is, you're the only one who can."

Tim looked solemnly off his desk. He reached out and retrieved a photo frame. Even from my faint childhood memories, I knew it was of a picture of my grandmother, Sally Sparrow.

"Your grandmother and I once stopped an end of humanity scenario from happening. A giant portal opening in the sky, a pandemic killing off the world. A few of our family and friends sacrificed everything to give us the chance to win." He placed the photo back on the table, reminiscing on the past. It seemed that saving the world was indeed in our family. "It all sounds like a fairy tale now. But if you really are where you are supposed to be, then I'm sure such a story won't surprise you."

I finished connecting the first tank to the Cryo-Tube. It would provide the liquid required to keep me in stasis for the next twenty odd years. Hopefully. I prepared the second tank, the one that would recycle and clean the same substance. Though I was not particularly excited about swimming in my own filth for two decades, my options were severely limited.

However, my grandfather raised up his left hand and I stopped my work again. Glowing white lines like that of circuitry began lighting up his entire forearm. At first, I thought they might be tattoos, but realised they were more akin to blood vessels bulging out from under his skin, the glow pulsing slightly at the pace of a breath. My mind worked to comprehend the event unfolding and I had to force myself to not see the arm as a special effect.

My grandfather started explaining, "This thing here, Milton, is what gives me the ability to predict the future. But more importantly, it allows

211

me to manipulate the Mist. It allows me to be immune to it. Your grandmother have something similar, and this was what allowed us to close the portal all those years ago." I continued to stare dumbfounded. I did not even notice I had managed to unload the second tank. I half-heartedly continued my work, though now more focused on the video. "Apparently, this is inherited. But uh...it skipped your mother and went straight down to you. So I'm guessing whatever problems you're facing that will end the world would likely have something to do with this."

I looked down at my good arm and called, "Bullshit."

The fact that I was not immune to Mist Poisoning and was still dying from it, constantly reminded of the shortened life by my prosthetic legs and broken right arm, raised doubts to his claims. But at the same time, the portal he described sounded disturbingly similar to the one that I was facing, spewing Mist out like an anorexic.

Like everyone I knew, as if reading my mind, he continued, "But yours is kind of latent. Not all there yet. We're not sure why. Leah has this whole, 'inactivate' theory. But I hope that you'll get it to work by the time this video reaches you." Again, he slumped to solemnity. "I'm really sorry to have put this on you, Milton. I hope you can find it in you to forgive me."

Forgive you for what? I thought. The man had given me a chance to live out my life. To see my daughter grow up and hug my grandchildren. His actions likely saved the world dozens of times over by giving our family a fighting chance. Yet, I could see in his eyes, the drooping dark bags that were under it, the flickering flames of the fight for life. I could sort of understand him now, as I too am tired of fighting a never ending battle against the dangers that life threw back at us.

"Grandpa! Grandpa!" I heard the familiarly strange voice come from off screen. I knew what happened next. I remembered.

Tim turned just in time for four years old me to jump into his embrace. "Grandpa! Do you have any new bikes!" It was a time when to me, Grandpa Tim was that cool mechanic with an awesome motorcycle collection. He'd never let me ride one of them, but would always find time to cycle around the block with me on his equally extensive bicycle collection.

The old man said to young me, "Well, let's go see, shall we?" He turned to the camera and winked to me, just as the last parts of the tank and pipe were coupled together. The Cryo-Tube was ready to go.

A searing pain shot into my guts and up into my lungs as I dropped my tools from the pain. The gears in my broken arm whirred as my brain tried to push it to grip at the pain. It was probably for the best that the prosthetic was not working. Given how hard my left hand was holding my chest, my robotic right would have likely ripped my skin off.

Through gritted teeth, I spat out, "Not now! Not! Fucking! Now!"

The pain subsided and I knew I was running out of time. Still in discomfort, but not enough to debilitate me, I quickly set the console to run on a timer for twenty years. The video continued to play in my left eye, my grandfather giving child-me a piggyback ride out of the room, their laughter echoing to the distance.

I climbed the old, rickety ladder up the machine and opened the hatch just as Agents G and Matthews had shown me all those years or days ago. Another round of hurt blasted through what's left of my legs and I fell, back first into the Cryo-Tube. Somehow, I had managed to pull the hatch close behind me and the isolated chamber was lit by the light from the old green button. I wondered if I had broken my spine during the fall, or if my nerves had been shot again, as I could not feel anything from it. Soon though, I realised neither of that was the case. My entire body was just in enough pain to overwrite my senses. Everything hurt equally.

"Hey, dad!" my mother greeted off-screen. They began chatting, but I could not hear them on the account of my own screams.

Reaching, grasping desperately, I got a hold of the oxygen mask and clumsily put it on. I felt I was on the verge of dying from pain itself. I lost count of the number of times I had almost passed out but was brought back to life by another pulse of heat through my body.

I reached for the button to start the machine. My hand fell to the floor. Wrong hand. I tried again. Success. Darkness engulfed me as I could feel the welcomed cool of the liquid filling the machine. The liquid seemed to be seeping into my body, numbing the pain from the outside in. Wrapping me. Engulfing me in blissful relief.

I heard young me shouting excitedly. "Let's play superheroes!"

For a moment, I wondered why the pain in my heart was the last to go.

Then my left hand glowed, lines of the same circuitry patterns that appeared on grandpa Tim's forearm now lit like neon light on the back of my hand. The line of light ran across my wrist, knuckle, and fingers,

213

wrapping around each joint like strings.

I stared at it, wide-eyed in disbelief. Only after what seemed like hours did I notice the liquid had been drained from the chamber and I was sitting, soaking wet, in the empty Cryo-Tube. I tore off my oxygen mask, wondering if something had went wrong.

The hatch above me flung opened and standing above me, hand reaching out, was my fellow time traveller, Pausa.

"Hello, Milton Jones," he greeted, his shadowed face backed by pale teal light. "Welcome to the end of the world."

Future, Part One

The dome had long since collapsed. A gaping hole in the ceiling revealed a Mist filled sky. Piles of broken support structures, cracked concrete, layers of dusts and random rubble covered what used to be Roagnark Park. I sat on perhaps the only bench left intact, wondering if the pond had dried up, been drained, or the water had just magically vanished one day as if it too had just travelled through time. The time traveller, Pausa, walked towards me.

"Here you go." He tossed a bottle of water to me.

I caught the drink with my one arm, the circuit-like lines still glowing gently on my forearm. "Thanks," I said, notching the bottle under my right armpit, I twisted the cap open with my left hand.

"Oh, don't thank me yet. That's all the water I have on me."

I looked to the time traveller quizzically. "And that's a bad thing why?"

"Because!" He jumped excitedly and pointed to the direction opposite me. "We'll be walking that way! About half a day."

"Why?" was my immediate reply.

"What do you mean? That's the way to the portal."

I recalled, after so long of having not fully delving on it, the portal that Professor Leah had once shown me. She had told me that at the end of my 139 years of freezing it would come in contact with the ground.

Regaining my thoughts, I said, "Right, right. Close the portal. Save the world." I had almost forgotten that. "How exactly am I suppose to do that again?"

He pointed to my glowing arm. "That right there is a bio-circuit capable of converting aether into energy, capable of executing a variety of meta-human abilities dependent on your gene sequence. You can use that to manipulate the fabric between the universe horizon and close the portal."

I stared back at him blankly, my mind trying to process his words before I replied, "Okay. That was good. Now speak to me like I'm ten."

"Ah. Um..." I could see him trying to rack his brain into dumbing the scientific information down for my pedestrian brain. "Your arm is magic."

Again, I stared. "Now speak to me like I'm five." Though it was no longer because I could not understand his explanation, but rather the reason themselves just seemed impossible.

Pausa sighed. "Okay, kid. You are what people from my time would call a Caster. A 'evolved human' basically. Someone who is capable of taking the Mist and using you body to convert it into energy. Energy that you could maybe shoot fireballs or teleport with." He then pointed to himself. "Or time travel. Or like your grandfather, predict the future."

"Whoa, wait a second here. You're saying I can control Mist?" He nodded. I gave a derisive snort. "How is that possible? If you recall, I am dying from Mist Poisoning?"

"Are you?" he countered. "Can you feel your arm? Can you feel pain? Can you feel the so called poison crawling through your veins?"

I reached for my chest and ran my nails over it. I could feel the scratch and the fabric of my shirt, the crawl of soft cotton only possible when provided by the sense of touch. I acknowledged that with the gaping hole in the ceiling, I was sitting in a Mist filled room, yet I was not retching. Again I looked to the glowing lines on my forearm and somewhere in my mind, I knew everything he said was true.

He continued, "You inherited an innate Caster gene from both your grandparents. And you had been cryogenically frozen for one hundred and thirty-nine years. If you think that your body will go through all that time without finding a way to immunise you from Mist Poisoning? You might be dumber than I gave you credit for."

"So I'm cured?" I continued to look at the glow of my arm. I tried to

216

look to Pausa, but the phenomenon continued to draw my attention like a magnet. "I can live my life."

"Yes."

"I can close the portal with this?" I waved my arm at the man.

"Yes."

Happily, I got to my feet and exclaimed. "I can save the world and live the rest of my life!"

Without hesitation, Pausa replied, "No."

I stood, stunned at the time traveller. "What do you mean, no?" My mood plummeted faster than a suicidal jumper.

Without his usual callousness, the man told me, "You can close the portal, or live your life. You can't do both."

"Y-you said my grandparents closed the first portal. They both lived."

"Your *grandmother* closed the first portal. And when she did it, she had the power of gods. You, you just got lucky. Your ability haven't even manifested itself yet," he explained. "It takes years for a Caster to even know how to use the Mist. You just became one. It's your first day."

"Okay." Desperate for a solution where I could survive, I suggested, "H-how about I wait a few years? I go explore the world. Do some backpacking or some shit and come back to close the portal when there's a better chance where I won't die?"

"The portal will touch the ground in two months, Milton."

I shouted, "So?" I could feel my face heat up with rage.

"Right now, the human race is living underground. The world above is completely desolate. Nothing survives there. The moment the portal touches the ground, it will spray Mist into the earth itself. It will kill the planet. Everyone will die within a year."

"Why don't you close it then?" I was ready to punch the man. He had rebutted every single one of my hopes and happiness in a matter of minutes. Sent me crashing harder than I had over the past century. "You're a Caster too, aren't you? How old are you?"

"Nine hundred and six."

"That's plenty of fucking experience! You close it!" I threw the empty bottle of water at him. He did not flinch, the container bouncing off his chest uneventfully.

217

"I can't. There's something else I have to do. Just like you, it's something only I can do. So I won't be there when the portal closes."

I wanted to slap my head, but my right arm, broken and unmoving, only whirred slightly, having been neglected of repair for decades. I was glad, for if I did hit my head with it, I would likely have broken my skull. Though at that moment, suicide was starting to seem like a less infuriating option.

"Son of a bitch," I cursed. "Son of a FUCKING BITCH!"

Pausa stood in silent respect. Even though up till then, I had mostly seen him make light of everything around him. It seemed the man knew the personal severity the choice was to me. My life or the world. A better man would have selflessly sacrificed himself for everyone else. But I am not a better man. Up till that point, I had assumed I would be dead, and that saving the world was just a pre-death bonus.

Angry, frustrated, confused, I started a rambling scream. "Why should I save the world? Huh? My family, my entire family, gave their lives to protect these stupid humans! But every time we turn around, someone, somewhere, makes shit worst!" I waved my arms, gesturing madly. I stepped away from Pausa, and looked gravely to my surrounding. My home. Roagnark. In ruins despite everything we've done in an attempt to protect it. "My wife protected everyone from the Mist. But The Forum had to have more power. They had start a war. My daughter tried to stop it and failed. Parker. Leah. Even my grandchildren managed to put a stop to Jason's madness. But every. Fucking. Time. We turn around, some new threat is knocking at the door! Does the world even deserve saving at this rate?"

To Pausa, I asked, "Nine hundred and six. Nine hundred and fucking six years! In all that time, how many wars have you seen? How many loved ones have you lost? Tell me, even if I close the portal, does the world ever find peace?"

Pausa looked to his feet and finally, took a seat on the bench. From above, the man looked shrunken, and I could see the weight that he had carried with him in his long life.

He began, "I lost my brother to war. I lost my best friend. Your grandfather lost his father and both his best friends. I have travelled through nine thousand years of time. Been a part of what? Seven wars now? I've seen billions of people die. I've lost count of it before I even turned thirty."

218

"Then what is the point?" I asked him. "Why keep fighting."

"For every battle, I see those few souls desperately trying to make the world a better place. I see the looks on their faces, the determination in their eyes." As he said that, I could picture the people I've met in my life. Joan. Leah. Leila. John. Milly. Lindsey. The Parkers. He looked up to me, conviction in his eyes. "How can I stand aside and watch as their efforts go to waste? They knew it would be next to impossible to bring peace but they all gave it their best shot. They all gave the world a chance to try. What about you, Milton Jones? Right now, you are the judge of humanity. The fate of the world lies solely in your hand. Do you think people deserve another chance?"

I looked away, not daring to meet his eyes. It held a fire that I had not seen before. Fierce, sagely, yet empathic and open. "Maybe it would be better if the world ended. Give the world a chance to start anew. Without all the damage people have caused."

He asked, "What about your great-great-great-granddaughter? Does she deserve a chance? Melissa Smith. John Smiths' great granddaughter. Living in one of the many underground cities, desperately trying to find a way to convert Mist into energy." He then snorted derisively. "Of course, such a technology is about seven thousand years before her time. She'll never make it."

"Melissa?" I asked, turning to him.

"Yeah. She's what? Twenty-eight? I don't know. I didn't check. She's not tied to the mistakes or duty of the past. Free to choose to make the world better on her own accord." He looked up to me, straight in the eyes. He asked, "That's what family's about, isn't it? Giving the next generation a clean slate and a hopefully better world. A chance to fix our wrongs. What's the kind of world you want to leave her?"

I looked around the dystopian park and up to the Mist filled sky where even sunlight could not pierce. ThenI stared down at the dead grass beneath my feet.

"Fuck," I cursed under my breath.

I might not be a good person, but never let it be said that I didn't care for family.

Future, Part Two

I had asked Pausa why he had not brought more water with him. He told me that there was no need to as the trip was one way. For both of us. I must admit that I nearly wet myself when he said that. It was the most ominous thing I've ever heard anyone said.

Ridge Valley was a city that existed before The Day of the Mist. According to history, it was the epicentre of the event where the main bulk of the Mist had came from. Now we knew why. It was the source of the portal.

The old city centre had succumbed to the onslaught of time and wind ages ago. Most buildings had long since collapsed, leaving our surroundings a pile of rubble and sand. Some of the base stood strong, like torn houses left after a hurricane. Wind cut through and twirled around us, the Mist swirling densely. A sandstorm of purplish-blue. A lone, burnt out neon sign jutted out from the earth, the words, 'HOTEL ALEX-'' barely readable. But the most striking sight was the portal just a stone throw away from the sign, hovering ominously above the ground.

Pausa voiced out, "That's so sci-fi yo."

The portal looked like a whirlpool in the sky, spewing out Mist like cold air rushing out of a freezer. Spinning and turning with arcs of energy sparking out. In the middle of it was a man-sized hole with a clear, albeit upside-down image of a tree on a hill. A picture within a frame. A mirror

220

to Wonderland. Despite the crazy atmosphere, the two of us stood with just the clothes on our backs, the Mist seemingly wrapping around us like a bubble does air, but never actually touching us. My arm pulsed a soft glow the entire time, as if it was a generator providing energy for the bubble shield.

"Sci-fi," I repeated the time traveller.

"I've seen the portal before, but never up close," Pausa noted. He started to walk towards it, a maddened glint of excitement and familiar curiosity in his eyes.

"Hey!" I shouted for him over the roaring winds. He stopped in his tracks. "What are you doing?"

"This is what I came to do! I came to see what's on the other side of the portal."

Confused, I asked, "Why?"

"What do you mean?" I wondered if it was becoming a common theme in our conversations, me asking questions and him answering. He continued, "It's a dangerous looking, poison spitting, spinning hole of death! If I don't poke it with a stick, who else is going to do it?"

I wanted to say that was not what I meant, but I felt my sense of the danger of the situation would not get through to the man. In fact, I had the inkling that his idea of a dangerous situation was so far off from mine I would be better off taking care of an alien.

Instead, I asked, "Before you go, can I ask you one thing?" He nodded and turned to me, the portal backing him like a screen effect. "My descendant, Melissa Smith. If I go through with this, what happens to her? What's her future like?"

Pausa folded his arms in contemplation and I could tell he was thinking whether he should reveal the information to me. There had to be rules to time travelling that even he could not break. From all the science fictions I've read as a kid, one of the most common one was to never tell people of their future.

"Come on! What happens to Melissa Smith?" I begged. "I'm about to die. You might as well tell me!"

Which was true. No matter what he said, I would not live pass the hour to talk about it. I did not intend to, and I doubted if I even could.

Instead of answering, he returned with a question. "Do you feel like a hero?"

"What?"

221

"Do you feel like hero?" he repeated with a steady gaze. For some reason, I felt tested, as if my entire journey had been for this one moment. This seemingly ordinary question. "Do you feel like the Hero of the Mist?"

I recalled my adventure. From the safety of the lab in Roagnark, to the dystopian, war-torn future that my grandchildren lived in. The little girl named Sally that spoke of hope from my story. But that was it the whole time. I was a story. I was not the protagonist of the tale. I was the lore of the world.

"No," I replied in earnest. "I feel like everyone else is the hero. Joan. Leila. The professor. My grandchildren. All of them have done more for this world than I have." My voice softened towards the end. For some reason, the wind slowed down, the howling quieting, as if in response to my tone. "Even you. Going off to god knows where on the opposite of that portal. All I've been able to do is watch. Watch my grandchildren save me. Watch Leila save me. Watch the doctor, the professor, the agents, my wife, all of them, saving me."

"And for the last century? The last two weeks of your life? What do you think you are."

I thought hard but not long, the answer knocking into my head with ease. "A bystander."

Our stares crossed and we watched each other in silence. For some reason, I thought of the passing of a baton in those old school sprint relays.

Finally, Pausa said, "You are a shadow, Milton. In the coming human history, you are forgotten. Not a single soul will remember you. In the tens of thousands of years of human history, your name will only be chanted during these one hundred and thirty-nine years, and not a day more." He opened his arms wide, gesturing to his surroundings. "This is your legacy. You, and your entire family. A dystopian, barren land. Everything they have ever done for the world, everything you are about to do, will be forgotten here. You will secure the entire future of the human race, yet no one will ever know who you are ever again."

I looked to him. He scanned my eyes, as if trying to find a defect through the windows to my soul, despite the windows being mechanical. When he did not continue, I pushed on. "What happens to Melissa Smith?" It did not matter if I did not leave a personal legacy. I just

222

wanted to know what happens to my family.

I could see it. Even from within the thick Mist, I could see his smile widening, a look of pride etched on his face.

"She goes on to live a happy life and finds work as a teacher. One of her students will invent a vaccine for Mist Poisoning until humans evolve into Casters." He grinned widely, teeth shining and all. "That, is what you leave behind. Your descendant, and the whole of the human race." He placed a hand over his heart. "We will forget you. But none of us will be here without you. Remember that."

I nodded at his answer. I did not really know why that was the question I asked, but it made me happy nonetheless. For some reason, the answer made me feel at peace with what I was about to do. What I was about to sacrifice.

He turned back to face the portal. After taking a deep breath, he started walking towards it again. This time, I did not attempt to stop him. Just before he stepped through the portal into the image of the inverted tree, he half-turned to me.

"I wonder what's on the other side?" He grinned.

And without a second look back, he stepped into the horizon, vanishing before my eyes and leaving me alone with the twirling, world-ending portal.

I looked to my robotic arm, then to Borris's watch still strapped to my wrist. I had never expected much from the end. After all, I always knew I would die. But I had always thought that I would be surrounded by people. Friends or family. A part of me even thought I might have fans. At the very least that there would be more drama or an exciting climax. But as I stood there, preparing to save the world, I realised how alone I was. It suited me well, I guess. I was never really a part of the action. My family was. I was just sort of there. It made sense that I took some responsibility and meet the end alone. No one else was going to get hurt.

I looked to Borris's watch again. "No one else," I said out loud.

Because we're fucking family you retarded fuck shit!

My arm glowed brighter than it ever did before. I could feel the energy flowing through it, as if whatever power it had was enhanced by the sheer thickness of the Mist around me. A burning sensation ran up my arm and I squinted and seethed slightly in pain. I knew instinctively then that when I activated whatever ability that would allow me to close the portal, my life would come to an end from that very same pain.

All families share a face. One day, I'll probably share your face too.

Somewhere, in the back of my mind, I could remember a picnic on a hill with my grandparents and parents. We sat under a tree, visiting my great-grandparents' graves. Joshua and Miranda Kleve, I think their names were. I wondered if that hill was the same as the one pictured inside the portal.

No widest sky, nor furthest seas, will part neither you nor me.

I raised my glowing hand to the portal, feeling the pins and needles that were running through my veins. I could feel hot liquid running from my eyes and down my cheeks but could not tell if they were blood or tears. The circuitry in my eyes had fried. I was once again blinded.

No death day due, or life lived lieu, will change my eternal love for you.

Reinforcing myself and to prevent me from screaming from the pain, I chanted, "My name is Milton Jones. Grandfather of Amelia and John Smith. Father of Leila Jones. Ancestor to Melissa Smith. Husband to Joan Jones."

The pain was almost unbearable but I held fast. The wind around me whirled louder and louder and I could hear an almost mechanical hum coming from the direction of the portal. Soft particles of dust landed on my skin, cold as snow.

I thought of Hillbury.

Favourite-test place. Ever.

There was no loud explosion. No burst of wind or scorching heat. Suddenly, the world just entered a state of immense quiet, like someone had muted the universe with the press of a remote. Even without my eyesight, I knew the portal had closed. My body ached. Everything screamed silently and I fell to my knees. I did not even have the strength to collapse properly as I knelt in the desolate wasteland.

I was sure I could smell flowers and feel the fresh breeze on my skin. My arm no longer burned, but only because it was no longer working. Both arms, robotic and skin, hung limply at my sides. My legs whirred to stand but the circuity too, had fried. I thought of Melissa, and wondered if I were to knock on her door at that moment, would she invite me in for a meal.

"Well," my voice croaked out, the water having dried from my body. I wished Pausa had brought a second bottle of water.

I could feel the last seconds of my life nearing. I wanted to say something cool. Some action hero phrase. A witty one-liner that would be remembered for the rest of eternity. I remembered how when I first met Agent Matthews, I noted that I should not face the apocalypse without one-liners.

My lips cracked a smile as I lazily finished, "Maybe next time."

Leah's ~~Report~~ Diary

[Report Log / Professor Leah Leslie Hullway]
[74 P.T / Project Dawn]
Username : LeahLH
Password : *************************
Log Entry : 139074
[/Start?]
[/Y]

Dear Diary,
I was told by Parker that all staff members
would now be required to keep yearly records. I'm
not sure why he was the one who announced and not
me, seeing as I am the senior lead on this
project. Well, I won't hold it against him, even
if he was the one who caused the incident last
summer after kicking the power cord in the
morning.

[Log Addendum 1 / Doctor Greene Parker] You know
I have to monitor and read these, right? And that
power cord was not there when I left the night
before. [End Addendum]

It's been two years since we brought Milton
out. We're working on the new design for the next
version of the Cryo-Tube and I've been closely
overseeing the engineers. Some of them told me I
should get a PhD in engineering, but I don't
think the qualification matters now if I can do
the job. Aside from that, nothing much happened
this year. Maintenance, meetings, maintenance,
meetings. Met a boy. Dated for a while, but that
didn't work out. Oh, Joan and G are finally
getting married! So exciting! Well, it has been
fun, but that's all for now. Until next time,
dear diary.
Love,
- Leah

[Log Addendum 2 / Doctor Greene Parker] This is a
serious report, Professor, not a teenage journal.
Please take the next one more seriously. [End
Addendum]

[Report Log / Professor Leah Leslie Hullway]
[77 P.T / Project Dawn]
Username : LeahLH
Password : *************************
Log Entry : 139128
[/Start?]
[/Y]

Dear Diary,
Has it been three years already? People sort
of just forgot about this report log. Even I did.
Guess it must be one of those things that the
higher-ups suggested just to make it look like
they were actually doing something by reading it.

[Log Addendum 3 / Doctor Greene Parker] People
did not forget about it. You're the only one who
never submitted anything in the past 2 years. How
you could be so competent at your work and
incompetent at managing your inbox is mind
boggling. You should hire a secretary. **[End
Addendum]**

Perhaps people just got busy, what with
bringing Milton out for the second time two years
ago, along with the installation, patches, and
updates of the new Cryo-Tube. I think we should
hold a over-the-weekend staff party for everyone.
I know we don't have much in the cohesion funds,
but I'm sure we could scrounge up enough for a
pizza buffet.
Love,
– Leah

[Log Addendum 4 / Doctor Greene Parker]
Professor, I'm starting to think you're just
having fun with me. This is a serious report,
please, no more of these 'Dear Diary' entries.
[End Addendum]

[Report Log / Professor Leah Leslie Hullway]
[78 P.T / Project Dawn]
Username : LeahLH
Password : ************************
Log Entry : 139239
[/Start?]
[/Y]

Dear Park-Park,
Lighten up. We're stuck with each other and
Milton for a few years, might as well make the
most of it.

[Log Addendum 5 / Doctor Greene Parker] Please,
not Park-Park. That's worst than Gee-Gee for
Agent Golph. **[End Addendum]**

I've told Joan about the party idea. I had
completely forgotten about it since the last
entry. She's really excited about it, and is even
willing to put some money for a live band. But if
we hire someone from the outside, we'll need to
find a public venue, seeing as everything here is
confidential. Maybe we could get the accounting
people? I heard they play gigs at cafes over
weekends.
Are you free next week? Me, G, Joan and Leila
are heading over to the new arcade for a day off.
Maybe you could join us, Park-Park?
Love,
- Leah

[Log Addendum 6 / Doctor Greene Parker] I am free
next weekend. But this isn't your personal
messaging platform. You see me all the time. Just
ask me face-to-face. **[End Addendum]**

[Report Log / Professor Leah Leslie Hullway]
[79 P.T / Project Dawn]
Username : LeahLH
Password : *************************
Log Entry : 139455
[/Start?]
[/Y]

Dear Park-Park,
I kind of like this idea of having a personal messaging platform, even if it is only once a year. It's a little like our own little secret, hidden underneath mountains of top-secret documents and opened to the prying eyes of curious politicians and army generals. Do you think anyone else actually bothers reading these? We should do a social experiment and see how long it takes for us to get fired!

[Log Addendum 7 / Doctor Greene Parker] Please don't. I actually need this job. **[End Addendum]**

Have you seen Leila? She's been coming in so often, running around, so excited about graduation next year. Once we have that party, we should definitely get Joan to bring her along. Maybe we could time it with one of Milton's wake-up call.
Love,
- Leah

[Log Addendum 8 / Doctor Greene Parker] That would be nice, having everyone together. But in the mean time, do remember to come for your medical check-ups. You're not a young woman anymore. You need to take better care of yourself. **[End Addendum]**

[Report Log / Professor Leah Leslie Hullway]
[80 P.T / Project Dawn]
Username : LeahLH
Password : *************************
Log Entry : 139675
[/Start?]
[/Y]

Dear Park-Park,
Oh, it's so nice to know that you care. I'll be sure to keep my body in tip-top condition, just for you!

[Log Addendum 9 / Doctor Greene Parker] Please don't make this weird. By the way, that entry was a year ago, and you still don't come for your check-ups on time. [End Addendum]

Isn't it great that Leila and Milton made up? It's so heart-warming to see father and daughter together again. Good work on these past few years. I must say, we wouldn't be able to make it this far without you.
Love,
- Leah

[Log Addendum 10 / Doctor Greene Parker] Thanks. But you're making it weird again. [End Addendum]

[Report Log / Professor Leah Leslie Hullway]
[83 P.T / Project Dawn]
Username : LeahLH
Password : *************************
Log Entry : 139888
[/Start?]
[/Y]

Dear Park-Park,
Have you seen the way Leila looks at that new engineer? I'm telling you, if he so much as touches a hair on our little Leila, I will make sure he gets it! I'm telling Joan! But have you heard that The Forum is planning on cutting all funding to Project Dawn? Madness!
Love,
- Leah

[**Log Addendum 11 / Doctor Greene Parker**] Please, Leah, you're a professor with 3 PhDs. Control yourself. And unless it's about my dashing smile and charming personality, leave your gossips out of the reports. [**End Addendum**]

[**Log Addendum 12 / Professor Leah Leslie Hullway**] Oh, doctor! Since when have you gotten so snappy? [**End Addendum**]

[**Log Addendum 13 / Doctor Greene Parker**] How did you access the addendum function? [**End Addendum**]

[**Log Addendum 14 / Professor Leah Leslie Hullway**] Please, Park-Park, I have 3 doctorates. How long do you think it took? [**End Addendum**]

[Report Log / Professor Leah Leslie Hullway]
[89 P.T / Project Dawn]
Username   : LeahLH
Password   : ************************
Log Entry : 139889
[/Start?]
[/Y]

    I don't feel good about this new direction The Forum is taking. Especially how they are now mass monitoring our communications. Ironically, this report might be the only safe place left for us, since I'm sure they have long since stopped checking them.

[Log Addendum 15 / Doctor Greene Parker] I agree. Even so, we should use this sparingly. We should wait and observe the result of the upcoming election before deciding anything. Perhaps the funding cancellation could be shot down. **[End Addendum]**

[Log Addendum 16 / Professor Leah Leslie Hullway] What about Milton's condition? I know there's a doctor-patient confidentiality and all, but we're all friends. I can tell, there's something about his condition you're not telling his family. The burden must be eating you. If you need it, I'm here, Park-Park. **[End Addendum]**

[Log Addendum 17 / Doctor Greene Parker] Thanks, but there's really not much else. I won't lie though, it's hard to think that once we pull Milton out, I'll only have 6 hours to do the surgery and stop the poison. Such a short time frame for such a complicated procedure. It's never been done before. I've been looking at the Vallertes Industry. They've been making quite a headway with bio-cybernetics. I'm going to push to get more funding through to them. With any luck, we'll have sufficient medical technology to make the operation in a decade or less. But for now, I wouldn't mind going for a drink. **[End Addendum]**

[Log Addendum 18 / Professor Leah Leslie Hullway] I dropped everyone a text. We'll go to Ander'z. **[End Addendum]**

[Log Addendum 19 / Doctor Greene Parker] Don't forget to come in for your check-up. Really. I'm worried about you too, and I don't need to have you on my mind as well. **[End Addendum]**

[Log Addendum 20 / Professor Leah Leslie Hullway] I'm on your mind? That's so sweet! I love you too! **[End Addendum]**

[Log Addendum 21 / Doctor Greene Parker] Thank goodness my wife can't see this. **[End Addendum]**

[Log Addendum 22 / Professor Leah Leslie Hullway] Don't worry, she knows how I am. **[End Addendum]**

[/Search / Log 139890 / Not Found]
[/Search / Log 139891 / Not Found]
[/Search / Log 139892 / Not Found]
[/Search / Log 139893 / Not Found]

[Report Log / Professor Leah Leslie Hullway]
[94 P.T / Project Dawn]
Username : LeahLH
Password : ************************
Log Entry : 139894
[/Start?]
[/Y]

   First Milton, now Joan. This Mist Poisoning is getting everyone. I'm really worried about Leila. She's been so down and stressed since everything. How is the research for Milton's treatment going? And did you delete the last four years of entries?

[Log Addendum 82 / Doctor Greene Parker] Yes, I deleted them. Had a little scare last week when the administration brought up the log. Turned out to be nothing, but I thought it'd be better to be safe. As for the research, things are fine. At this rate, we can do the surgery early next year. I just hope there's enough time for Joan. **[End Addendum]**

[Log Addendum 83 / Professor Leah Leslie Hullway] Good call on the deletion. Nice job, Park-Park. **[End Addendum]**

[Log Addendum 84 / Doctor Greene Parker] Can I get a new nickname? You've changed G's to Golfie. **[End Addendum]**

[Log Addendum 85 / Professor Leah Leslie Hullway] Nope. Park-Park is nice. **[End Addendum]**

[Report Log / Doctor Greene Parker]
[99 P.T / Project Dawn]
Username : DrParkerG
Password : ************
Log Entry : 139895
[/Start?]
[/Y]

Dear Leah,
We buried G today. It's been three years since
Joan, and a year since you passed. Now, G's gone
on too. I'm kicking myself for being younger than
all of you. But it's not all death and gloom. I
got to hold my grandchild today. Little baby
Clover. Leila's thinking of having another child.
Not sure if she would with the world as messed up
as this. I hope she does. We need more kids if
we're going to have any future.
You know, this was one of the things I missed
with you. You once said these reports were like
our own secret conversation that no one else
knew. You were right, of course, as always. But
the fact that there were only the two of us here
and now one of us is gone just kills me.
Anyway, we'll be moving Milton out to the
falls in a couple of years time, depending on how
this revolution swings. Our funding has been
slashed and we're only keeping up with outside
help from Penstine and Lucinda. Once we move,
we're not coming back to Roagnark any more. We
won't be able to visit any of your graves either.
I think, for me, at least, I deserve this
outcome. Younger, I was brash, proud, and
disrespectful. It seems now I will have to face
the end of my life alone. Maybe that's fitting.
But don't worry about Milton. He's in good
hands. For now, all of you can rest easy. I'll
make sure of it.
Sincerely,
- Greene Parker

[Report Log / Doctor Greene Parker]
[113 P.T / Project Dawn]
Username : DrParkerG
Password : ************
Log Entry : 139896
[/Start?]
[/Y]

Dear Leah,
Who knew I'd live this long? Clover has a
heart condition and it got worse a while back. I
had no choice but to return to Roagnark to seek
medical help. They agreed, on the condition that
I worked the rest of my life for them. Imagine my
surprise when I got back that these logs were
still here. I'm getting old, and my memory isn't
what it used to be. I'm happy to have the chance
to relive old times.
It's been two years since I came back and I
miss all of you. More so than my youth. Clover is
fine now, and from last I heard, Amelia and John
are doing their best as well. Maybe it's time we
leave the future to the kids and move on. It
would be nice to finally be able to rest again.
Yes. Rest sounds nice right about now.
Love,
- Park-Park

[10 Minutes To Automatic Log-Off]
[Press ENTER To Resume Session]
[5 Minutes To Automatic Log-Off]
[Press ENTER To Resume Session]
[2 Minutes To Automatic Log-Off]
[Press ENTER To Resume Session]
[30 Seconds To Automatic Log-Off]
[Press ENTER To Resume Session]
[10 Seconds To Automatic Log-Off]
[Press ENTER To Resume Session]
[Session Ended]

<<<<>>>>